Haunted Gem

by

Gabriella Lucas

A River Styx Mystery

Cover Art by *Lisa Dawn MacDonald*

The Wild Rose Press, Inc.
PO Box 708
Adams Basin, NY 14410-0708
Visit us at www.thewildrosepress.com

Publishing History
First Edition, 2025
Trade Paperback ISBN 978-1-5092-6041-6
Digital ISBN 978-1-5092-6042-3

A River Styx Mystery
Published in the United States of America

Dedication

To my wonderful first readers, Susie Kemp, Adrienne Deckman, Rae Griffin, and Leah Hunter.

Special thanks to Jason and Leah for all your work on the website—I love you.

Special thanks to freelance editor Amy Tipton at Feral Girl Books, and to Kaycee John, my Wild Rose Press editor, without whom this book would never have been published.

As always, a shout out to my love, Michael.

Prologue

Gemma Martelli was just seven years old the first time a ghost spoke to her.

She was in the attic—a place full of wonder to a little girl. She saw an old mantel clock that was laden with gray dust, and albums filled with photographs of Italy where her grandparents were born. She sat in the rocking chair where her grandmother sat as she knitted sweaters and mittens. She found a box full of ribbons—awards that her mother earned when she played flute in high school competitions.

She played dress-up with clothes she found in an old chest and twirled in front of an antique cheval mirror. She picked up a necklace, a silver pendant with magical symbols on a long chain. When she fastened it around her neck, she heard a woman's voice that seemed vaguely familiar.

The woman said, *"Bona jurnata, Gemma."*

Because her grandparents often spoke their native language, Gemma knew this was Sicilian for 'good day.'

"Who are you?" she asked.

"Madre di Gina."

The voice was her maternal grandmother's. But she had been dead for several years.

Gemma didn't think it was normal to hear voices in her head. She ran downstairs to tell her mother. She expected her mother to scold her for rummaging through things in the attic instead of picking up her room. But her mother smiled and patted the sofa cushion. When Gemma sat down, her mother put her arm across her shoulders. "Gemma, did she say who she was?"

Gemma repeated the words in broken Italian but got her point across.

Her mom smiled. "You heard my mother? What were you doing right before you heard this, Gemma?"

"I had on this hat," she said, pointing up to the black pillbox that her grandmother had often worn to church. "And I put this on," she added, reaching up to her neck to touch the amulet.

Her mother smiled again. "That was your grandmother's, Gemma. It's an Italian charm that keeps away the evil eye." She kissed Gemma's forehead. "Wow, honey, you have a special gift."

Gemma swept her bangs to one side of her forehead. "But it's weird, Mom. No one will understand. I'll never have a boyfriend."

Her mother laughed. "The right person will understand, honey. And Gemma, every ghost has a secret. Think about it. You will be a keeper of secrets. Maybe even secrets that can help solve mysteries or crimes."

"But it's not normal," Gemma said, wiping a tear from her cheek.

Her mother gently wrapped a finger through one of Gemma's chestnut brown tendrils. "Oh, Gemma, it's normal for you."

Chapter One

Seventeen Years Later

Gemma yanked the wheel of her car to the left and rocketed up the long driveway leading to the farmhouse. Her brakes screeched as she jerked to a stop. Heart racing, her hands clammy, she threw open the door and jumped out. Then she bolted toward the old, gnarled tree.

Twirling in a circle, she whispered, "Talk to me, Marjorie. Is this the place? Am I in the right place?"

She dropped to her knees and started to scratch at the dirt. "It's here," she mumbled. "It has to be here."

A stream of stomach-turning images and sounds pulsed through her head. A whack with the butt of a handgun. Three shots and blood pooling on the ground, on the very spot where Gemma knelt. The sound of a shovel smacking the ground, dirt grinding and flying in all directions like a gray fog. The thump of the body being tossed into the grave. A tree sapling with a smooth, gray trunk in an open field.

That tree had grown into a sturdy pine tree with crackling bark and long, pointy needles. As Gemma knelt beneath it, the woody, slightly sweet scent conjured up Christmas celebrations with her family. How odd.

"Hey!" a man called out.

She froze, sucked in a breath, and looked up.

The end of a pitchfork was inches from her face. His

jaw hardened. "Who the hell are you, and what are you doing on my farm?"

She tried to present a calm front, but her pulse quickened at the hollow of her throat as her gaze dropped to the sharp metal tines. She swallowed hard. She couldn't find her voice.

"Answer me, or I'm going to call the police."

She extended her arm and lifted her hand to stop him from moving closer, but he jerked the pitchfork even closer to her face. She put both hands up in the air, then slowly reached into the side pocket of her blazer. She pulled out a business card. "Yes, call the police. Here, call this number."

The man's eyes narrowed. "Get up."

Her heart hammering against her chest, her hand trembling, she gave him the card.

"Please. Just call."

He would call, and then he would understand.

She hoped.

Chapter Two

"You know where all the bodies are buried, Gemma. Literally."

Detective Shakespeare Williams' words swirled in her mind.

"That means I was right. You found her, Shake?"

"We did. What's left of her. After over forty years, Marjorie Hobbs can have a decent burial, thanks to you."

"You're sure it's her?"

"Well, not until we do DNA tests, but she was wearing a wedding ring with her initials, and her sister identified a necklace as one she gave to Marjorie. It appears that you just helped me solve a decades-old cold case."

It had been over a week since Shake had convinced the family of a woman who'd been missing for years to loan him a pair of the woman's earrings. They were tiny gold squares, nothing very pretentious or expensive. Jewelry of a farmer's wife.

Once they were in Gemma's possession, the dreams, visions, and whispers assaulted her brain night and day. Her mind was battered with images and tiny clues. Marjorie's cries crackling and roaring like thunder after lightning. The nauseating, metallic taste of blood. A word here, a murmur of sobs there, a soup of putrid smells, a glimpse of a gnarled pine tree. Gemma also had a strange recurring nightmare of a building with legs that propelled itself across a field. She knew that the only way that all this would stop was to find the body.

By themselves, these things meant nothing, but it all clicked into a full picture as she drove past the cornfield. That was why she veered off the road and got out of her car. When Gemma's feet hit the ground, she knew exactly what had happened. Marjorie's husband, who had always claimed that his wife deserted him, had killed her and buried her in a grave next to his barn. He planted a tree there. That was where the remains were found—under the tree, next to where the old barn once stood. He sold the farm not long after she disappeared, and the present owner of the farm razed the old barn and built a new one farther away from the house.

How odd that when all was said and done, that crazy nightmare of the big building with legs that marched across the field actually made sense.

She exhaled slowly. "So, Shake, did the farmer wonder who the heck I was?"

Shake laughed. "He did. He asked me who the tiny brunette with the sad, brown cow eyes was. You do realize that you shouldn't have gone to the farm by yourself, right? What if he'd had a gun and decided you were a trespasser? Well, you *were* a trespasser. I told him that you were a CI."

"A what?"

"A confidential informant. He didn't ask any more questions. Next time, just do as I ask. Promise me that you won't play amateur detective. A little more caution would be prudent, you know? What were you thinking?" He sighed. "Look, Gemma, I'm responsible for you. I mean, this . . .." He stuttered, like he was groping for words. "This relationship we have is off the books, but I still can't let anything happen to you. What would I tell your mother? My niece?"

Gemma and his niece Jasmine had been friends since kindergarten.

"I appreciate your concern, Shake, but—"

"Say you're sorry, Gummy Bear. Admit that he's right."

It was the voice of her late brother's spirit—Peppi had always been her moral compass; he had always been her North Star, and as usual, though he'd been dead for several years, he was still guiding her, protecting her.

Okay, Peppi. I get it.

She hesitated for a moment, then said, "I'm sorry, Shake."

"I'll admit that I'm pretty gobsmacked that you figured it out," Shake said. "Now we just have to find her husband. He's an old man now."

She looked out the window. All of a sudden, the storm that was brewing cut loose, dumping buckets of rain that pounded against her windowpanes. It had been like this for weeks and weeks with no sign of let-up. This year, spring was her reluctant reflection—stubborn in coming, slow and sullen, its batteries desperately needing to be charged. Its constant gray clouds had carried a heavy burden; they seemed unable to move, always ready to collapse or burst.

It was exactly how Gemma felt . . . tired, stuck in place, and carrying a burden that sometimes got to be too much. "Shake, why do you do this?"

"Do what?"

"What you do. Open up cold cases? Search for killers that are long gone?"

The pause was long but telling. Finally, he said,

"Sometimes there's a case that begs for closure. It's like the whole story was only partly unearthed. And then I get to thinking about the people who have done unspeakable things and gotten away with them. There's no justice. By the time I get the case, the perp has probably had a comfy, cozy death."

She bit back the questions that sprang to her lips, as well as the retort that skipped to the tip of her tongue. She almost asked, "Is any death ever really comfy cozy?"

"I don't like the idea of that, Gemma. Of no reckoning. Not when they should be in the fiery pits of hell."

Her pulse quickened as she thought about the man who should definitely be in hell for what he did. "The man who murdered Marjorie—he won't know anything about—"

"About you?" he interrupted. "No, of course not. The plan is to say that an anonymous tip led us to the grave. I'm not going to advertise that I used a psychic, Gemma. You won't be in any danger. *This* time," he added.

The night was quiet, except for the silver nails of rain pinging off the roof, the train whistling in the distance, and the hammering of her pulse. She looked down at her T-shirt and could see her heart pounding. Perhaps Shake was right, but Gemma still felt a heaviness in her chest.

"Get some sleep now, Gemma," Shake said. "And thank you."

"I'm glad I could help, Shake. Good night."

She meant it; she was happy to help, and she did it with a precision of detail that surprised her, but it still filled her with overwhelming sadness. Her particular skill set wasn't one she had ever wished for. She paced in her kitchen, her hands shaking as she nursed a glass of red wine. She always had trouble sleeping after these events. Not that Gemma Martelli's sleep was ever deep. It never allowed her mind to relax entirely, especially since she'd started to use her gift to help on cold cases.

In Chicago, Gemma could fly under the radar when she consulted with law enforcement. But now that she lived in the village of River Styx again? Everyone knew everybody's business, and it would be harder to fade into the woodwork. She was also convinced that the one person in the world that she really hoped would understand her probably never would.

Reverend Dr. Luke Bailey.

Based on the only one-on-one conversation they'd had on the subject of the afterlife at a recent funeral, it was clear that she and Luke saw spirits in a very different light. Her view was 'the road less traveled,' one that Luke undoubtedly thought was full of potholes and mile-wide cracks.

How to explain to Luke what she could do? In her limited experience, most ghosts went their merry way once they accomplished their goals. Anchored souls haunted because they had loose ends to tie up. They sought justice or forgiveness or wanted their remains found . . . whatever it took to have RIP on a headstone and really mean it. But until that happened, Gemma lived with their voices in her head. Her gift was a speed bump in her attempt to lead a normal life, especially in the romance department.

She filled the coffee maker with water and a filter with coffee grounds and set the time for seven a.m. She grabbed a bottle of water from the refrigerator, walked to the bedroom, tossed her slacks and T-shirt into the hamper, and hung up her blazer. She put on an oversized red-and-gray college sweatshirt, which had belonged to her late brother. She gulped down half the bottle of water, put the cap back on the bottle, set it on her nightstand, and picked up her cell phone.

As she climbed into bed, she couldn't shake the chill despite the muggy night. She yanked up the crazy quilt. A lump beneath it moved. "C'mere, silly," she said to her white Persian cat that formed the bump beneath the covers at the foot of the bed. "C'mon on up here."

Fantasma—named by her mother, Italian for phantom or ghost—slithered toward her, found Gemma's stomach, and perched herself on it. Reaching out from beneath the covers, she checked her cell phone for messages. '*You have one new message and six saved messages.*'

"Hi, Gem. This is Luke Bailey."

Luke called? He'd never called her before. He'd left a message that he wanted to stop by her jewelry store in the morning; he needed a gift for someone.

"Who do you think Luke Bailey needs a gift for?" she asked the cat. *Hopefully not another woman.*

She hadn't heard any rumors about Luke seeing someone, and in the village of River Styx, gossip about the town's handsome minister would take off like a runaway train.

When he was still a Catholic priest, she'd barely spoken to him even when she was home on break from college or for a holiday, because she didn't attend his church. Maybe a 'hello' on the street or at the grocery store. But that had changed.

Now he was a minister at her church, an eligible

bachelor, and since she'd moved back home, she found herself scheming out ways to run into him. Luke was clearly different from her deceased boyfriend—Antonio was flamboyant and reckless, always on a breathless quest for the next adrenaline high, and that killed him. Luke was gentle and stable. But his background was a mystery. What she did know about him, she liked very much, especially the way he laughed and the way he dressed—usually jeans and a graphic tee, in a maverick's disregard for small-town expectations. She felt invigorated, a little dizzy, and off her axis when he was around.

Fine, just admit you really like him, even though you didn't expect to be fascinated by anyone in your little hometown.

Petting Fantasma, and soothed by her purring, Gemma listened to Luke's voice mail message again, then turned off the light and closed her eyes. She tried to tune everything out. The case was over, practically solved. But she couldn't suppress the shivers that ran down her spine, and she couldn't control the way her hands trembled.

The damn building with legs didn't want to park itself somewhere else.

Chapter Three

The next morning, unwilling to move and wanting to savor a few more minutes of peace, Gemma raised her arm in front of her eyes to stop the sunlight that roared through her bedroom like a leaping flame. She continued to rest her cheek tenderly against the soft pillow, but the slanted rays of light didn't retreat, and she finally forced her eyes to open.

For a brief moment when she woke, she wasn't sure where she was. Sometimes, she scanned the room because she still expected to wake up in her apartment in Chicago. It was as if everything went off the grid while she slept. She would mentally trace the room, pinpointing where the bed was, where the light switch was, where the chest of drawers was.

She missed her apartment, but being back in the village had its plus side. Each morning, she inhaled the sweet scents of lilacs, and old-time petunias, and alyssum, and apple blossoms. They reminded her of the lazy summer days of her childhood, spent playing in the nearby woods with her best friend, her only friend, or sitting under a tree with a good book. The last few months had been very chaotic. Her mother remarried and moved. She talked herself into moving back so that the family jewelry business would continue. But it was more difficult to settle back into the rhythm of the hamlet than she thought it would be. Sometimes these fragrances were all that allowed her to think that untroubled peace was possible.

She closed her eyes again and sank back into the pillow for a moment, savoring the rich aroma of the coffee that filled her apartment. Lying there, silently welcoming the blue skies, the dazzle of the sun against the windowpane, and the fact that spring had finally arrived with its pledge of summer, she was in no rush to get up. But her eyes shot open when she remembered. *Luke called yesterday. He is coming to see me today.*

Brightened by this thought, she threw off the covers and sat up. She pushed ghosts and bodies and murder cases from her mind. She wanted today to be a normal day, one without messages from beyond, without spirits whispering in her ears. Today, the ex-priest she'd found herself crushing on was coming to her jewelry store.

She yawned and stretched, reminding herself that things were finally jelling. She was getting the hang of running the store by herself. Earlier that week, she'd sold a piece of vintage costume jewelry, a choker necklace created by Miriam Haskell from the early 1950s, for over three hundred dollars. And she and Jasmine, her dearest friend, were making plans for the weekend.

After she hopped out of bed, she went to the kitchen to disarm the security alarm. She watered the plants on her balcony and breathed in the faint scent of the salvia bush and fiesta red hibiscus shrubs that 'Nonno,' her grandfather, had planted in pots to attract hummingbirds. After her grandmother passed, Nonno was uncomfortable in the home they had shared for many decades, and he moved back into this apartment over the jewelry store, where he, her grandmother, and her father had lived when the family first moved to River Styx some fifty years ago. They lived there until he bought a house with some land.

She was about to go back inside when one of the little birds shifted his position to allow her to glimpse a flash of bright emerald green and brilliant red, its feathers glittering like jewels in the sunlight. It filled her with a flood of thoughts, especially memories of Nonno glancing out the window of the workroom at the back of the store, watching his little friends take nectar as he repaired watches and jewelry.

She fed the cat and poured herself a cup of coffee. She sipped it as her eyes followed the huge, white clouds that slowly drifted across an electric sky, a welcome change after weeks of rain and hail and gray clouds.

After her shower, she refilled her coffee mug, applied a hint of makeup, and dried her hair. Leaning closer to the mirror, she made a face. *What's with the 'elevens' between my eyebrows? Time for Botox? No, you're only twenty-four years old.* She looked at her face more closely and wished that someone would describe her tired brown eyes as Jane Austen had described Elizabeth Bennett's— "She had fine eyes."

She smiled when her poet brother's spirit whispered in her ear—*"No, Gummy Bear, your eyes are like the cognac left behind in the glass when Nonno went to bed."*

"You're sweet, Peppi."

Gemma removed her late brother's Italian horn from her neck and took off the earrings that her dead boyfriend Antonio gave her. She knew Peppi's spirit stuck around to look after her, to keep her safe, even from the grave, but Antonio's ghost was just a pest. She hoped that if she didn't wear their jewelry today, they'd stay away.

"Take a vacation day, boys. I need normal today."

Standing in front of her closet, she dragged her fingertips across dresses and blouses. She shook her head. In her apartment in Chicago, she had a huge closet. In the house she grew up in, the one her father had built, she had a walk-in. This was more like her college dorm, only worse because back then, she mostly wore T- shirts and jeans to classes. Now she crammed dresses, blouses, pants, and blazers into the world's smallest closet.

"Okay, what to wear for Luke," she sighed. Then she scolded herself again. "Stop it, Gemma Martelli. It doesn't matter what you wear today. It's not a date. Luke is just coming in to shop. He's a customer, not the love of your life."

But she did find herself studying Luke all the time. He seemed very friendly and kind, but he shared little about his past. Even the town gossips didn't seem to know much about him. When she saw him with elderly people or with the youth group, her heart melted. But she was dying to know why he left the priesthood to become an Episcopalian minister, and she wanted to know what made him tick.

****

Luke was six years older than Gemma; he had just turned thirty. He was slim, toned, and every muscle of his over-six-foot frame was firm. He was most comfortable in a graphic T-shirt under a dark blue blazer and jeans. Every time she saw him, she took note of another aspect of Luke Bailey. He had a strong chin, an easy smile, an even easier laugh, and his eyes were like lanterns of light, the color of pure water blue. He had sun-toasted skin and light hair. He made her think of California surfers. Nothing about him suggested that he had ever been a priest or that he was currently pastor of the village's Episcopalian church. At least, he didn't conform to her perception of how a priest, or a minister should look, as in staid and a little stuffy, definitely reserved, standoffish, even. Certainly not like the village's biggest heart throb.

With his broad shoulders, toned biceps, and small waist, Luke had a classic swimmer's athletic body, and Jasmine had mentioned to her that Luke swam at the rec center almost every morning—Jaz saw him when she ran the track. She said that when he walked by, he smelled of chlorine. Gemma wanted to sneak in and see him in a bathing suit, but it seemed wildly inappropriate, so she only fantasized about him in spandex. But she had no doubt others surrendered to their curiosity because she was definitely not the only one whose heart did cartwheels around him. If he were still a priest, she was certain that every girl within a hundred-mile radius of River Styx would line up for confession on a daily basis. As it was, every girl over the age of twelve and every woman under the age of eighty eagerly volunteered to help him out at the church or on mission trips or pretty much whatever he asked.

****

Pushing everything but one dress to the side, she ran her fingers over the lace at the top of a yellow sundress. This one always made her feel pretty. But she'd save it for the church picnic and raffle. She was an entrepreneur now; she had her own business, and she should look the part.

She decided on a blue dress that hugged her body in all the right places, slipped on the matching bolero, pulled on nylons, and slid her feet into a pair of dark blue kitten heels.

Fantasma swiped at her ankles, her usual greeting, and a sharp claw snagged her nylons. People often remarked how beautiful she was, but beneath her fluffy, white fur, there were some wicked claws. Sometimes she was anything but sweet.

"Darn it, Fan. That is why Jasmine calls you Demon Spawn, you know."

With coffee in a large thermos, she went downstairs to her shop and read the 'Word of the Day' in the paper. *Paroxysm*—defined as 'a sudden attack or violent expression of a particular emotion or activity.' She sucked in a breath because that precisely described her reaction when a spirit reached out to her and walked her through its final corporeal moments.

When she opened a few windows, she heard Luke's laughter in the distance. She walked to the front door of the shop. So that he wouldn't see her spying, instead of standing at the large front window, she dragged the stool that she used to reach high shelves to the front door. She stepped up and peeked through the transom window near the top of the door. She saw Luke, who was deep in conversation with Mrs. Bloom, the owner of the florist shop across the street.

Bonita Bloom was one of her favorite people in the village. Waif-thin and elderly, she had a glorious tumble of hair that was the color of an artificial silver Christmas tree. Since Gemma's return to River Styx, she'd come to be a substitute grandmother.

As she watched Luke now, a spring breeze lifted his hair. It reminded her of the desert—a rolling wave of thick, butter-gold sand, a bit windswept. She thought she saw a wry smile touch the corners of Luke's mouth when he nodded as Mrs. Bloom told him whatever little story she wanted to share.

But she did wonder why Luke Bailey needed to buy flowers from the town florist.

It had to be Luke because he'd messed up his leg in a car wreck many years ago, and she could always tell it was him by his gait.

"You expecting someone?"

She rolled her eyes. "Well, this is a store, Shake. And Luke Bailey said he'd stop by."

Pretending not to be excited, she looked away. She didn't want Shake's radar to go up. She wasn't great at being coy—in fact, more than once her lack of diplomacy had gotten her into trouble. She just didn't want anyone to know about this thing she had for the local minister. One of the reasons she'd hesitated to leave Chicago and move back to the village was that it was such a small town with such a big rumor mill.

"Go ahead, Gem. Can't keep Father waiting."

Wrinkling her face, she corrected him. "Shake, he's an ex-priest." Emphasis on 'ex.' "He's an Episcopalian minister now, remember?"

This was an important distinction. Catholic priests were celibate.

But Shake attended St. Mary Ascension, and he knew Luke from when he still served as a priest at that church. He couldn't seem to let go of the 'Father' title.

"Listen, Gem, don't tell him I'm here. Okay?"

Puzzled, she shook her head. "Why would I? Help yourself," she said, pointing to a plate of muffins near the coffee thermos. "Mrs. Bloom baked them yesterday."

She went out to the store, trying to hide the blush on her cheeks.

"Hey, Gemma," Luke said.

She felt all of her anxiety and fatigue, all the insanity that came with being who she was, simply drain out of her. *Wow*, she thought. No matter how vexed she was,

Luke brought her a strange kind of calm.

"Do you have a minute?"

"Sure. I saw you with Mrs. Bloom. I haven't checked on her today. Is she okay?"

"She's fine. I was arranging for flowers for the church on Mother's Day."

"Ah. Well, what can I do for you, Dr. Luke?"

He waved a hand and made a face. "Luke, just Luke." He cleared his throat. "I see you changed the sign?"

She nodded. "Yeah. It was a really hard decision, because last year was the one hundredth anniversary of the Martelli & Sons business, but there aren't any Martelli sons now." *And I wanted to really make it my own.* "I thought Gem's Gems had a nice ring to it."

He smiled. "It does. And there's nothing wrong with progress. So, anyway, I want to look for something special for my mom for Mother's Day."

Note to self. That's the sign of a sweet and wonderful son.

"Well, Dr. . . . Luke, I'm still getting my bearings here in the store. Give me an idea what you're looking for, and I'll try to help."

"Nothing too expensive," he said. "But everybody says people come from all over to buy estate jewelry from you. Mom likes antique things. Vintage stuff."

"Does she like certain gems? Are her ears pierced?"

"I don't know," he admitted. He swore under his breath and looked down. His perfectly sculpted cheeks flamed. "Sorry."

She smiled. Additional note to self. She liked a minister who occasionally cursed. It made him human.

"She likes emeralds. And, yeah, I think she has

pierced ears." He pulled on his ear. "Just those little ones. Studs?

"She used to have an emerald ring, too. It was worth—well, it was very, very valuable."

His face clouded as he said this. She wondered why.

"But emeralds are way out of my league, Gem."

He doesn't know vintage stuff can be expensive, too, she thought.

He walked around the store, glancing at jewelry in the display cases. Usually, she loved being around him, but she kept thinking about that mystery piece of jewelry in Shake's little velvet bag. It was calling to her.

"You know my mom closed the store for a couple months after her wedding to give me time to think about whether I really wanted to move back here and take it over. I still don't know the store very well. But I do know that we carry estate jewelry. If I find something that isn't priced in the vicinity of the Crown Jewels, I can bring it by the church later."

"That would be great, thanks." His hand was on the doorknob, but he turned and winked at her. "You cut your hair."

In a self-conscious gesture, she reached up to touch her hair and batted her long bangs to one side. Her hair had been waist-length, but she cut it to her shoulders because she wanted to look more professional.

"I like it," he said. "And a new color?"

"Hmm, not really," she lied. She did, in fact, have gold and red highlights added to her mousy brown hair.

"It looks nice, Gem. Matches your eyes." His gaze locked with hers. He seemed to stare right through her. His eyes crinkled up as he smiled. "Don't they say the eyes are a mirror to the soul? Yours are like the forest—

27

deep and dark and a little mystifying, but with just a bit of light shining through."

She felt the blush coming on again. "Is that a good thing?"

"Yeah."

His smile vanished, replaced by shadows, as though something dark and buried had swelled to the top and snuffed out the joy. She was certain that there was something in his past that he had not reconciled with his present.

He tilted his head, then turned to look out the front window.

"Yeah, that's a very good thing. I love the forest. I like to walk there," he said, his voice low. "It's one of the things I like about this place—being close to the woods. You know, for one sweet moment, the world is quiet. If you listen, sometimes you can even hear the dragonflies and the faint ripples at the lake. I go early sometimes and wait for the pools of light hanging between the trees. But honestly, I could spend the whole day waiting for the next move of a grasshopper or watching the ups and downs of a blade of grass. Nature makes you bury your grief when you see the sunrise and—"

He stopped mid-sentence.

She sucked in a quick breath.

As he turned back to face her, his smile reappeared. He laughed and shrugged. "Whoa, sorry. But yeah, the forest is a good thing."

"You sound like a poet, Luke."

"Do I? Then I must be sad and troubled, huh?" He chuckled. "Once upon a time, I thought that's what I'd be. A sad and troubled poet." He gave her a weak smile and opened the door. "Well, see you later, Gemma."

She had a lump in her throat when he left. She watched him walk up the street toward the church, thinking of the first time she met him. She was home from college on spring break. She went to church with her mom and other women to sort through clothes which had been donated for a homeless shelter. Luke was a priest at the Catholic church at that time, but he pitched in. She'd recently lost Antonio and was not remotely interested in romance. Besides, Luke was a priest then. But none of that dissuaded her from wanting this handsome young man to like her. A singular moment that day struck her. His eyes drifted away, fixed on something only he could see. And then he stepped back, away from the others, and leaned against the wall, like boys who were too shy to mingle at a school dance.

Perhaps she was attracted to him because she felt they were kindred spirits. Beneath the good looks and cheerful style, she sensed a loneliness, an 'otherness' in him with which she was all too familiar. Luke had memories, she thought, that bumped up against each other and drove in so deep, it was like a physical pain. She knew because she'd experienced this herself too many times.

Luke's sermons were often self-deprecating. He was clearly capable of experiencing those profound moments of revelation of his own mistakes and failures . . . and he dwelled on them. In one sermon, he said it was important to thirst for criticism of ourselves, to long for what is good in us, so we can strengthen it, and to learn what needs work and rid ourselves of it. She remembered that he said that "being eager for flattery shouldn't be the goal; instead we should seek authentic criticism . . . you don't call a doctor to tell you that you have great bones; you call him to set the fracture within."

Like Gemma, Luke seemed to be feeling his way in the dark, trying to find the light.

She saw him cross the square and slowly march up the church steps. A tiny voice in her head sent up a red flag. This man is complicated. *Then again, so am I.*

She dashed back to Shake, reached into the bag, and pulled out a large ring.

In that moment, in that fraction of a second, the day changed.

Chapter Six

An invisible hand clapped over the gaping mouth of the village, smothering all the sounds and smells that made it quaint and peaceful.

Ensnared in pain, a flurry of emotions rushed over Gemma. It was like hearing the crackle when you step on a twig in the woods and then you hear the snap. You realize that you've triggered a trap, and the strong metal jaws snap shut around your limb. There's no way out.

She hunched over and moaned. All she wanted to do was curl up into a fetal position. Within seconds, a voice in her head screamed, "Let it go! What have you gotten yourself into?"

Shake's voice seemed smothered, muffled, and distant, as he asked over and over, "Gem, are you okay?" He sounded frazzled. Shake never sounded frazzled.

She expelled a breath. No, she was not okay. She felt dizzy, as though all the blood was draining from her body. She knew that she needed to rein in her galloping pulse. She grabbed the edge of the table, then found the chair and sank into it. Her legs felt heavy, like she was crawling through mud. Her stomach twisted into a pretzel, and her throat rattled as she suppressed a scream. Then it was as if a strange creature was crawling over her, prowling around her brain. Still gripping the ring, she winced as she felt a sharp object twist into her lungs. A stabbing pain, like an eagle's talons striking her chest.

She'd never felt agony quite like this.

There was a feeling of paralyzed hopelessness right before she saw the image of an auburn-haired girl falling to the pavement, knowing she could do nothing.

Finally, she locked her eyes on Shake's.

"Gem . . . Gem, what can I do?"

The stabbing pain in her chest again. Though there was no water, she was drowning. Gasping, choking, she clutched her chest and tried to grab air as if it were the most precious thing in the world. Seized by the appalling cramps in her chest, she held her wounded self close. A murmur of sobs, then a whisper, tears on her cheek that weren't really there.

Trembling, she inhaled deeply, swayed a little, then gripped the sides of the chair.

Shake—cool, calm, collected Shake—rushed toward her and steadied her. "Gem, you're white, gray actually. Give me the ring. Forget this, just—"

"No. No. I'm okay." She rose and dragged herself to the sink and filled a glass with water. After she gulped it down, she turned and lifted her eyes to meet his. "It was a painful death, Shake. But quick."

She told him what she saw and felt. Then she went to the sink, filled her glass again, and drained it quickly. Her bangs fluttered as she blew out a breath. She smoothed them back into place.

Staring at the empty glass, she turned to Shake. "It was just . . . really intense this time. Did the victim drown? I felt like—"

"No," Shake said, "but the autopsy report shows that she was stabbed, then drowned in her own blood."

Her own blood. The pain, the piercing pain and the feeling of water swamping her lungs made sense.

"That ring matches a photo of a ring that belonged to a young woman who was murdered five years ago. We never found the perp. The police thought it was a robbery that went south. A few days ago, someone tried to pawn the victim's engagement ring, this ring, at a pawnshop in Cleveland. I couldn't let Father Luke see this."

"Why?"

"The victim was a young woman, a nurse. And, Gemma, she was Father Bailey's fiancée."

Her mouth fell open.

****

It took a moment for her to process this. Dr. Luke was engaged? So, is that why he left the priesthood? This really threw her off kilter. *So much for having a normal day*, she thought.

"Luke was engaged?"

Shake nodded. "Several years ago. Apparently, he planned to leave the priesthood for her. And he did anyway, even though she—well . . .." He inhaled and coughed. "So, do you think you'll get some of your . . . you know, insight? Something that will help me find her killer? Are you even sure you want to do this?"

"Yes, I want to do this. Can I hang on to it?"

Of course, he should not leave the ring with her— but he would.

"Bless your heart, Gem, because no one has looked into this case for a couple years. Like I said, they wrote it off as a botched robbery, but I'm not so sure. Why is the ring just popping up now? I gotta find out."

"You said she was killed five years ago."

"Right."

That's when Luke came to River Styx.

Shake started to tell her more about the case, but she

interrupted him. "I have to get my info from the source." *Because otherwise, no one believes me.* "If I do need more information to follow up on something, I'll let you know."

She put the ring on the velvet platform and took out her loupe, the jeweler's magnifying glass that she used to inspect the gems for inclusions—imperfections—and slight color changes.

"Okay," she said and took a deep breath. Her hands still shaking, she measured the emerald, the main stone, and the round diamonds in the ring. She peered through the loupe and then turned to her computer to do some quick research online.

"Shake, you're looking at an antique Art Deco 2.5 carat Columbian emerald flanked by almost flawless diamonds. These gems are high quality, and they're set in platinum. There's a unique filigree carving on the band. I'd sell this ring for a minimum of twenty-eight to thirty thousand dollars. I doubt Dr. Luke could afford to buy this ring for anyone."

"I know."

He walked over to the sink to get her some more water and banged his head on a cupboard. "Damn," he muttered.

Stifling a laugh, she said, "Shake, I swear, you're as tall as a pro basketball player."

"Got some of them by an inch, in fact. I should have stuck with the basketball career."

He checked his watch and gulped down his coffee. "I have to go. Are you sure you're all right?"

She studied his face. His eyes were tired. His face was worn. "Yes, but are you?"

He whispered, "Yeah."

It occurred to her that the exhilaration he felt when he closed an old case was surely joined by all the angst that he couldn't distinctly separate from it—all the months or years of looking through his own kind of lens and reframing the case and the world of the victim. He saw into the heart and soul of the victims and their families, as well as the killer's; he identified the flaws and omissions in the original investigation and assembled all the evidence again to solve the case. Surely each humble new discovery inspired him to soldier on, but it wore him down. The cost to his psyche had to be immeasurable.

She placed the ring back into the pouch and put it into the safe. "You take care, Shake."

He patted her shoulder. "You, too."

"I'll call you in a day or so, okay?"

He nodded, but he still seemed vexed, and all the calm the vibrant spring weather had brought her disappeared for her as well.

"We'll get to the bottom of it, Shake."

"Of course we will," he replied, but she detected uncertainty in his voice.

She walked him out to the main part of the store, and as he grabbed the doorknob, she said, "Wait, Shake."

He turned.

"Was Luke a suspect?"

"Father Bailey?" He shook his head. "No, no. I mean, sure, we always look at husbands, jilted boyfriends . . . but he had an ironclad alibi. When she was killed, he was with a dying patient in a nursing home on the other side of town giving the Last Rites. That was confirmed. Father isn't on the list of suspects. Not that we even have any sort of a list."

She let out a breath. "Thanks."

When he left, she went outside for some fresh air and looked up at the new sign over the door. She liked that it said Gem's Gems now. All the Martelli men were gone now. It was just Gemma Elena Martelli. She smiled, thinking of her clever mom, making her initials spell out G E M. *I need to give her a call*, she thought.

The last time they spoke, her mother had promised she'd send a plane ticket so Gemma could visit at Christmas, if not before. "I will shower you with designer fashions and Broadway shows," she'd said. Gemma told her mom that depended on whether she was in the middle of another paranormal investigation.

"Murderers and ghosts don't take the holidays off, Mom, but hopefully they won't be paying me visits at Christmas time."

"Hopefully not, honey. You aren't Ebenezer Scrooge."

Murderers and ghosts.

She tried to think of anything but what was in the safe, but good luck with that kind of elephant in the room.

Try not to think of it, and it's all that messes with your brain.

****

Gemma went back to the little room behind the store. A stairway led from this back room to the second-floor apartment. After working on appraisals for a few hours, she flipped the front door sign to "Closed," and locked up the store to go upstairs to have lunch.

She made a tuna sandwich and sat down on the one chair that had a wobbly leg. Every time she forgot and sat in it, she was sure it was going to tip over. She switched chairs and broke off little bits of tuna for Fantasma. She tried to eat, but her chest was painful, and her heart kept racing.

All of a sudden, thoughts, not her own, bombarded her again. The victim inhabited her head, forcing a blizzard of her memories to snow into Gemma's brain. Suddenly she knew that the ring had once belonged to Luke's mother, who gave it to him to give to his girl.

She looked at Fantasma, stared into her intense blue eyes. But it was Luke's fiancée's blue eyes that she saw.

And suddenly she knew that the dead girl's name was Judith.

Chapter Seven

Luke patiently looked on as Mrs. Bloom showed him photos of different arrangements and combinations from which to choose a floral array for the altar for the Mother's Day service. He nodded, but his mind was elsewhere.

Though he'd known Gemma Martelli for several years, it was only since she'd returned to River Styx that he'd really noticed her. Luke's predecessor, Reverend Epley, had told him, "You couldn't find siblings that close anywhere on the planet. Peppi took her everywhere with him. And her grandfather and her dad adored her."

She was pretty and kind. How many twenty-somethings would check on the elderly lady across the street every morning? How many would find the inner fortitude to paste on a smile despite all of her losses?

But she seemed distracted earlier in the day. Maybe he was reading into things, projecting even. He was distracted himself.

For days, he'd felt like someone was following him. He imagined footsteps in the hallway. He thought he heard whispers. He felt it in the church, in the pastoral residence, in the woods, even at the rec center while he was swimming.

The Presence. That's what he called it, and for the last few days, it was very close.

"Which one speaks to you, Dr. Luke?" Mrs. Bloom

asked. "Chancel flowers should symbolize something, don't you think?"

Blinking, he asked, "I'm sorry, what did you say, Mrs. Bloom?"

She frowned. "I asked which one you like and that I think they should represent something."

Forcing himself to pay attention, he agreed. "Absolutely, Mrs. Bloom. So, what symbolizes motherhood?"

"I'm partial to carnations. But then there's anemones. They're wispy and fragile and blow gracefully on the wind."

"I kind of hope there's no wind blowing through our sanctuary, Mrs. Bloom."

"True. But they symbolize love, and they're in season in May."

"How about both then—some carnations and some anemones? What color are they, anyway?"

"Anemones? They come in a range of colors," she explained. "Red, pink, icy blue, white, deep purple."

"Icy blue," he whispered. He immediately thought of Judith's eyes. "How about white carnations and the blue anemones? And whatever else you think."

"Perfect," she said, beaming. "I'll make it beautiful."

****

When Mrs. Bloom left, Luke glanced around the small church office. He remembered the first time he'd been there to see his predecessor, Ralph Epley. The credenza was covered with family photos, and the window sills were cramped with African violets and orchids, all well-maintained by Ralph's wife.

Now it was pretty stark. The flowers and photos

were gone. There were two wing chairs, a desk and chair, and a floor lamp tucked in a corner as an afterthought. A box of tissues sat at the corner of his desk, which was covered with books and magazines, and various reports he needed to review. His office lacked warmth; it wasn't soothing, even though many of his visitors showed up distressed, even hysterical, and in need of calming and counseling.

He thumbed through the stack of magazines and books on his desk—some of them were about supernatural experiences, and some contained articles about religious men, icons, in fact, who believed in ghosts and didn't think it controverted their faith at all. He'd been reading a lot about that lately.

One author mentioned that St. Thomas Aquinas thought that ghosts were real. He said he'd had had several ghostly encounters, and once, he reported that the ghost of a close friend visited him, one he did not even know had passed away yet.

He opened the magazine to the article he'd been reading. The author, a Catholic theologian named Collins, said that separated souls sometimes come forth from their abode and appear to men. He described three types of ghosts: sad and wispy; malicious and deceptive; and bright and happy. The bright, happy ones, he said, are spirits of deceased friends or family members who appear at God's behest to bring messages of hope and love.

He closed his eyes and thought about that for a moment. *If I have a ghost here, which type is it?*

Luke read the article again, for the tenth time, and tried to grasp that this theologian saw no contradiction between believing in ghosts and what Luke believed in.

He wrote believing in heaven didn't mean that spirits didn't exist on Earth. Ghosts, he said, may be in heaven, or purgatory, or hell, but subsequently be able to appear on Earth for some reason. He also proposed that ghosts might make their presence known because they're needy. 'They need something. They're in pain, and they need help.'

Luke's reflection was interrupted by the young couple who had come to see him about final wedding ceremony preparations. He ushered them in, offered coffee, and went over the things that still needed to be done before their wedding. But his mind kept drifting back to spirits.

"Dr. Luke?" the bride-to-be said.

He blinked back to reality.

"I'm sorry, you were saying?"

"Mrs. Bloom is doing all of our flower arrangements for the wedding. Can we get into the church that morning to help with putting the ribbons on the pews and all that?"

"Sure, of course. I'll make a note to myself to be sure the sanctuary is open for you."

"Are you okay?" the young woman asked. "You seem a little distracted."

That's what I said about Gemma, he thought. *But if she really hunts ghosts, like her friend said, why wouldn't she be? More than distracted, in fact. How about petrified like I am?*

"I'm sorry," he said.

He rose with a sigh, saw them out, and then walked back to the desk with the intention of attacking those reports. But he caught the scent of flowers. His gaze drifted to where Mrs. Epley's collection used to be, expecting to see a row of beautiful blossoms on the sill. It was gone, of course.

For crying out loud, why is everything about flowers this morning?

"Roses. I definitely smell roses," he whispered. He went to the church sanctuary and sat down in the first pew. He bowed his head and tried to quiet his thoughts and fears.

But when he felt a light touch on his shoulder, he shivered. He even turned around to see who had entered the church. But no one was there.

Chapter Eight

Gemma didn't feel like eating. Nervously playing with her hair, she made a quick cup of fresh coffee and went back downstairs to the store. After she flipped the door sign over to Open, she started looking through a collection of vintage costume jewelry, hoping to find something that Luke could afford to buy for his mom. Not emeralds, certainly.

In one display case, her mother placed costume jewelry of value. "Most costume jewelry is worthless, Gemma, but there are certain designers whose pieces have become collector's items from people like Coco Chanel," her mom told her. Her mom taught her what to watch for at estate sales, and she intended to add more of those brands to the costume jewelry collection.

Just before her mother went to New York with Dylan, her new husband, she'd sold a signed vintage Chanel Gripoix brooch for almost forty-five hundred dollars, and it didn't have a single valuable gem in it. But the lady who bought it collected Chanel Gripoix. "Beauty is in the eye of the beholder," her mom said.

She opened the display case and took out several pieces of Trifari jewelry that she liked a lot. She found something that might interest Luke, a brooch pin, and matching earrings. She placed this set, and a few other pieces, into a tote. She stopped for a moment. It was recess time. Kids chattering in the playground, lawn mowers and weedwhackers. She went to the workroom again and opened a window. Once again, she inhaled the aroma of the delicate white-and-pink blossoms on the crooked limbs of the apple tree on the lawn of the school. The scent was faintly reminiscent of fresh apple pie. One of the few things she remembered about her nana was the scent of fresh baked bread and apple pies that always filled her grandparents' home.

She felt a chill, a vague feeling of being watched, and she took several deep breaths, willing her fretfulness to a faint ripple. But she knew that this new case could lead to nights of terror and days of confusion again.

She blew up her bangs and swept them sideways. "Stop," she whispered. "You know you're going to do it. Just stop agonizing over it. It's a lovely spring day."

She walked to the square toward St. Aidan Emmanuel Church, Dr. Luke's church. She approached the middle of the square. The rain had stopped, so she sat on a bench near the gazebo and cast her eyes skyward. She glanced up and down the streets leading into the square.

****

The village of River Styx was a quaint township in northern Ohio surrounded by farm country. Less than five thousand people lived there. There wasn't a lot to do, and as a kid, Gemma wondered why her grandfather opened a store there, but he said that he wanted to raise his family away from the city.

Gemma could drive for miles and miles and see nothing but cornstalks and wheat in the summer. In the fall, its treeless vistas and dark, empty meadows were suddenly forgiven by a cheery red silo or a plain, white Amish farmhouse with crisp white, cotton curtains, an

44

oil lamp in the kitchen window, and smoke puffing through the chimney.

She decided to take advantage of the warm, dry weather and strolled up and down the streets. On the main street were her jewelry store, the quilt and fabric shop owned by Jasmine's mom, a vacant building where they used to sell tires, and the courthouse at the corner. She walked down Titan Street, peeking into the windows of the antique shops, and then turned on to Charon, "Church Row," with its three churches: the Catholic parish behind her shop, Luke's Episcopalian church, and a Protestant congregation. Meandering past the funeral home, the small rec center, the town's one gas station, a drug store, a grocery store, a diner, and the post office, she began to see the town slightly differently. It really did have a lot of charm.

As a teen, she often thought it was like an island— and there was no way off. Now it was more like someone had stepped out of a time machine to a slower, easier time. Maybe leaving Chicago wasn't so terrible after all.

When she got to Rockin' Boots, one of the two bars in town and the only one that featured country line dancing, she leaned closer to study the images on a poster in the window. "Line dancing lessons on Friday Night."

Hmm, could Luke dance with that injured leg?

"Maybe you should ask him."

Her head swiveled as the female voice spoke. Despite the rays of sun warming her face, a cold chill rippled through her because there was no one there.

The woman's voice was calm. Young and sweet. With that looping through her mind, Gemma came to a dead stop and turned around. Trying to wrap her mind around the possibilities, she picked up her pace and walked briskly toward the church. When she got to the front steps, she ran into Mrs. Bloom. "Hi, Gem. You on your way to see Dr. Luke?"

"Yes, Mrs. Bloom."

"I helped him pick out floral arrangements for the Mother's Day service. You know, in case enough people don't donate in honor of their mothers. Which," she added, "wouldn't surprise me with some of the thoughtless people around here these days."

"Anyone in particular, Mrs. Bloom?" Gemma teased.

Her eyes narrowing, Mrs. Bloom replied, "Oh, you know how Mrs. Ratty is. She's a burr in my butt. So are a few other book club members. You saw the torrent of protests at our last meeting about paying for an author's lodging. Especially from Acantha Ratty. But I have great news!"

"Which is?"

"Some relatives of your friend Jasmine are moving here soon, and one of them knows an author—a bestselling author, no less—and, apparently, she has relatives near here. She's going to come and speak to us in August at no charge."

"That is great news, Mrs. Bloom. Very exciting!"

Mrs. Bloom shook her head back and forth. "You know, I realize that Acantha Ratty is going through a rough time, but—"

"But?" Gemma asked.

"She and her sister are looking after their mother—she fell and broke her ankle. Acantha is spewing a bunch of sibling rivalry baloney to that poor old woman. Trying to make her mother feel bad that her sister Clio was her favorite or something." She shook her head again. "It's just so . . . Acantha."

Gemma smiled. Mrs. Bloom's bubbly outlook, her songbird-sweet voice, her ladylike temperament all masked the stubborn, get-her-done, no-nonsense approach to her floral business and leading her little book club. Bonita Bloom took no prisoners, and Gemma adored her.

"Anyway, enough of that. Dr. Luke said that he is going to diplomatically mention the floral fund next Sunday. Isn't he just the nicest young man, Gemma? I do miss Reverend Epley, but I must say, Dr. Luke is very easy on the eyes, isn't he?"

Gemma blushed and agreed.

"You know, now that he isn't a priest anymore, he'd be quite a catch for the right young woman." She nodded slightly. "Quite the catch. And wouldn't you be the most beautiful bride?"

Gemma's cheeks reddened even more.

"You have a good day, Gemma." She hugged her and then hurried away.

****

Gemma stood at the bottom of the church steps and looked up at the slender steeple and bell tower. It was hardly a cathedral, but its history was not lost on her. It was the oldest building in town, and the most majestic. Constructed over one hundred seventy-five years ago of white stone, it was practically ancient to her. As she gazed up, the wind whipped her hair, and she pushed it away from her eyes. The sunlight beamed through the stained-glass windows as if some unknown source directed it.

Her parents were married there. Her mom and her

new husband said their vows there.

She inhaled deeply, took the steps two at a time, and opened the front door to the church. Blue carpeting led to the altar, behind which was a large, white cross. There were two pulpits, worn, wooden pews, some stained-glass windows, and banners that changed with the seasons.

Standing behind the last row of pews, she did a double take as images of the coffins she'd seen in that sanctuary barraged her brain. This was where services for all four of her grandparents, her father, and her brother took place. After the last funeral, her dad's, she'd vowed never to step foot in the church again. But she couldn't bring herself to miss her mom's second wedding just before Christmas, and she'd been attending church ever since—mostly to see Luke though she didn't want to admit that was the driving force.

Gemma stepped into the center aisle and saw Luke sitting in the pew nearest to the altar, clearly lost in prayer. She pondered whether to turn around, but then heard the soft voice in her head. It was the same voice she'd just heard while walking to the church. It was feminine and youthful, but it was also a mule kick to Gemma's stomach. *"He's still praying for forgiveness."*

"Judith?" she whispered. "It's you whispering to me, isn't it?"

The spirit didn't respond, but a scene played out in her head like a movie reel, as if Judith filmed it and was playing it back for her. She had never experienced anything quite like this.

****

She heard the ticking of a distant clock. Faint, like it was on a wall in the distance. She started to take a step, but her feet felt like they were on slippery stones, and she grabbed a pew to steady herself. She brushed her fringe back and waited.

Her mind staggered from image to image. A toe tag. Pink toenails. Fingernails, clean and short. A flash of auburn hair.

Then came the glint of surgical instruments on a tray—scalpels, scissors, toothed forceps, and oscillating saws, large knives, and rib shears.

She saw the clock. One o'clock. The afternoon after Judith was murdered? She gripped the back of the last wooden pew. "Oh, God," she whispered. *I'm seeing an autopsy suite.* Gemma held her breath. *This can't be happening.*

Judith lay on a cold, steel table. Her hair spilled in loose ringlets over the sides of the shiny table. Even now, she could have been sleeping.

Her eyes were closed. It was easy to imagine the spray of roses on her cheeks on a crisp, autumn day or one trinkling streamlet escaping her eyes as she held the hand of a dying patient.

But her skin was gray and lifeless, her arms limp. She was the worn-out rag doll that your mother tosses in the trash when you aren't looking.

She heard a man's voice. "She left work a few minutes after eleven, after her shift, and she was found in the parking lot of a Catholic church. She was stabbed with a knife."

Another man said, "We won't know the weapon was a knife until I finish my postmortem. This your first homicide?"

Gemma could see the young detective and the medical examiner now.

"Yeah," the detective answered. "And we think it was a knife.

"Her name is Judith Walsh. She was wearing a black sweater under a thick red vest when she was stabbed, and the people who found her say the wound produced only a small amount of visible blood. The single knife tear within her clothing wasn't immediately obvious. The people who found her initially thought that she either fainted or experienced a seizure.

"She was transported to the clinic," he explained. "She worked there as a nurse, by the way. A doctor saw blood seeping through her clothing while two paramedics continued to perform CPR. He immediately ordered them to stop. Her blood-soaked bra was cut from her body to reveal a single stab wound. She was pronounced dead by a physician at 12:49 a.m."

As he looked down at the body, a single tear leaked out of the corner of his eye. "I've seen her before. My aunt was there at the clinic a few months ago. This girl took care of her. She was nice."

The medical examiner catalogued her personal effects.

Her clothing. A watch. A cross around her neck.

He examined her body. "No scars, no tattoos, or other marks except abrasions near her left ear. There is no evidence to show any form of sexual assault."

He made a few humming sounds. He cleared his throat. With his hands deep inside the chest cavity, he looked at the detective. "The knife penetrated the breastbone, piercing the right ventricle of the heart and severing her pulmonary artery, causing extensive hemorrhaging into her chest cavity. She would have been unable to scream for help because essentially, she drowned in her own blood. Death occurred within five minutes."

At this point, Gemma felt faint and dropped her tote to the floor. She gripped the top of the pew as hard as she could.

She wanted this connection to end. But it didn't.

Her brain was disappearing as Judith's own memories washed over her. It was as if she was in the room, standing there, looking down at Judith lifeless body. That paroxysm, that 'sudden attack or violent expression of a particular emotion' she'd read about—that's exactly what she felt.

The ME stepped back, rubbing his chin. He moved his head side to side, stretching his neck, then made a gesture with his right hand. "The assailant was facing the patient when he stabbed her, and he or she was right-handed."

Gemma heard the clock again. Tick, tick, tick.

Now, the ME stood next to Judith's body with a tape recorder. "This is Dr. Thomas Patel. The date is October 2, 2019, and I have conducted the autopsy of Judith Walsh. She was a Caucasian female, age twenty-six, killed by a single stab wound to . . .." His voice faded.

Twenty-six. Just a little older than I am, Gemma thought.

The only sounds above the awful stillness were the steady drip, drip, drip of a leaky faucet and the slow tick of the clock. She tried to blink it all away. It didn't work. She blinked again and again. No dice.

She didn't want Luke to see her like this. She picked up her tote and dashed to the ladies' room near the entrance to the church. Her fingers went white as she gripped the sink. Judith's memories were dark and disturbing—the kind that gave Gemma nightmares. It might be hard for an anchored soul to watch her own autopsy, but it was not pleasant for Gemma either.

Please don't make me see any more!

She shook her head back and forth as if she could shake it away. Like one of her grandfather's old records, the brain movie had jumped a groove, and more ominous images and smells and sounds stabbed at her. A flash of Judith lying in a satin-lined coffin, her nurse's cap tucked into a corner, her ashy, pale fingers wrapped around a rosary and crucifix. The sickening scent of too many flowers, all of them too sweet, all of them a day or two away from wilting. The stifled sobs of mourners.

Deep in her chest, Gemma sensed malevolence. Somehow, she knew that the deeper she delved into this case, the more real the evil would become.

"Judith," she whispered, "You're on Fast Forward. I need you to go back to just before you were killed. I need to know about the assailant. It's the only way we can give you peace."

Nothing.

Still wobbling, she inhaled deeply. Willing her heart to slow and her blood to warm, she made her way back to the sanctuary.

About to tiptoe out of the church, she saw Luke rise and turn his head.

Chapter Nine

Luke gave the church a slow sweep, not sure what he expected to see. Then he saw Gemma.

"Gem!" he called. "I heard footsteps, and I thought . . . never mind. C'mon up." He waved her toward the front pew.

When she reached him, he asked, "You okay? You look out of breath."

She nodded. "I'm fine."

"You look a little gray around the gills, Gem."

Her voice faltered. "So do you." She lifted her tote. "So, um, I. . . well, I brought some jewelry for you to look at," she stuttered.

"But, if this isn't a good time—"

"No, it's fine," he said, waving her toward the front of the church. "Let's go to my office."

She followed him to his office; he gestured to the blue armchair next to his desk. She sat down and rolled out a velvet rectangle.

"Do you want a coffee or something?" he asked.

She licked her dry lips, then searched her purse for lip balm. She pressed the stick to her lips. Then she rubbed her hands up and down her arms.

"Are you cold?" he asked. "The AC isn't on. Do you want some coffee or hot cocoa or tea or something?"

As she lifted her chin, the corners of her mouth turned up into a slight smile. "I'm okay. But could I have some water?"

He got a bottle of water from a mini fridge and handed it to her. She gulped down half of the bottle. She recapped the bottle and gripped it with both hands. He detected a slight twitch in her eyelids, a change in her body language. Tension and anxiety rolled off of her. He hadn't noticed any of this when he visited the shop, and he wondered what on earth was bothering her.

"You sure you're okay, Gem? You really do look a little pale."

She lowered her eyes for a moment, then looked up and flashed a smile. But her voice quivered. "Do I? No, I'm fine."

She inhaled deeply. Her fingers twitched as she placed some jewelry on the velvet. "I brought you some vintage jewelry. Real gems—you know, emeralds and diamonds and such—that's expensive. But some vintage costume jewelry is pricey, too."

He flicked a glance at the jewelry. "It is?"

She nodded. "Some of it. Certain brands are in demand by collectors. Depending on the name of the designer—if they were famous—some pieces are worth a thousand dollars or more. It's all about supply and demand."

"Well, a thousand dollars is too much for my coin purse."

"I know—I mean I figured you didn't want to spend that much. But I brought a variety for you just to look at and have an idea of what qualifies as a collector's item, not your run-of-the-mill costume stuff." She pointed to a piece on the velvet. "Here's a vintage piece from the Crown Trifari collection. It's from the 1940s. It's called a pink coronation brooch with a jelly belly paste crown.

It costs eight hundred."

He whistled. "I had no idea costume jewelry could cost that much." He picked up a piece which to him looked like a brooch, something a woman would wear on the lapel of her coat or blazer. "How much is this?"

"That one is very rare. Circa 1941. Mom said to price it at a thousand dollars. It's a signed vintage piece, a Jelly Belly Lucite Sailfish Fur Clip Brooch."

"Jelly belly?" he asked.

"The bellies of the featured animals were always made of colorful Lucite. And this particular collection of faux pearl jewelry looked like the real thing. In fact, a former first lady wore a Trifari pearl choker to her husband's inaugural ball. That was the first time that costume jewelry was worn at a presidential inaugural event.

"I just wanted you to know that even if it's costume jewelry, it isn't necessarily cheap or crappy."

He put it back down. "A thousand dollars is way out of my league."

He looked at a few more pieces, then asked, "How'd you learn all this? At that gem school you went to?"

"No. Well, yes. I learned a lot when I was working at a store in Chicago after I graduated, but mostly from Mom and from Nonno before he died."

"That's very cool, Gem."

They locked in a stare. She was close enough for him to catch the slight scent of her cologne—a mixture of roses and glycerin. He recognized the scent because it was one of Judith's favorites.

She looked away, then down at the jewelry. She picked up a couple of pieces. "I was thinking of this for your mother. It's a vintage set, a brooch, and earrings.

It's called Peas in a Pod. They're not emeralds or real pearls—the pearls in the pod are faux pearls. But it has the green you said she likes, and it's valuable."

"How valuable?"

"My mother had priced it at . . .."

"At?" he asked after she stopped speaking.

"I'll sell it to you at cost. A hundred dollars."

"Gem, what is it really worth?"

"Mom priced it at around three fifty, but like I said. A hundred dollars."

"Which means you're giving me a deal. And you don't have to do that."

She tilted her head and smiled. "And so what if I am? If you like it, I'll wrap it up nicely for you."

He grinned. "I can bring a check over tomorrow. I think Mom would really like this."

"You said she has emerald earrings. Does your dad buy her expensive gifts?"

"My dad is an—" He stopped short. He despised his father. They had not spoken in years.

"Well, this set may not be emeralds, but it's coming from the heart. I'm sure she'll love it."

"Thanks, I'm sure she will."

She put the jewelry back into boxes, rolled up the velvet, and stuffed everything into her tote bag.

"You sure you don't want a coffee?" he asked. "I make a pretty mean latté."

She tipped her head to the side. "Rain check?"

He tried not to show his disappointment. There were things he wanted to talk with her about—things that had nothing to do with costume jewelry. "Sure."

"I'll come by tomorrow with the gift, Luke. I'll have it all wrapped and ready, and you can give me a check and a latté. Does that work?"

"Absolutely. Say, around six? After you close the store?"

"Okay, I'll see you then."

"I'll just see you out," he said. He walked back to his desk to get his coffee mug and gestured for her to go first. She took two steps toward the hallway. He gripped the mug tightly, then reached out to touch her arm. "Wait, Gem?"

She whipped around to face him. "Yes?"

She was an inch away, and he felt his breath hitch. He opened his mouth to ask her to dinner but thought better of it. Memories served to sabotage his effort to move on. His gaze settled on her ears. "Um, your earrings—the ones you're wearing . . . a replica of Monet?"

She nodded as her fingers went up to the drop earrings she was wearing. "Right, replicas of his *Water Lilies* painting. I got them at the Smithsonian in DC."

"Well, anyone who wears Monet has class."

She tilted her head and said, "Thanks."

"And Gem, I was just thinking . . . I was wondering . . .."

"Yes, Luke?"

"Um, nothing," he said, shifting his feet. "Have a good evening."

Is that disappointment on her face?

"You, too, Luke. See you tomorrow."

She disappeared out the door, and he let out a shaky breath. The truth was that ever since Gemma had returned to the village, she had been in his thoughts almost daily. Uncharacteristically, he went out of his way to talk to her at church gatherings or if he ran into her anywhere—sometimes he even crossed the street to bump into her on purpose. He often wondered if she had figured that out.

He hadn't had any relationship since Judith—except the one he had with the bottle that nearly got him killed. A thousand times he mulled over why he went ahead with his plans to leave the priesthood after Judith died. But a bit of therapy had convinced him he had never really considered leaving just to be with her. He wasn't cut out for his vocation. He hadn't entered it for the right reason. His therapist told him he probably would never 'get over' losing Judith, but he did encourage Luke to move forward, to pursue a life that would make him happy. He told him, "It's clear that you don't want to be celibate. That you want a home and a wife and kids."

He was right. It was why he enjoyed working with the church youth group so much. He liked playing guitar with the kids and talking out problems with them. He loved going on the annual trip with them to Appalachia to build and repair homes, supervising the teens, but also getting to know them better and having an open-door policy if they wanted to talk. He was pretty sure that, given the chance, he'd be a much better father than the one he'd had.

Gemma was still in college when he first met her, but that had changed. She was a lovely young woman now, running a business on her own, confident, and strong. Even if she didn't have an ability to speak with spirits—if indeed there was any truth to that—she would have intrigued him.

He picked up one of the magazines he'd been leafing through before she arrived but shifted his attention to the window so that he could watch Gemma cross the square.

How strange was it that he was ready to spill his guts to her about this presence that he felt was hovering over him.

The temptation to run after Gem was frighteningly strong, but he pushed it away. Getting involved with someone meant getting hurt again. He wasn't ready for that.

Chapter Ten

When she got back to her shop, Gemma saw that someone had slipped an envelope under the door. She unlocked the door, picked up the envelope, and ripped it open. Inside was a note from Shake and a certificate. She locked the door again.

Shake wrote, *This is a copy of the certificate of authenticity that was submitted to the insurance company. Just wanted you to see it.*

She went to the back room, and, still shaky, she took several deep breaths and splashed water on her face. She unlocked the safe, retrieved the ring, and went upstairs. Her stomach rumbled, so she took her half-eaten tuna sandwich from the refrigerator and made another cup of coffee.

As she sipped her coffee, she heard Judith's voice again.

"He's going to ask you to dinner."

"How do you know that?" Gemma whispered.

"Because that's exactly how he tried to ask me out the first time. It took him like ten more times."

"Well, then, one down, nine to go."

"Be patient," Judith urged.

Gemma sat at the table, wiped her sweaty forehead with a tissue, pushed her bangs from her eyes, and tucked her curls behind her ears. She twisted her hair into a bun and secured it with a claw she found in her purse.

Munching on her sandwich and holding the ring in her other hand, she perused the certificate.

Mineral type – Natural Beryl – Emerald. Color – Green. Shape – Square Cushion. Measurements – 8.97 x 8.95 x 4.89.

A diagram appeared on the left side of the certificate.

Cutting Style – Step cut. Set in 14K gold with six round diamonds.

A second diagram also appeared on the left side of the certificate. 'It is the opinion of this laboratory that the origin of this material would be classified as Columbia. This is an antique certified Columbian Emerald and Old Mine Cut Diamond Ring, circa 1890.'

The certificate was dated September 10, 2000.

"2000," she said to herself. "Luke would have been about six."

She took her cell phone from my purse and called Shake. "Hey, I got the certificate you put under my door."

"Yeah, I forgot to give it to you."

She was about to ask how much the insurance company paid Luke when Judith's voice intruded. *"Not Luke. His father . . . pay-out. But Luke's mother gave the ring . . ."*

Gemma felt her jaw begin to twitch. "But Luke's father was the insured on the ring?"

"Yes, that's right. Father Bailey's dad. How did you know that? Never mind," he added quickly. "You were right about the ring, Gem. They actually paid out more— almost forty grand. But Luke's mother gave him the ring so he could give it to Judith.

"According to notes in the case file, it was originally

a gift from his dad to his mom," Shake advised. "But the insurance on the ring was never changed. So, for insurance purposes, it was the old man's property."

"Was he a suspect? In Judith's murder, I mean?"

"Not really. I did a little digging. He does seem to be on the shady side, and while forty grand would be motive for a lot of people, his record is clean. Plus, he's loaded. Nothing whatsoever ties him to the murder. He and the wife had been divorced for years, and according to all the statements I've read, he didn't even know that Father Bailey was thinking of leaving the priesthood or that he had a girl or any of that. According to a statement Father Bailey made at the time, his dad wasn't aware that his ex-wife gave the ring to Father Luke. They were estranged. He said his dad never met Judith, that he didn't know anything about her or the engagement."

Given what Luke said, that didn't surprise her.

"The ring was in my purse," Judith whispered.

"Shake, I've been told that the ring wasn't on her finger. It was in her purse."

"Which is one reason that it got written off as a robbery gone bad. The killer fled the scene. The empty handbag was found in a dumpster, but there were no fingerprints other than the victim's. Same with the ring when we got it from the pawnshop. Whoever stole it wasn't stupid."

"The insurance company wouldn't have known it was in her purse, but they paid anyway?"

"True, but according to statements from all of her co-workers at the clinic where she was a nurse, she did wear it to work, but she took it off during her shift. Her things went into her locker."

"So, it was assumed that she just wasn't wearing it?"

"I suppose it could have been on her finger—but there was no sign of a struggle, Gem. We also searched her apartment end to end. No ring there. Based on the statements from her co-workers, the insurance company paid the claim."

"I was giving it back."

Judith was giving the ring back? Whoa.

"Shake, I gotta go. Talk soon."

"Wait, Gemma. You need to be aware that Judith's killer is still out there. If there's more to this than a one-off robbery and he finds out that we're investigating . . . that you are involved in it in any way . . . look, it's different than the cornfield corpse. We're pretty sure we know who killed Marjorie, and I found out just this morning that her husband is in a nursing home—wigged out, in a memory unit. But right now, Judith's killer knows nothing about you. I want it to stay that way. You funnel everything back through me. Understand?"

"Understood."

****

Gemma kept waiting for Judith to say more. She sat at her kitchen table playing with Fantasma, who leaped and pounced at her favorite toy—a fake feather tied to a long rope. Gemma tugged on the rope to make the feather wiggle and slide while the cat pounced and jumped at it.

Fantasma tired of playing and made it clear she wanted food. She nudged her bowl, then buried her nose in it and turned to Gemma, flashing her baby blues with urgency. Gemma appeased her with fresh water and a full food bowl. Then she sat down again, and as the hours ticked by, she kept mulling the situation over in her mind, begging Judith to intrude. But she didn't.

Finally, she warmed up a can of soup, ate, changed for bed, and turned on the news.

She put Peppi's Italian horn and Antonio's diamond studs back on as she often felt naked without them. Putting the earrings back on tonight proved to be a mistake. The mattress depressed in the spot next to her on the bed.

"Caro, you need to rest."

"Don't 'beloved' me, Antonio. And what is it about you being here that leads you to think that will be restful?"

"It worries me when you can't sleep. When you have all these problems on your mind."

"Maybe if you hadn't decided to be Evel Knievel on that ski slope in Italy, I wouldn't be so uneasy all the time. I'd have you to come home to, to talk to, wouldn't I? But Antonio, you're gone. Why don't you just make yourself really be gone?"

"Because I worry about you. And I am sorry I left you, my Gemma."

She sighed. It was hard enough to deal with the fact that she would never see her lover again, let alone that he wasn't really quite gone, and she never knew when he'd invade her thoughts . . . when he'd move a piece of clothing or sneak into her dreams and make her feel like he was still in her arms. But she didn't really know what she'd feel if he completely disappeared.

"Amata, ragazza amata—"

"What did I just say? I'm not your 'love' anymore. You died. Peppi died, and Nonno, and Dad. And then Mom went off to New York. It's pretty lonely these days. Just piss off."

The mattress bounced back to shape.

Good. He knows I'm in no mood to deal with him.

****

It was lonely—especially since she could tell only a few people about her gift. If word got out, it would spread like wildfire. When she was growing up, some people suspected she was 'different,' and Luke already knew a little about her belief in ghosts. They'd had a chat about it a little while back at the funeral of Mr. Finch, who'd been the local funeral director. That had been a strange conversation.

Finch's son, who would take over the funeral home, said something about St. Joseph of Arimathea being the patron saint of undertakers.

"Wow. Is there a patron saint for everything?" Gemma asked.

Luke said, "Yes, there pretty much is. You don't believe in saints?"

"I didn't say that."

Her sassy friend Jaz, who was sitting with them at the time, opened her big mouth. "It's a two-way street, though."

"What do you mean?" Luke asked.

"Well, people ask saints for help but—"

"But what?" Luke asked.

Though Gemma shot daggers at her, Jaz went on her merry way. "Ghosts often ask Gemma for her help. She helps them get closure."

Gemma wanted to strangle her. She never advertised her gift.

At first, Luke stared at Gemma, then began to probe. She didn't elaborate a great deal. She glossed over her gift, but from the questions he asked and the posture of his body language, she was certain he had trouble with the concept. That was no surprise.

Later, when she got Jaz alone, she screamed, "What came over you? What were you thinking?"

Jaz simply shrugged. "I've dreamed of the two of you together. He'll find out some time. He'll be okay with it."

Gemma highly doubted that. Though her mother always told her the "right person will understand," she could count on one hand the number of people who actually did embrace her gift. Her mother, her brother, Jaz, Antonio, and, recently, Shake.

A few days later, at a church raffle, Luke brought it up again. He said people were talking about Shake being at her shop. The whole town was curious about why he would pay her a visit, speculating what "that Gemma Martelli might have done." She didn't betray any details of the investigation, but she told Luke that sometimes she received little pieces of information about cases that help the police.

"That sounds awfully cloak and dagger," he said. "And this supernatural stuff that Jaz mentioned . . . you're not saying you're a psychic, are you?"

She stiffened and clenched her jaw.

It didn't surprise her that most people, especially police officers, had misconceptions about people like Gemma—tarot card readers, psychics, ghost hunters. Some were carnival grifters. Some were scam artists. Some genuinely wanted to aid bereaved lost souls on Earth, or like Gemma, wanted to help not only the spirit but the police if there'd been a crime. If her unique, little niche helped the police catch robbers or killers, all the better.

Unfortunately, it was not as easy as Hollywood

portrayed it. Few mediums actually saw ghosts. Few heard an entire story. Her mom just saw a misty kind of fog. The spirits never solved the case, and neither did Gemma. The spirits could just give so much, and she, in turn, could just relay that, nothing more.

She and Luke quickly called a tenuous truce and changed the subject, but he was clearly skeptical. He dropped it then—and it hadn't come up since. Now, with the investigation into Judith's death being reopened, if he discovered she was involved, she had the feeling it would not go well.

Chapter Eleven

After a restless night, Gemma dragged herself out of bed, showered, and dressed in business casual for a jewelry trade show in Dayton, Ohio. There were a ton of these all over the state throughout the year, and her mom often traveled to most of them. It was one of these expos that brought Dylan, her new stepdad, to Ohio.

He was a buyer for a big jeweler in New York City and traveled all over the place, looking for gems for custom settings. He was also an avid country line dancer, and when a friend who lived near River Styx recommended Rockin' Boots, he met Gemma's mom there.

Not long after he met her mother, he asked her to marry him. Gemma dropped her jaw when she saw the engagement ring. She often thought a rock that size would send a woman straight down to the ocean floor if she went overboard on a cruise.

After Gemma gave Fantasma her breakfast, she gulped down a bowl of oatmeal and got on the road to Dayton. Since the drive would take about two hours, she hoped that Judith would intrude into her thoughts and give her a few more clues.

She was about halfway to the show when she heard Judith's gentle voice, this time in snippets—a word here, a word there. *"Clare"* . . . *"Pawn"* . . . *"Fence"* . . .

None of it meant anything . . . yet.

When her cell phone rang, she jumped. She glanced at the number—it was Shake.

"So, anything yet?" he asked.

"Your impatience is showing."

"So, you haven't—"

At times like this, Gemma would have given her right arm for a tornado of words swirling into her head, but the messages from most spirits came to the medium in quiet whispers, in bits and pieces, like a short clip from someone's entire speech or a short preview of a movie. There were only small clues to the pain and deep-seated anger or bewilderment that they channeled through whispers instead of screams.

"Shake," she said with infinite patience, "standard operating procedure for spirits is a hint here, a clue there. Getting a complete story is unusual."

"Sorry. It's just that you definitely seemed on to something when you first held the ring."

The fact that she'd heard actual complete sentences from Judith the previous day and that she was able to see and feel some of the woman's memories—very traumatic ones, like the attack and the autopsy—was highly unusual. She thought that perhaps it was her connection to Luke that gave Judith the strength to communicate with more clarity.

"Yeah, but that was yesterday. Judith isn't on a strong audio frequency on Spirit Radio today."

His gasp came through the lines loud and clear. "You know her name?"

"Yes, I do."

"But I didn't tell you."

"Nope. Hang in there, Shake. I'll be in touch, promise."

She hung up and sighed. She didn't have the ring with her, and she wasn't with Luke. Was that why Judith was AWOL?

****

One of the parts that was most difficult for Gemma was the sitting-still-and-being-quiet part that her mother always urged. She thought back to when Judith came through loud and clear—in the church, with Luke nearby. And again, when Gemma had the ring in one hand and the provenance in the other. Both times, it was quiet, peaceful, still . . . and she was listening. "No matter how strange the message is, you need to listen," her mother told her, "even if it doesn't make sense at the time."

I'm really missing you these days, Mom.

Gemma exhaled slowly. "Judith, I know that you want to give me hints I can build on. I promise I'll help you do that. I'm listening."

As she continued on her drive, she turned off the radio. She tried to blank everything out. But she was getting nothing, and her mind wandered to Luke.

I'm just thankful that Luke still talks to me, she thought. *But I wonder—as this case proceeds, what will I need to reveal to him? What secrets must I try to get out of him? Will he be completely turned off if he finds out the extent to which I use my gift? The last thing I want is for him to be afraid of me.*

****

Doing what she did definitely made her strange . . . a freak. The idea of communicating with ghosts frightened most people. There were a few people who'd experienced something of a spiritual awakening about her gift. She counted Shake and a couple of police officers back in Chicago among them. They were willing to search in unorthodox ways for answers to the questions they had. But in the past, and even now, psychics and mediums were seen as evil. In times past, they were labeled as witches and were often burned at the stake, just for having a rare gift.

Her own maternal grandmother refused to speak with anyone about her gifts except Gemma's mother. Her mom said it was because as a child in Sicily, Nana was often shunned, called a *strega*, or witch. Her Randazzo family from the northeastern part of Sicily near Mount Etna boasted a long line of *stregas*. The so-called witchcraft of her grandmother was her use of herbal remedies, and the spirits came to her in the form of dreams, much like her friend Jasmine experienced. Some people had revered her nana, but most feared her. She, and her mother before her, wore an amulet, a *cimaruta*, the one that Gemma found in the attic as a child when she first encountered her grandmother's ghost. She still wore it sometimes.

****

The trade show was pretty successful. She saw some jewelry buddies and had coffee with a few. She picked up some nice costume pieces for her customers who were collectors. She made some new contacts, which could make all the difference in the world when you run a small jewelry business.

One gal named Pam told her about a scary moment a few weeks before. She also had a small jewelry store in an upscale suburb. A young guy, dressed in a hoodie, came into the store, refused to take off his sunglasses, and tried to sell her a pretty expensive ring.

"My radar went up," Pam said. "He wouldn't take

his sunglasses off. I told him I needed to see his face. He got all fidgety and belligerent. He had his hands tucked into the front pocket of his sweatshirt, and I thought, 'This dude's got a gun.'

"He didn't, but he threatened me—you know, one of those 'you better watch your back because I'm watching you' spiels. I called the cops, and they picked him up, and sure enough, he was trying to fence the ring he stole."

When she said, "trying to fence the ring," Judith's words came back. Someone had tried to fence Judith's ring. Maybe that was where this was leading her. Gemma decided she needed to learn more about pawnshops and jewelry thieves.

Chapter Twelve

On the way home, Gemma stopped by the quilt shop to see if Jaz wanted to have coffee. Jasmine Laveau had been her BFF since grade school. They were both 'freaks' to the kids at school. She would 'talk to herself' when she was communicating with a ghost, usually her nana. Jaz interpreted dreams and 'granted' wishes that often came true. Gemma had had her working on one for a long time—making Luke notice her.

She pulled into the driveway of the quilt shop Jaz ran with her mom. Gemma couldn't sew a straight line, but she loved walking up and down the aisles to look at the beautiful fabrics, especially the ones Jaz found in other countries. She had the best job ever—she traveled around the world to purchase unusual fabrics for the shop and to sell them online. Oriental fabrics, French toiles, colorful Kente cloth, a fabric with a basket-like pattern that mostly came from Ghana.

Jaz charmed everyone she met. She had managed to overcome the fact that she was different from most people because of her dream interpretations, and the fact that she was part of Shake Williams' extended family, the first Black family that moved into the outskirts of the township.

Jaz greeted Gemma at the door with a hug. As usual, she wore her hair in tight, waist-length braids with some purple streaks. Today, she wore a raspberry African-print body-hugging blouse over black slacks, sky-high black heels, and huge gold hoop earrings. Her long nails matched her blouse.

Gemma followed her through the shop. Halfway down an aisle, a bolt of fabric flew off a shelf and, suspended in the air, floated in front of her, blocking the way. It was embroidered tulle with mirror sequins. It glittered and shimmered in the light. She'd heard rumors about 'that strange fabric shop,' but though Gemma had been in the shop a hundred times, nothing like this had ever happened.

"What the—"

Jaz turned. "Well, look at that," she said, calmly putting the fabric back on the shelf. Her fingers lingered on the material. "This will drape well," she said. "The sequin lines will be easy to work with."

She grabbed a pair of scissors, snipped off a corner of the fabric, and handed it to Gemma. "This is a new row of fabrics, specialty fabrics for brides and bridesmaids. Our cousins from Louisiana are moving in next door. One of the girls is an excellent seamstress, and she's going to do some tailoring and also make dresses for weddings—for brides and bridesmaids. This one chose you."

"Chose me? Did you say the fabric chose me?"

"According to Mom, when a prospective bride comes in, the fabrics she should use for her dress and her attendants will reach out to her."

"But Jaz, I'm not a prospective bride."

"Yet," she chuckled. "Hang on to this fabric swatch. You'll need it someday."

The idea of being a bride mentioned in the space of a couple of days, first Mrs. Bloom and now Jaz . . .

Weird, Gemma thought. Shaking her head, she put the piece of fabric in her purse and followed Jaz to the back room where her mother, Lisette Laveau, was teaching a class. Everyone called her Lady Laveau.

The sewing room had every kind of sewing machine, a longarm quilting machine, and huge tables for cutting and assembling quilts. Gemma waved to Lady Laveau, then she and Jaz continued to the small kitchen in the next room.

Gemma's decision to stop by was spur-of-the-moment, but the table was set for tea.

"I guess that you dreamed I was coming, huh?"

Jaz nodded. "I've had a lot of dreams about you lately, girl."

Gemma sat down across from her. "Now tell me all about your trip to New Orleans."

Jaz grinned and poured two cups of tea. "It was fabulous. I went to all the fabric stores and to the French Quarter, of course. I loved the French Market. I went into MS Rau—it's an antique and jewelry boutique. You'd love it.

"I had coffee and beignets every morning," she bragged. "Those are fritters, and I want to try making some. And I finally got to visit my ancestor's grave in St. Louis Cemetery. It's only a block from the French Quarter. It was easy to find."

She was referring to the tomb of the famous Marie Laveau, the "Voodoo Queen," in New Orleans. Marie was an herbalist, healer, and midwife, and also a so-called practitioner of voodoo, even though she was a devout Catholic—a unique mixture of faith traditions handed down through the ages. Jasmine's family continued that tradition, and Jaz knew Luke well before

Gemma did because Jasmine's family attended the Catholic church next to the park behind the jewelry store—the church where Luke was a deacon while he was a seminary student and for a brief time after that.

Gemma leaned forward. "What was the tomb like?"

"Exciting. I mean, she was really famous."

"And the cemetery itself?" Gemma asked. She and Jaz often enjoyed strolling through old cemeteries to check out the archaic tombstones.

"Very cool, Gem."

"All the movies make cemeteries in New Orleans look really spooky." Gem chewed her lip. "Was it?"

"Very sinister." Jaz nodded. "It feels ancient, for one thing. It's eerily quiet even in the daytime, but especially as dusk falls. I mean, there are broken tomb shells and cobblestones, crumbling above-ground crypts. It's a labyrinth with no orderly layout at all. A lot of the tombs have cryptic, pardon the pun, symbols on them. It's cloaked in age and death no matter where you walk.

"Most vaults were constructed in the eighteenth and nineteenth centuries, and there are tons of famous people buried there, not just Marie Laveau. There's even one of Jean Lafitte's pirates."

Gem reached over to pick up a cookie. "I'd love to go there."

"Well, I told you to come with me!"

"I only just inherited the store, Jaz, so—"

"I know, I know.

"I'm convinced the cemetery is haunted," Jaz continued. "For sure by my great-great, whatever great she is, grandmother, Marie. People have seen her in the French Quarter, especially near her old house on St. Ann Street. She wears, they say, a red-and-white turban tucked around her hair, and brilliantly colored clothes, and she just vanishes. In the cemetery, people have seen her walking around the tombs. If you're there and you mock her powers, you get scratched, pinched, or shoved to the ground."

"Then, not exactly Casper the Friendly Ghost."

Jaz shook her head. "People mark her tomb with three Xs and ask her to help them make a wish come true."

"Is that where your gift comes from, do you think? From Marie?"

She shrugged. "Maybe. Weird, huh?"

Gemma laughed. "Not really."

She drank some tea, imagining what it would be like to visit this place, and regretting that she'd decided it wasn't a good time to take a trip with Jaz.

She took another bite of cookie but stopped mid-swallow when Jaz asked, "So, how are things with you and Dr. Luke?"

Gemma swallowed the cookie, washed it down, and wiped her mouth with a napkin. She swept her bangs off her forehead. "He came into my store and asked me to find something for his mom for Mother's Day. I'm going over to the church in a little while to deliver it."

Smiling, Jaz said, "That's progress. But—" A sudden frown swept over her face.

"But?"

Jaz thought for a moment. "But you're wearing that?"

Gem looked down at her business suit.

"Not sexy. You have a great figure. You have great legs, even though they're on the short side," she teased. "Lose the suit, Gem. Show a little cleavage, and a lot of leg."

Gemma laughed and felt the heat in her cheeks.

Jaz's lips turned down again. She scooted her chair to be next to Gemma and took her hand. "But Gem—"

"What? Another but?"

"Well, it's just that you need to be sure you're over losing Antonio. I don't want you to jump into something if you aren't ready. You know, rebounds don't work out most of the time."

"First of all, Antonio died four years ago and I'm not jumping into anything. Luke bought some jewelry, that's all."

"Here's the thing . . . I'd hate to see you be involved with someone who is going to duck and dive."

Nodding, Gemma agreed. "I know. If he gets to know just how involved I am in—well, I think he's already wary of me and the whole psychic thing, and if he knew everything, the cheese might slide even farther off the cracker."

"Not to mention—" Jaz stopped mid-sentence.

"Spill," Gemma said.

"Well, you know I said at that funeral that I've dreamed of you two together. But like I said, while I was away, I did have a lot of dreams about you. And about him. And also about you and him."

Uncomfortable, Gemma shifted in her seat. "And?"

"Remember, dreams are symbolic. I don't see what's actually going to happen. It's like you—I get snippets."

"And?" Gem asked again.

"I've seen you falling, in slow motion into nothingness. Ditto Dr. Luke."

"Which means?"

"Impending disaster. You were at a gate. It could be literal, like you actually being at a gate of some kind. Or a gate might represent an entrance or an exit, a beginning, or an end. But everything is black. It was like images from an apocalyptic movie, like post nuclear war or something. That's a sign of evil and darkness."

Gem shivered.

"Do you have a new case?"

Gemma shifted her eyes to the floor.

"Do you have a new case from Uncle Shake?"

"You know I can't talk about cases, Jaz."

"I ran into my dear uncle this morning and heard about finding the grave on the farm. I asked about you, and he was evasive. That usually means something is up. Be careful, okay? There's danger, evil all around you."

Gem pushed away from the table and stood up. "Well, I'm on my way to church, so I'll ask for a little help, huh?"

Jasmine's face clouded. "I'm dead serious about this. I don't have dreams like this too often. They're disturbing."

Gemma touched her hand. "I'm fine, Jaz. Don't worry."

"Don't be so complacent. In my dreams, Luke is surrounded by the black cloud." She leaned back for a moment, then smiled. "I'm just being, you know—me. Are you guys getting along okay?"

"Yeah, I think we are. He actually complimented my hair the other day."

She laughed. "Then you're practically engaged."

"But he's . . . I don't know, Jaz. I think that he has a lot of things that bother him—things from his past. Things I'm not sure he can get past. And then there's me and my whole . . . thing."

"You should be proud of your whole thing, baby girl. You're special."

"So are you. Ya know, I really, really missed you when I lived in Chicago."

"Yeah, well, I really, really miss visiting you and shopping on the Magnificent Mile."

"You'll just have to come with me when I visit Mom in New York."

"Deal."

Gem threw her a big smile, gave her a hug, and was on her way.

On the way home, Jasmine's words churned in her brain. Dark things. Evil things. The case wreaked of them. Ghosts, spooky old cemeteries, and frightening dreams could be unsettling, but images of the way Judith died, seeing her on the autopsy slab, knowing that Judith simply could not rest, took creepy to a whole new level.

****

It was too late to bother opening up the store, so Gemma placed the gift for Luke's mother in the store's signature red box. She wrapped it with silver-foil paper and tied a neat ribbon around the box.

She was about to leave when it occurred to her again that everything about this case became more clear when she had the ring in her hand, or she was in the church with Luke. Why not try both?

She rummaged through the cubbyhole where she stored things she usually needed for vacations—like compression cubes and travel size toiletries. She found what she was looking for—a small pouch that she could fasten to a bra and hide under a shirt with credit cards and some cash. She was almost robbed while on a trip with Jaz—they'd been warned that pickpockets were magicians and could get inside zipped pockets, or even tight-fitting jeans, and they'd never know it until it was too late.

Gemma ran downstairs and took the ring from the safe. Per Jasmine's instructions, before she changed into tight jeans, a flattering T-shirt, and a pair of faux leather sandals, she put the ring into her 'bra stash wallet.' She looked at the watch on her wrist, an over-the-top birthday gift from her stepdad, and realized she needed to get going.

She was about to walk out the door when she suddenly recalled Jaz's dream. She sat down behind a counter and folded her arms. What could it mean—black gates and all that? Her friend's dreams always carried symbols and meanings. You couldn't be a descendant of the Queen of Voodoo and not inherit some kind of supernatural talent.

But she felt sparks ignite when she was around Luke. Not a wildfire, not what she'd felt with Antonio. This was more like slow, sizzling embers that warm a whole room. And she hoped for more. She didn't want Jasmine's squishy predictions or the investigation to foreclose that possibility.

She locked the door behind her and headed to the church.

All the way there, she mumbled, "Talk to me, Judith."

Chapter Thirteen

With his feet up on his desk, ankles crossed, Luke sipped a cup of coffee and surveyed his redecorated office. He had spent the morning hanging artwork on the walls, arranging books and some photos of his mother and his favorite uncle, may he rest in peace, on the credenza behind his desk, and parking some planters he'd bought from Mrs. Bloom here and there. His heart a bit lighter than it had been, he took some time that morning to decide what to wear, too. He wore khakis and a blue-and-white striped, button-down shirt with the sleeves rolled up. If he decided to ask Gemma to dinner, he thought he should wear something other than his usual daytime uniform—a T-shirt and jeans.

Engrossed in a magazine article, he didn't hear Gemma walking down the hall. When she knocked on the open door, he nearly tumbled out of his chair. He looked up, dropped the magazine on his desk, and scrambled to his feet. He pulled the sleeves of his shirt down to his wrists. "Hi, Gem. I didn't hear you come into the church. Usually, the sound of footsteps echo down the hallway."

She pointed to the pile of magazines and books that blanketed his desk. "Whatever you're reading must be interesting. You seemed totally engrossed. Is it some gripping mystery?"

He adjusted the stack of magazines and books on his

desk and then tapped the cover of the magazine. "Actually, that's not far off. I've been reading some thought-provoking articles, some you'd be interested in, I think." He pointed to a chair next to his. "Have a seat."

As she sank into the wing chair next to his desk, he said, "So, confession time."

"I thought confessions were a thing of your past."

"Well, me listening to them is, yeah. But, well—"

"Well?"

"I've been reading the opinion of a priest who writes about ghosts."

She lowered her head once in a nod. "Ghosts," she repeated. She touched the Italian horn at her neck, and her eyes took on a faraway look that puzzled him.

"Yes, ghosts," Luke said.

She blinked a few times but remained silent.

"Gemma," he said as he sat down in the matching wing chair. "Here's the thing. I feel like I'm being followed or watched."

"Like stalked or—?"

"I don't know how to explain it, but it has me thinking about what you and Jaz said at the funeral home and then at the raffle. About the whole spirit and haunting stuff and—"

She grimaced and stopped him. "Wait. You mean about ghosts reaching out? Jaz had no business talking about that, and I don't want to—"

"Just bear with me a minute here." He related the essence of the articles and books he'd been reading. Then he held up a magazine. "There's a priest who says that ghosts are real, and he reminds us that we . . . my former church communicates with saints. Intercession and all that. I mean, people ask saints for help, right?"

"Right, like you've said before. Like that saint who finds things."

"Saint Anthony."

"Right." She paused for a few seconds. "And people bury a statue of some saint upside down to sell a house. Mom did that."

"That's exactly right, Gem. Saint Joseph. Not the undertaker's patron saint. The other Joseph. And we've all heard of Christoper, the patron saint of travelers."

"Okay, so—"

"So then, religious people are really just trying to communicate with spirits, aren't they?" he asked. "Maybe it's kind of like that movie with the sacred tree where people can talk to ancestors?"

Feeling agitated, on uneven footing, he rose and walked back and forth as he spoke. "The Tree of Souls, I think it was."

Gemma said, "Right."

He chose his next words with care. "Anyway, this priest mentions all the ghosts that are referred to in the Bible." He tapped on the magazine again. "And St. Thomas Aquinas said the ghost of a close friend visited him before Thomas even knew he had died."

She fell silent for a moment.

"What? What are you thinking?" he asked.

"I have this very specific memory of an encounter like Saint Thomas describes." She placed her hand on the edge of the desk and leaned forward. "When my dad died . . . well, I didn't know he'd died yet because the hospital hadn't called . . . I saw his favorite rocking chair rocking back and forth. Later, when we went to the hospital, we found out that he passed at that exact moment."

"Hmm, do you think your father needed something

from you?"

"No, I think it was just his way of saying, 'Goodbye,' " she said. Then she leaned back in the chair. "Luke, why are you talking to me about this?"

Luke saw her expression change, as if she were listening to someone whispering in her ear. He noticed a flicker of recognition in her eyes. She squirmed in her chair and fidgeted with her hair.

He walked over and stood right in front of her. "This theologian says that ghosts actually support our belief in an afterlife, not the opposite, because they confirm the existence of a life after death. Isn't that interesting?"

He looked over her shoulder and stared out the window. He felt his eyes tear up. He cleared his throat and looked at her again.

Gemma looked stunned.

He sat down again, this time next to her. "I know this is . . . very curious coming from me. But this feeling is extremely strong, and I'm trying very hard to understand it. Your point of view . . . this, these possibilities."

"Like we talked about at the funeral a while back, Luke, we ask them—our ancestors, saints, whatever moniker you want to put on it—for help. And sometimes they ask us for help. Where are you going with this?"

"I'm really not sure," he answered.

She stared at him and then suddenly burst from the chair. "Can you hold that thought?" Without waiting for a response, she bolted from the room.

Surprised, he threw his hands into the air. "Shit," he mumbled. "I spooked her."

Then he laughed at the fact that it was probably a spook that was driving him a little insane.

Chapter Fourteen

Gemma rushed down the hall to the ladies' room. Once inside, she locked the door and slid down the wall to the floor. Her body curled over her knees, she rested her head on her kneecaps, rubbing her temples with the heels of her hands.

While Luke was speaking to her, a darkness, like dusk deepening, cast a shadow over the room. She'd heard Judith's voice. *"He feels me. Because of the ring. Because of you. He feels my presence."*

Gemma rocked on the cold floor tiles. This was the worst possible time for her to make contact . . . while she was there in the church with Luke . . . with him just a few feet down the corridor. She couldn't think straight.

"He misses his lady," Antonio said. *"As I miss you."*

She'd weathered his interruptions at the most inopportune times before, but at this particular moment, she didn't want to think about his spunk or his strength or his comic way of approaching things that bothered him.

She shook her head and pounded her fist on the floor. "Antonio, get out of my head."

"I am always in your head, caro. Don't let him confuse you."

She reached inside her top to grasp the pouch that held the ring. "Judith, what do you mean he feels your presence?" she whispered.

"I need to make him understand."

She shuddered. "Look, whatever it is that you need to tell him, we can get to that, but I need to help Shake—the police solve your murder. I really need your help with this, Judith."

Once again, she heard Judith say, *"Clare"* . . . *"Pawn"* . . . *"Fence."*

"I can ask Shake about it, Judith. Are you talking about the person who tried to fence the ring at the pawnshop? Who is Clare? Is she the person who was trying to get money for the ring? Or is your killer named Clare?"

"He needs to understand."

"You mentioned he's praying for forgiveness. Why?"

No response.

She pounded her head against the wall. She wanted to scream or punch something. "I promise you, Judith, I'll find a way to let him know whatever it is you want to tell him. But first help me find your killer. Please."

She waited a few minutes. Nothing.

But Peppi popped into her head. *"Tell him, 'We are such stuff as dreams are made on, and our little life is rounded with a sleep.' "*

"Peppi, now is not a good time."

"He doesn't really believe in ghosts, Gummy Bear," Peppi said. *"He isn't ever going to understand. Just tell him that life is ephemeral, a dream, and death is the final sleep that completes the circle of existence. Then he won't bother you."*

"Bother me?"

"He's going to pick your brain about ghosts, Sis.

And it's going to get into a whole big thing that will make you nuts."

She stood up, slammed a fist into the wall, and whispered, "You don't know that. He may be a sensitive. I think he feels Judith. But you are making me nuts. You and Antonio. I gotta work this out for myself. Just bug off already!"

The idea that Luke might begin to understand her lifted her spirits. This was huge. He was telling her that he was beginning to see her point of view and, more importantly, he was starting to accept that their views were not mutually exclusive, that they didn't have to be an obstacle. That what he believed and what she believed and knew to be true didn't have to cancel each other out. Perhaps his beliefs and hers could coexist.

But how to help him get through it? The last thing he probably needed was another crisis in faith.

Expelling a breath, she splashed water on her face and smoothed her bangs. Still a little wobbly when she returned to Luke's office, she inhaled deeply again and willed her heart to slow and her blood to warm.

****

"Hey," she said when she returned to Luke's office.

Luke turned from the window.

"Are you okay, Gemma? I mean, did I upset you or—"

"Yeah. I mean, no. I just had a long drive from Dayton, and then I had tea with Jaz and didn't stop to . . . never mind. You did throw me a bit. Tell me more."

His face brightened. "Okay, then. Sit down."

She took a seat again.

"Here's the thing. For a few days, I've been feeling—well, it's hard to explain. I feel like someone I care about, someone who is not with us anymore, is near."

"So, you feel that . . . you're trying to tell me that you think that someone who is dead is haunting you?"

He nodded. "That's right, I guess. I . . . I feel like she—like this person is hovering. Like I've got a helicopter ghost or something."

She heaved a huge sigh. "Look, if there really is a spirit around and you can feel it, it means you have some sensitivity."

"Sensitivity," he repeated.

"Luke, if you are feeling this . . . presence, you may be—" She groped for words. "Will you promise me that you'll just listen—and not interrupt or call for the guys in the white coats to come pick me up?"

He sat down again. "It's hard for me, Gemma, I'll admit. I feel like I've closed my account at the Bank of Sanity. Like I'm whack-a-doodle. But I'm listening."

"Okay," she said, exhaling. "First of all, do you actually see anything? Do you hear anything?"

He shook his head.

"Hmm. Well, there are definitely varying degrees of paranormal sensitivity. My mother knows when a ghost is present, but she sees only a misty form."

"Your mom—she's . . . you're saying that you and she—"

"It's kind of a family thing, yeah. She never hears them or actually sees them, but somehow, she knows why the ghost is stuck on planet Earth. She was the first to realize that my brother Peppi's spirit lingered. As for me, with jewelry, I hear the spirit's voice, but I've never seen one.

"Mom told me once, 'Ghosts come to us in all

shapes and forms. We just cross our fingers that they aren't malevolent spirits and that their problems can be resolved.' "

Since she had no idea where Luke was on the gray scale of the Ghost Communication Network, right about now, she felt like she should be telling him, "Every time you walk into a room, be prepared. Seriously, be prepared to do a double take the next time you walk into a room that appears to be empty."

She shifted in the chair and fidgeted with the hem of her T-shirt. "So, you felt this . . . presence, and you've read these articles, and now you're convinced that maybe souls do anchor themselves here?"

Luke inhaled, and his eyebrows quirked. She couldn't figure out what he was thinking—but clearly, he needed to suss this out. This 'feeling' he had seemed to be driving him crazy.

"I wouldn't say I'm convinced, Gemma. Maybe I just want to believe it even if it's ridiculous. No offense. I've never given this paranormal stuff any thought before."

The way he looked at her, she sensed that he was clearly waiting for something concrete even though he was venturing into a world that was anything but tangible or definite.

"See, if you really do have some potential as a sensitive, which is a person who has increased sensitivity to a paranormal or spiritual energy, then you can experience things beyond the realm of normal human experience. An empath. Sort of."

He played with a pencil. He closed his eyes for a moment.

"Look, Gem, I'm trying to have an open mind about

it because this feeling is incredibly strong. And reading these articles made me feel like it's actually okay to take a look at the possibility. To not be too quick to judge what I don't understand. I mean, even if I cannot see the sun, I know it exists. As a priest . . . well, now as a pastor, I ask people to believe in things they cannot see, things that they cannot touch or smell or hear. Don't I?"

His voice suddenly was more urgent. These new thoughts and feelings, and Judith's presence, had to be clawing at him, shaking his very core.

"Right. Are you asking me to help you with that? Or—"

"I'm not sure, honestly. I guess I wouldn't mind exploring it with you. I mean if you don't mind."

"No, I don't mind. Not at all."

It about killed her not to tell him that Judith truly was hovering and that she had something she needed to tell him. This wasn't the right moment, and the last thing she should talk about right now was Shake's renewed investigation but getting him to talk about why he left the priesthood might lead to more information about Judith that she could use.

"But first, before we forget," she said, pointing to the box on his desk, "there's your mom's present."

"Oh, yeah, I completely forgot about that. I have a check for you."

He opened a desk drawer and handed her the check, and their eyes met.

"Thanks," she said as she put the check in her purse. "And I actually have some questions to run by you, too."

"About heaven or the afterlife or—"

"No, no. I've been curious about how you became an Episcopalian minister. Not why you left the priesthood or any of that," she lied. She hoped if she got him talking about his journey, maybe she could pry more out of him about Judith along the way. "Just the mechanics of it. I know you were a deacon briefly at St. Mary Ascension, and then all of a sudden you were here, doing the whole youth ministry thing, and then you took over as pastor after Reverend Epley left. I just wonder what that all entails."

"Oh—like what I needed to learn about to make the transition?"

"Yeah. Just curious."

He glanced at his watch. "But I wanted to ask you more about—no, never mind." He sighed. "Look, it's almost six, and I'm starving. And there's this Amish restaurant I really like down the road about twenty miles."

"Miller's Farmhouse Kitchen."

"Yeah, that's the one. Would you like to come with me and get something to eat and we can talk more?"

She didn't want to sound too eager. But she certainly didn't want to say no. "You're asking me to dinner?"

"Well, yeah."

"Then . . . yes, I'd love to." She looked down at her beige tee, blue jeans, and sandals. "I'm not exactly dressed for dinner out, though, am I?"

"Me either. But, Miller's is casual."

"Oh, tell her she is beautiful, Priest."

"What did you say?" Luke said, his eyes narrowing on her face.

Oh, my God, did Luke just hear Antonio? Maybe he is more sensitive than he thinks he is.

She squeezed her eyes tight and chewed her lip. *Antonio, just stop.*

She hoped Antonio realized she would have been screaming and throwing dishes at him right now if he were still alive.

"Tell her you think she always looks like an angel and that you think about her all through the day and that you wonder what it would be like to hold her. That is what such a woman deserves."

Antonio, you are incorrigible.

But when Luke looked at her, smiled, and said, "You look great, Gem. You always look great," she wondered if maybe Luke actually heard the nudging.

"Let me go lock up," he added, "and I'll meet you in the parking lot in five minutes."

"Sure, great."

Judith, you're on deck. Help me figure out how to help him. . . and you.

Chapter Fifteen

Luke drove his ten-year-old family-friendly sedan as if it were a high-performance racer and turned the ride into a thrilling escape. The country roads were curvy and hilly, and if you drove too fast, you caught a lot of 'air' and likely lost your stomach contents. Thundering on, he watched his navigation screen for alerts to construction and police. No need to spot flashing lights or hear the wail of a siren this evening.

He kept time with his fingers, drumming on the wheel, to a rock song. Gemma sang along and patted her knees in time with the music.

He wore a pair of aviator sunglasses that slipped down his nose, so he adjusted them now and then. Relaxed, he propped his elbow on the window frame as he navigated the winding country roads to the restaurant. He never tired of the landscape.

The fiery red sun began its descent, bathing the countryside with soft hues. Slow, billowy bells of clouds drifted overhead. He enjoyed driving past the smoldering gold pastures where dairy cows and horses grazed, where rows and rows of corn and soybeans were growing, and pine and oak and spruce dotted the fields.

He wondered what the farmers were doing right now after a hard day's work in the fields. He wondered about the Amish families in the area. He knew they were humble and lived simple lives, that they thought the secular world polluted innocence and promoted too much pride, greed, and materialism. They believed in faith and good works and peace. They avoided television, radios, computers, and modern appliances. What was it like to sever yourself from the electrical grid, from the Internet, from the fast lane of society? Sometimes that was precisely what he thought he needed.

He'd accepted long ago that he was never going to get rich as a priest or as a minister, and that was fine. Greed had turned his father into a monster. But he did love his rock music and his car and modern conveniences. Those would be hard to relinquish.

He glanced at Gemma and caught her sneaking a peek at him. It brought a smile to his face. Father Fowler had chided Luke for being too 'flirtatious.' He accused Luke of speaking his mind way too frequently, and not 'looking like a priest.' Maybe he didn't look like a minister either. He knew it was hard for people to shed their preconceived notions of what they should look like. A celibate, off-limits man wasn't supposed to be vain or rebellious, and he knew that he was guilty on both counts.

They stopped first at the outdoor pavilion to feed the ducks and fish, and he watched her as she ripped off chunks of bread and tossed them into the pond. She was an intriguing combination . . . young and exuberant and enthusiastic, inquisitive and in love with life, and very mature—light-years more mature than the kids in his youth group even though she was only five or six years older than some of them. He patted her arm. "Okay, we fed them. Let's go feed us."

The restaurant was a huge building that looked like

a rustic barn with wood beams and rough-hewn flooring. They went straight to the salad bar and the serve-yourself buffet that had everything from beef and beets to pies and puddings, not to mention the best biscuits and honey butter this side of the Mississippi. They filled their plates and quickly dived into the food, but his brow knitted, he put down his fork. "I never thought to ask you—would you have preferred a restaurant where we could get wine or beer or something?"

Gemma shook her head. "No, no. This is a great restaurant. I love the food here."

"Next time, we'll start with a nice wine."

"A buttery white," she mused. "Or something golden and aromatic."

He grinned. "Something tells me you know your wines."

Smiling, she nodded. "My grandparents on one side came from a little village in Sicily and on the other side, from Genoa. Their ancestors raised grapes and made wine. I'm partial to red wines—I like the light, fruity kinds, or the really deep, rich ones. There's something about a nice wine . . . a pale red or a rich maroon. Each has its own aroma, a unique taste. I love to slide into a bubble bath, nurse a glass of wine, put on some great classical music, and be surrounded by candles and—"

She stopped and looked away.

"That sounds nice. Soothing. Tranquil. Romantic."

They locked in a gaze. "My mom says the best things in life are simple," he said. "A little wine, candles, and a big tub to soak in. She used to do that in the evening after work. I wasn't allowed to come in, of course, but I'd sit cross-legged outside the bathroom door, and we would talk about her day."

"What did she do, your mom?""

"She's Irish, like my father, and they both worked for an Irish guy—they met when he was a dock worker, and she worked in the office. She's always done secretarial work. She still does."

When Luke fell silent, Gemma changed the subject. "Wines."

"Huh?"

"We were talking about wines," she said. "When I was a kid, my grandfather would sneak me a sip during dinner. I thought I'd grow up to be a professional wine taster. That I'd travel around the world, dressed up all the time, show people how to taste and savor, and that I'd taste every single kind before I die."

"That is an ambitious goal and not one this place will help you fulfill. I'm sorry it wasn't the right choice for my wine connoisseur. Next time we go out, I'll take you to a wine tasting," he added. "How does that sound?"

She rested her elbows on the table and linked her fingers. "Oh, okay," she agreed without giving him much of a clue how she really felt.

****

Halfway through dinner, he said, "You know, Gem, when I first came to River Styx, you were just a kid. You were still in college, right? I remember you had a ponytail down to your butt."

She blushed. "I did, didn't I?"

"I was a new priest, and I only saw you once in a while when you were home in the summers from college. And at a couple funerals."

She looked down. "I was a senior in high school when Peppi passed away. Then my grandfather died in my freshman year of college, and my dad passed later that year. It was a lot, and I almost dropped out. I thought Mom needed help at the store. I worried about her taking care of the house all by herself. I worried about her, period."

He reached over to briefly place his hand on hers. His nerve endings tingled, and he withdrew his hands. "I'm sorry, Gem. You really have suffered a lot of losses."

She rested her elbows on the table and propped her chin. "Mom wouldn't hear of me dropping out of school. I think she just wanted to keep her excuse for visiting me at Northwestern and buzzing into Chicago to go shopping on the Magnificent Mile."

He laughed. "I take it your mom loves clothes."

"Definitely. Now that she's married to Dylan and living in New York, she's taking that city by storm."

He whistled and laughed again. "Did you really want to come back here and take over the store after she moved? I mean, after living in Chicago—"

"Oh, I'm not here because I feel obligated, if that's what you mean," she insisted. "But I did like Chicago. I loved taking long walks by the lake—you know, there's a lakefront trail there."

He shook his head. "I've never been there."

"It's a great city. Every Sunday, during the spring and summer, I made it a point to walk along the lakefront, sometimes as far as Navy Pier. The trail is like eighteen miles long or something, and people jog and walk and cycle and skateboard. You can get to all the parks from it, and I used to stop at the zoo—it's on the path. And at the Field Museum and Shedd Aquarium and Soldier Field."

"Oh," he said putting down his fork. "Soldier Field,

now that I'd be interested in. I'd love to see a Bears game there."

"You should go," she said, reaching out to touch his hand.

He felt sparks again. Just that slight brush against her hand sent a zing through his body. Surprised at the physical response he was having to her, he willed his adrenaline not to spike.

"And you should go to Wrigley Field, too, for a baseball game," she urged. "I'm not a baseball fan, but before I left for college, when I was doing campus tours, Dad took me to a game there. You can feel the electricity."

"Sounds like you really liked Chicago. It must have been hard to come home."

"I liked it. But River Styx is home. I was raised here; my best friend is here. I don't like big jewelry store chains, actually. Which is what I was working in. Now that I look back on it, I think I'd have come home eventually even if Mom hadn't moved away."

"Really?"

She nodded.

"Well, I'm glad you're here and that you're . . . well, all grown up. You know, Gem, I feel like I know you," he added.

"Huh? I've only been back a couple months. I wasn't around much when I was in college. And I hardly ever went to church."

"Yes, but your friend Jasmine goes to Saint Mary Ascension, and she worked with the teens whenever she could. She talked about you and your family all the time."

"Whoa, I'm afraid to ask what she had to say."

"All good, believe me. You have a really dear friend there. And I envied both of you."

"Envied?"

"For having such a great friendship. Having someone to talk to about everything. I really never had that until—well, for most of my life. Part of what I missed as a priest was the opportunity to be really close to a person. To know them. To have them know me."

"But surely you had friends growing up?"

"I come from a background of shadows, Gem."

She stared at him but didn't speak.

"And I haven't exactly fit in here in River Styx."

"It had to be hard. Being a priest, I mean. People kind of put you on a pedestal, don't they, Luke?"

He put down his knife and fork. "I hope not. But I don't think it was just that. I never felt that I fit in. Like anywhere."

He picked up his fork again and ate a few bites of potato salad, then said, "You're a beautiful, young woman. I'm surprised no one has snagged you yet."

"I was engaged. Well, actually, almost engaged. But my guy was killed in an accident when we were juniors in college."

"Another loss," he said. "Good Lord, that's what? Four loved ones in the space of a few years? Your grandfather, your dad, your brother." He hesitated. "And your fiancé. I can't imagine."

"You can't?" she asked, tilting her head. "I mean, I'm sure you've lost someone you love."

He hesitated again and dodged the topic. "What happened to him?"

"A skiing accident."

"I'm sorry. I don't know how you got over all of it,"

he said, glancing away.

"You don't get over it. You get through it. People would say, 'in a year or so, you'll get over this.' You don't get over losing someone you love. You push past it, with a lot of work. You . . . you deal with it and—"

"But doesn't dealing with it, doesn't moving on mean you just, well, you just forget the person?"

"No!" she cried. "Moving on doesn't mean forgetting. It means finding a way to go on, knowing that your life is forever different but that it didn't end. You grieve, and you carry pain around—maybe forever, because that person is part of who you are. But if they loved you, then you know they'd want you to be happy." She tilted her head and added, "Anyhow that's what a shrink will tell you."

He leaned back and gazed at her. "You really have thought it all through."

"Like I said, I had a little help from a shrink."

Then he picked up his fork again and added, "But most shrinks haven't actually experienced what makes you need therapy—just like priests are clueless about having a wife and kids but are expected to counsel about it. It's always stuck in my craw."

She laughed. "I guess." She put down her fork and asked, "What about you?"

"Me?"

"You left the priesthood for some reason, but you still ended up in a church in River Styx. Priests go where they're told to go, right? Or did you have a choice?"

"Well, no, we . . . they . . . priests don't have a choice, but I had connections. Someone who pulled strings for me."

"I don't understand."

"My uncle—my father's brother—ran the old tire place—you know, it used to be next to the quilt shop?"

"Yeah, I know—I mean, I never went into it, but I know it was there."

"Well, Mom liked my uncle," he continued, "and even after the divorce, we would visit him. I loved the village, and when my father found out I had entered the priesthood, he made some phone calls. He has this strange affection for the priesthood, and in his weird way, he wanted me to be happy in my vocation. He knew I loved the town and being close to the national park."

"You're kidding! Even though you two aren't close, he helped?"

"Yeah."

"But how—I mean, how do you pull strings to place a priest where he wants to go?"

"Let's just say it's amazing how many people my father knows—and how many people owe him something."

"You make him sound like a mob boss or something."

His eyes narrowed, and he felt the shadow of his past. "Wealthy, powerful people can pull a lot of strings. They can influence people. Mayors, cops, corporate execs. Bishops."

They fell silent for a while after that. As they finished dinner, she asked, "This . . . this presence you feel. Do you think it's a relative? A sister? Grandmother?"

"I was hoping you might help me with that. I mean, you have this. . . gift."

"My gift is a little quirky. I need a piece of the person's jewelry to connect."

"You have limitations?"

"It's not like in the movies, Luke. But, of course, I'll help if I can. Try to tell me what you feel."

"Like I'm being watched. Or like someone is in the room with me. And when it happens, I think I hear her . . . just in my head. A familiar voice."

"But you don't know for sure who it is?"

"Honestly, it's not so much the who as the why. Why the person—the spirit would need to reach out to me. Is that something—I mean, are you able to figure out something like that?"

"Like I mentioned—there are limitations. At least for me."

She explained the jewelry thing in more detail, and then they continued eating dinner in an awkward silence.

After they snagged dessert, he asked, "You wanted to know about my leaving the priesthood and becoming a minister, right?"

"Only if you don't mind talking about it."

He tilted his head. "No, it's okay. I started college when I was seventeen, got my bachelor's in philosophy, and then entered seminary. I started working on a master's and then a doctorate. I was a deacon during my last few months in seminary—at St. Mary Ascension. The priest there, Father Fowler—he was . . . very, very old school."

"So I've heard."

His eyebrows scrunched up. "Huh? How?"

"My best friend Jaz—"

"Oh, of course."

"Her family loved you, though. And they like the new young priest."

"Father Dunlap."

"Right. But they don't like Father Fowler much. They say he's stuck in the Dark Ages and that he's mean."

"Well, working with him sucked." Luke chuckled. "I had moments I wasn't sure I'd survive. One of my duties was to visit the sick from our parish at hospitals, and that I did like. A lot."

She twirled her hair and got that inexplicable faraway look that made him wonder again what was going on inside her head.

"When I decided to leave the priesthood," Luke continued, "I went to talk to Reverend Epley, your old minister. I'd heard he could use some help. He pulled strings for me, too, I guess. Ralph gave me the youth ministry job at his church while I took the courses I needed to become an Episcopalian minister. There's a seminary around twenty miles from River Styx, and I went to classes there and took courses online. It took less than two years, and then Ralph retired. I did a lot of interviews with committees and filled out a lot of forms, but in the end, he must have held some sway, and they accepted his recommendation.

"I was very lucky to find a church in River Styx because I love it here and it was a fairly easy transition."

"So then it wasn't that hard to stop being a priest."

"I didn't say that, Gemma. It was hard. You see, once you're a priest, you're always a priest."

She bit her lip. "But you left. I mean, you stopped being a priest."

"No, I'm still a priest, Gem." He touched his chest. "In here."

He exhaled slowly. It was always difficult to talk to anyone about his decisions. He bowed his head, then said, "And I ask for forgiveness for breaking my vows every single day."

Chapter Sixteen

He sat back in his chair and tossed his napkin on the table. His eyes closed for a moment and then he looked straight at her. "See, here's the thing. A priest can never stop being a priest, Gem."

"I still don't understand."

"Holy Orders is a sacrament; Holy Orders stick."

She pushed back her plate. "But you left. You—"

"It's complicated. Sacraments like marriage, baptism, Holy Orders are supposed to be forever. Once a priest, always a priest. Like I said, complicated."

"But you have a new church," she reminded him. "Why do you still feel tethered?"

His speech was halted, careful. "Look, I love what I do. I really do. I'm happy in my new role. I love the kids I work with, the choir, and the congregation. I love the town I live in. But I guess I wasn't cut out to be a priest. I'm sort of a man of the cloth who didn't want everything that goes with that particular cloth."

She leaned forward, her elbows on the table, hands under her chin. "And you're still conflicted."

"That's a mild way to put it. I realized I wanted to have a wife and kids. That avenue was totally off-limits to me before. Now it's not. But—" He stopped and sighed.

Gemma cupped Luke's hands in hers. Right now, he just needed a friend. Someone to listen. "I'm not very wise. I'm barely beyond being a kid but—"

He rubbed the top of her hand. "I disagree. You're an old soul. One who carries things that others cannot see."

She inhaled and went on. "There you go, being a poet again."

He smiled. "I think that your song remains unsung, Gemma. There is a part of you that remains ineffable."

"Ineffable?"

"Beyond words."

She gave an uneasy laugh. "Oh, I missed that word in my daily Word of the Day ritual. And as for being an old soul or whatever, sometimes I take two steps forward, three steps back. Sometimes I trip and do a face plant."

"Don't we all?"

"But if I've learned anything, Luke, it's that you just have to accept who you are and keep moving. Otherwise you can't face whatever is ahead." She let out a long breath. "I know that some people strongly believe that marriage—and the priesthood are forever. One and done. And that's fine. But it just seems to me that if you realized you couldn't be the kind of priest that you needed to be, that if you want a family—a wife and kids and a picket fence and a dog named Spot, and shelves and shelves of books of poetry—"

He smiled. "Yeah, all that stuff."

She squeezed his hands. "Then you have to accept who you are, right? My brother Peppi used to recite poems to me—he loved Shel Silverstein's poem that goes something like, 'There is a voice inside of you,' and he'd tell me that if it felt right, to listen to it.

"I'm not a shrink—but I had a good one," she added,

"and the world's best brother."

He smiled widely. "Me, too. The shrink part."

Her eyes widened. "You have?"

"Everyone needs a shrink on their contact list. On speed dial, even."

She laughed. "Definitely. But what I'm saying is, can't you find a way to love your new life—this new life you've chosen? You're good for the community. And you're wrong that you don't fit in."

"Oh, I don't know about that."

Again, she reached over and held his hands. "Luke, people love you. They do.

"By the way, my brother wanted to be a poet, too. I remember this one thing by Emerson that he'd quote. 'Do not go where the path may lead, go instead where there is no path and leave a trail.' "

He tilted his head and smiled at her. His eyes glistened. "You're saying I should close the book on old things."

"Yes." She shook her head. "No, not all of them. We all have memories we cherish, and we all have baggage. Mom always says we should try to learn from the past, so we don't trip up on the same stuff over and over. I'm just saying maybe you could open your heart to new things. We all make mistakes, don't we? Look, your mom is divorced. You don't hold that against her, do you?"

"Of course not."

"She needed something else, and she went after it. So, shouldn't you allow yourself to have that opportunity, too? To course correct? Shouldn't you?"

She held her breath, waiting for an answer from Luke and for something new from Judith.

None came.

****

Conversation throughout the rest of dinner was a bit lighter. They talked about the town, about some of the people—those they liked, those they didn't—and were very much on the same page in that regard. They talked sports—well, he did because she knew zilch except for a little bit about baseball which her dad loved. They shared places from their "I Want to Travel To" lists—again, very much the same, and he was interested in her trip to Spain with Jaz because he wanted to go there one day.

"You'd be out of your mind, Luke," she said. "We went to a monastery up in the mountains because Jaz wanted to see the Black Madonna. The square going up to the church has sculptures, and the main altar is decorated with enamel and alabaster—biblical scenes, like *The Last Supper*. The cross is from the fifteenth century, and there are some beautiful paintings in the chancel. It's amazing."

"I'll get there some day. I want to travel."

Finally, it was time for dessert, and they couldn't resist. Luke ordered a variety of delicious, sweet endings and forced her to share. "Desserts here are out of this world. Warm apple pie, sponge cakes drizzled with chocolate or butterscotch, pound cakes bursting with berries and whipped cream, and those little cupcakes with little flowers made out of sugar. Those are almost too pretty to eat—almost," he laughed.

"I think I've had my fill of sugar with all the honey I let dribble on the biscuits, Luke! I need to watch my waistline. If I keep eating here, I'll need to wear those elastic waist pants that Mrs. Bloom wears."

He laughed out loud again. "I kind of like your waist

just the way it is. You'd look pretty hilarious in Mrs. Bloom's bloomers."

She grinned.

"But I wouldn't change a thing about Mrs. Bloom."

"Neither would I," she agreed.

He scooped up some apple pie and whipped cream and said, "Open wide."

She complied, and he held out the spoon.

She bit into the sweet confection, and their eyes held. Blushing, she looked down and then gazed at him again as she swallowed and then ran her tongue across her lips.

"You like it?"

She nodded.

"Or you," he said.

"Or me, what?"

"I wouldn't change a thing about Mrs. Bloom—not even her waistline or her hips. And I wouldn't change a thing about you, Gemma Martelli. Not one."

By the time they headed back to River Styx, the sun was setting. The sky had turned grit-gray and brooding; rain was on the way again. They didn't talk much; she felt like there was this alien serenity between them—like they stepped up to a line and then backed up and did it again.

She touched her fingers to her T-shirt. Beneath it was Judith's engagement ring. *Talk to me, Judith, please. He's right here. I'm right here.*

She heard the same words. *Fence. Pawn. Clare.* But this time, Judith added two new ones. *Poor* and *sister.*

It was progress, but not nearly enough.

As they drove home, her mind swirled with everything they had talked about throughout dinner and all the things they didn't talk about. She had desperately wanted to return the sympathy, the compassion he showed when she spoke about the loved ones she had lost. But she wasn't supposed to know anything about Judith Walsh, deceased fiancée of Luke Bailey.

When she told Luke about Antonio, his ghost had touched her hand. She had squeezed her eyes shut, thinking, *Your timing sucks, Antonio.* It always did! She had pushed Antonio out of her head and tried to gently probe, hoping Luke would spill his guts after she bared her soul. She thought he might confide that he'd lost a lover himself, that he'd start to share his own feelings about Judith's death. But he clammed up on that front.

It was clear he felt guilty about breaking his vows. And probably about falling for her. That's what Judith meant when she said he was praying for forgiveness.

****

Luke walked her to the back door of her building to make sure she got in all right, and they said good night. He was halfway across the patio when she turned to him. "Luke!"

He whirled around to face her.

She quickly walked toward him, stopped inches away, and looked up at him. She said his name again in a whisper. "Luke, it's not a sin to have desires. It's not a sin to make mistakes. You're a mere human like the rest of us. Stop beating yourself up for being human. And as for this presence you feel—I know that it's unsettling. But you'll—we'll work through that, okay?" She heaved a sigh. She had trouble finding the words.

"I don't understand this . . . this gift you say you have, Gem." He ran a finger down her jaw and cupped her cheek with his hand. "But you are a really beautiful human being."

She thought he might kiss her and wasn't sure how she would respond.

Instead, he said, "Good night," again, crossed the patio, turned the corner, and was out of sight.

A complicated man, she thought. *More complicated than I imagined.*

****

As she walked toward the back steps to her apartment, thunder split the vault-like silence and lightning buzzed and crackled across the sky. A moment later, a gush of rain sent her running up the steps. She had just stepped inside when Judith's voice sounded in her ear. This time the words were in a different order. *Pawn, fence, sister, poor, Clare.*

She put the pouch with the ring on the kitchen table and slid into a chair. Trance-like, she fixed her concentration on it, waiting for Judith to say more. But all was quiet again.

For the next hour, the only sounds in the room were the humming of a fluorescent light from the bathroom, the clapping and growling of thunder, and the zig and wriggle of lightning as it whipped across the black sky. She finally turned to her computer. She needed to know about pawnshops. She needed to know a lot more. And she hated to admit it, but she needed to talk to Shake or she knew she couldn't help him the way she wanted to. She curled her hands into fists of frustration and pounded the kitchen table. "Damn it!"

After she was exhausted from researching pawnshops, she turned back to the ring. She did not take her eyes off it, and she promised herself that she would not allow sleep to come until Judith gave her more clues.

112

It wasn't just about solving Judith's murder. It was about preventing Luke from slipping into insanity. After all, the presence of ghosts drove *her* batty, and she understood and accepted the concept.

Finally, she fell asleep with her head on the table without hearing Judith's voice again.

Fantasma curled around her feet.

Chapter Seventeen

Before dawn the next morning, Gemma found herself tapping the fingers of one hand on the table and chewing on the end of the pencil as she read about a program called LeadsOnLine.

She put down the pencil on the kitchen table, and it rolled to the right, off the table, and to the floor. This reminded her that her little apartment needed work. The floor in the kitchen was slanted; the cupboards needed to be stripped and restained; and all the windows should be replaced.

She rose to open a window to get some fresh air, and she placed a heavy wooden pole between the bottom of the window and the sill to hold it up. The windows in the old building were the old-fashioned kind with ropes, sash cords, and weights. The ropes were broken, and the only way she could keep a window open was by sticking a pole between the bottom of the window and the sill.

She sighed. Her grandfather had kept his home in perfect condition—it was well-maintained, organized, pristine. But after Nana Martelli passed away and he sold their house, he didn't seem to care very much about his surroundings.

Leaning back in her chair, Gemma wondered, "Will I ever have someone I share everything with and can't bear to be without?"

She took a break, picked up her coffee cup, and

wandered into the bedroom. She realized she had given no thought to interior decorating since she moved in.

The plaster ceiling needed to be repaired, and the old wallpaper needed to go. She went over to a corner and scratched at a seam that looked like it was about to split apart and mentally put this project on her long 'To Do' list.

She touched the old blue paisley drapes. "These are definitely not my jam," she told Fantasma.

Why don't I make any time for any of this?

"You know why," her brother whispered. *"Admit it. It's because you'd rather be chasing down faceless murderers."*

Gemma went into the bathroom. Looking around, she made a mental note to fix this room up, too. The walls were painted in an agreeable pale gray, appropriately called 'Ghost Gray Light,' but the linoleum was old. A few pops of black or red towels and accessories would most definitely have slicked it up a bit.

Fantasma meowed and lashed at her with a paw, as if to say, "Get back to work."

Right, she thought. *Because that really is what's important.*

She sat down at her computer.

****

She found that most pawnshops were not the sleazy, back-alley dives seen on television. Owners generally played by the rules; they let the police know if you suspected someone of trying to pawn something that doesn't belong to them.

According to everything Gemma read, the pawnbroker assumed the risk if he took possession of stolen property. Usually, they'd ask info on the item, like model, serial number, that kind of thing and for identification, like a driver's license. Some states required a holding period to allow time for law enforcement to track and identify stolen items.

She read out loud to Fantasma. "Each night the information gets uploaded into a site called LeadsOnLine, and the police have access to it. They can see what the pawnshop took in on a particular day, and the person's info who sold or pawned the item. If the police get a hit, they ask the pawn manager to put the item on hold, and the item can't be released to anyone but the police. Conviction of pawning stolen property is a felony in some states, and a pawnbroker can also be charged for accepting it."

She looked at the cat. "This is a good thing, right, Fan? Police get an alert, and pawnbrokers know better than to take stolen goods. And that's why Shake got involved in this case again."

Fan opened her mouth wide in a disinterested yawn and walked away. She wrinkled her nose. "Well, see if I give you a treat anytime soon. Pfft."

The cat pushed the pencil across the floor until it bumped into Gemma's foot. She picked it up and muttered, "Thank you for your service."

She turned back to her computer. She knew that if you lost an item or it was stolen, you filed an insurance claim for the loss, and the insurer reimbursed you for the loss.

But what would happen if the stolen property turned up? From her research, she learned that the insurance company would ask you to either return the insurance money paid on the claim, or the item so that the company could sell it as salvage to recoup their loss.

The police department recovered the ring, but the insurance company paid Luke's dad for it long ago. Once the case was solved, the ring would belong to the insurance company.

So many questions here. The big one wouldn't go away. Was the ring being pawned really involved in the original crime? Was this crime random after all? Or was there some nefarious motive involving the woman whom Luke loved?

She picked up the phone. It was just after seven, and she wondered if she should disturb Shake. Then again, she knew that he was an 'Up at Zero Dark Thirty' kind of guy.

Pacing as the phone rang, she tossed cold coffee into the sink and poured another cup. She felt a breath on her shoulder.

"La mia, amata. You own a jewelry shop. You're not a police officer."

She lifted her shoulders as if to shrug him away and hissed, "You're not helping, Antonio. Go away."

Finally, Shake picked up. "How y'all doing?"

"Okay, but I have questions."

"Shoot."

"Tell me about this pawnshop."

"Uncle Pauly's Pawnshop, over on the east side of Cleveland," he answered.

"And the pawnbroker—did he ask for information? For ID?"

"He said the woman gave him a driver's license, described her as dressed to the nines, very pretty. He remembered that she was a redhead, but she wore sunglasses and a face mask. She told him she was being careful because she didn't want to catch the virus again.

But from what he could see of her face, she looked like the photo on the driver's license."

"Okay," she said with a sigh. Pacing, she asked, "What did he do?"

"When she wouldn't take off the glasses or mask, he became suspicious. When she showed him the ring, he got really suspicious. Then she asked to see Sully, the prior owner of the pawnshop. This guy we interviewed, Paul Neely, is new, just bought the place. Sully—the former owner—fenced more than fourteen thousand items on eBay to the tune of almost seven hundred thousand dollars and is now serving twenty months in jail, no option for parole. The judge ordered him to pay a one hundred thousand dollar fine and forfeit to the government the money he got from the eBay sales."

Curious, she slumped into a chair and quickly searched for articles about a pawnbroker who fenced merchandise on eBay. Fantasma started to swipe playfully at her feet. She shoved her away as she tried to listen to Shake. Putting her hand over the receiver, she whispered, "Shoo, Fan. Go on. You're more distracting than Antonio, and that's going some."

"What did you say, Gem?" Shake asked.

"Nothing. Go ahead, Shake."

"This guy's scheme ran from around 2014 to 2020. Since the woman with the ring asked for Sully, we think that she thought she could fence the ring, that she didn't know Sully had gone to jail. When the new guy asked for her fingerprint, she bolted. Didn't even grab the ring or the driver's license on the way out."

"But he held on to the license?"

"Right. She was in one helluva hurry to get the flock out of there."

"You traced the license?" she asked as she hopped up on the counter to avoid Fantasma's persistent paws.

"Yeah. It had expired. It belonged to a woman named Sile MacDonald. It's spelled 'S I L E,' but it's pronounced Sheila. Old Irish name, I'm told."

"You talked to her?"

"I actually thought about asking for a warrant to arrest her, but the prosecutor told me we didn't have a solid case. We went to her address, her old address on the license, and talked to her mother. Her mother told us she had an ironclad alibi. The woman, this Sile, only communicated with me through the Mother Abbess."

"Come again?"

"Sile MacDonald is now a—what did she call it—a novice at the convent of the Poor Clares. She's in her early twenties, and she's been at the convent several years. She went there straight from high school, I think. Her license was in a purse, which was stolen not long before she entered the order."

Fence, pawn, Clare, poor, and sister.

Oh, my God! Finally, your clues make some sense, Judith!

The woman with the ring thought she was taking it to a *pawnbroker* who would *fence* it. And the driver's license belonged to a nun—a *Sister* of the Order of *Poor Clares*.

Thank you, Judith, she thought. *Now we're getting somewhere. But we're just at the tip of the iceberg. The cops already know all of this. We need more.*

"Did Sile . . . what's she called now?"

"Sister Mary Evangeline."

"Okay, how did Sister Mary Evangeline say that her purse was stolen? What were the circumstances?"

"Just that it was stolen, Gem. These nuns don't talk. Like, at all. They only speak to each other for about an hour each day. They only speak to family members or friends a few times a year, and that's through some kind of gate or grate or something."

Gate. Jaz talked about a gate. A black gate.

"I only got any information at all through the Mother Abbess," Shake said. "Look, somebody got hold of her license and tried to use it. That's all we know."

"Do you think she would speak to me? Or maybe to a priest?"

"I don't want Father Bailey to know about where this is going right now. Because it still isn't going anywhere. We still have no solid new leads. All we have is the ring that someone tried to pawn; and we know that someone used a stolen driver's license as an ID."

"It's not a dead end. Sister. Sister," Judith urged.

"Judith disagrees, Shake. I'll be in touch."

She opened the shop later that morning but had only one customer. She wasn't disappointed. All she really wanted to do was work on Shake's case, anyway. She couldn't shake the feeling that Judith's words were going to crack the case—if only she could put it all together.

****

Gemma glanced out the window. The sky continued to look ominous, and she heard thunder in the distance. Fantasma hated storms, so Gem wasn't sure if the cat was whining from fear, because she was hungry, or just to be a pest. As she swiped at her ankles again, Gemma gave her some treats. This seemed to satisfy her for the moment.

As she bounced around websites, she thought about her relationship with Shake. Jaz was the one who got

Gemma into all this. Shortly after she moved back to River Styx, he was having trouble with a cold case and Jaz told him about Gemma. He scoffed. Gemma was pissed that Jaz broke the confidence, and even more so because he summarily dismissed the possibility that a psychic could help law enforcement.

But not long after that, Shake went to a cop convention and sat in on a seminar about the use of psychics in police work. He called Gemma and asked her to lunch.

Gemma remained silent while he launched into a soliloquy about his work and this police thing with psychics and what he'd learned.

****

For one thing, one of the speakers talked about a study conducted by a federal agency on how to explore the value of using mediums. Out of eleven officers at different police agencies interviewed, eight said using a psychic provided them with otherwise unknown information. Three out of those eight officers had found the bodies of missing persons through the use of a psychic.

One of the speakers mentioned certain psychics specifically. One was Kathy Richter and her involvement with the 1989 murder of Renee Johnson, who was found in her apartment bludgeoned to death. Richter had a vision from which the police sketch artist created a picture that exactly matched the person who was ultimately convicted. She also consulted with police about the disappearance of a ten-year-old girl after she had visions of a windmill and feathers which led police to find the girl's body in a field near a chicken ranch. A police detective called her 'the real deal.'

Another detective told the story of a homicide case where the police had no clue where to find a missing person. He contacted a psychic. While the person wasn't found at the time, her body was found later at exactly the location described by the psychic. His opinion was, "Use every resource available—because, why not?"

Other speakers were less favorable. One came right out and said, "Don't believe so-called psychics are of any use. Never, ever in a million years would I use that crap."

Gemma didn't have an opinion as to whether other psychics were effective. She just knew what she could do.

After she helped Shake find the body in the cornfield, they created a fiction where he and his department figured it all out on their own—on an anonymous tip or a newly discovered piece of evidence. She was fine with that. She didn't want any limelight.

She wished she could have attended that convention. She'd have taught them a thing or two about ghosts who whisper clues that can be useful to law enforcement. There was no black and white in this world; she knew that. Dr. Luke's vision of the afterlife wasn't crystal clear. Neither was hers. She just tried to take her gift for what it was. She didn't have much choice.

****

Gemma looked out the window again. The rain came down hard; the sky was filled with doom-black clouds, and the bone-white hailstones sounded like a machine gun as they hit the roof. Holding the window up with her left hand to keep it from slamming down, she removed the pole carefully with her right hand and lowered the window.

There was a single vein of lightning at first, but then

branches of lightning buzzed and hissed and streaked like silver forks. They seemed to crackle with anger at being shackled to the sky instead of crashing down to scorch the pavement.

Fantasma jumped into her lap, shaking. Gemma petted her from her head to her tail and then pulled her close. "It's okay, baby. But you're such a wuss, Fan."

She kicked off her shoes and stretched her arms above her head.

"I wish I were there to rub your feet, caro," Antonio told her. *"I miss being with you."*

"Right," she scoffed. "You are the one who always had to go zero to sixty in nano seconds. You could still be here, you know."

"And now you look to another to keep you warm and happy."

"Yeah, as a matter of fact, I do."

"But a priest, caro?"

She shook her head. "Ex-priest, you twerp."

She pondered the Damascene moment that Luke seemed to be having. She had been hoping for one, waiting for him to realize that he could look at things differently and that might lead to a change in how he saw her.

But it wasn't turning out quite the way she'd hoped. Judith's spirit was hovering around, just like Antonio's ghost, and that was not the unexpected event she had hoped would cause Luke to suddenly see things in a new light and decide to take a different path.

No, instead, it just confirmed that he wasn't over Judith—not even close. And she knew that Judith had something she desperately needed. She'd help Shake find the killer and close the case. Then Judith's spirit could rest. Then maybe she could figure out a way to help Luke move on.

Do I tell him that Judith was giving back the ring, probably breaking the engagement? How would that help? But if he's guilty about something, maybe he needs to hear that.

She touched the diamond studs in her ears, the ones that Antonio gave her for her twentieth birthday. His spirit's ability to stick around was a slight deviation from the normal course of things. Antonio didn't wear earrings . . . but the diamonds came from a ring he had inherited from his late, very wealthy father. He took two flawless, colorless diamonds, two carats each, from the ring and had them fashioned into the earrings. He told her the next step would be to remove the rest of the stones from his dad's ring to have them made into an engagement ring. "But not until you finish college, caro," he'd said.

Then the fool went and wiped out on a ski slope in Italy. He was visiting his family in Italy for the Christmas holiday. One wintry afternoon, he went skiing with friends. When they all returned to warm up and have drinks—his favorite was a yellowish and caramel-colored liqueur from Livorno in Tuscany, his hometown—he went out for one more run by himself on a tree-lined slope and smacked into a tree.

His mother told Gemma he looked like he'd been bludgeoned to death. She was glad she could not see his apparition. She didn't want to remember him that way.

The curtains moved, as if touched by a gentle breeze. Fantasma let out a nasty growl and jumped from her lap, her claws digging into her thighs as she leapt. Spirits got under her skin.

"Tempo per dormire, amore," Antonio whispered.

"I'm not tired, Antonio."

"Dimentica tutto, dormire."

"Forget everything, huh? Just sleep. Easy for you to say. I have a murder to solve."

But she was actually exhausted. She crawled into bed and cuddled a pillow. She could almost smell the cedarwood scent of his favorite cologne. A tear slipped from her eye. She still missed him.

Chapter Eighteen

It was only six thirty a.m. when she dragged herself out of bed. The last of the morning stars were spent, flashing their last light, and fading in the dawn sky, and a sliver of pale moon lingered over River Styx like a ghostly guardian. Shards of sunlight were just beginning to peak through. The comforting cocoon of silence was broken by a flock of birds gripping their perches on the wires way above the ground, as well as squealing children who were dropped off early by parents on their way to work. They played on the jungle gym, the slide, the swings, and crawl tubes in the park behind the shop.

Looking out the window at the park, she saw that the rain had stopped, and everything looked green and fresh. The leaves on the trees shimmered with raindrops left behind, but the fine, powdery pollen of the oak trees, almost in full bloom, dispersed in the wind like yellow snowflakes. It was time to start watching for the songbirds that perched in the trees and feasted on pollen-covered insects.

She fed Fantasma and petted her. A purr rumbled through the cat's body. "I slept the day away yesterday, Fan. That's unacceptable." She ran her hand down the cat's back. "What shall we do today, Fan? Catch a killer?"

Before she went downstairs to the shop, she checked her voice mail. She hadn't bothered the entire day before.

There were two messages.

The first, to her surprise, was Luke. "Hi, Gem. I just wanted to tell you that I really enjoyed having dinner with you. I hope you didn't mind me asking questions about—"

He paused. "About, you know. I'm probably just imagining things. Anyway, I'd like to see you again. I mean, not just around the shop or at church. I mean, like dinner. Bye."

Her heart jumped, and her stomach lurched. Of course, she wanted to have dinner with him again, but things seemed so thorny right now.

The second voice mail was from Shake. "Gemma, you say that the nun is not a dead end. I don't see it—she was just unlucky to have her purse stolen. But anyway, for what it's worth, she lived in Cleveland on Elton Avenue—that's near 78th and Lorain. Her mother, Dervla MacDonald, works at a pub near there—The Old Cork. The daughter, Sile, was born in 2001. Hope that helps, but don't do anything stupid."

Hmm, don't do anything stupid, huh? As in alert him to all new information but don't follow up myself? Fat chance, that. I'm into it now.

Shake said that detective work was seventy percent legwork and paper chase, twenty percent new leaps in forensics, ten percent luck. It wasn't all cops and robbers, guns blazing, people jumping on moving trains or some version of parkour—jumping between buildings and up walls and off roofs. Even Gemma's part in it involved tracking down clues more than physically following some suspect.

He told her that he'd just read about a cold case— more like an icy, frigid case—where a twenty-five-year-old mother went missing in 1968. Nearly twenty years later, construction workers uncovered a body in a shallow grave on a beach. But it wasn't until recently that an investigator took DNA samples from family members and got a match using genetic genealogy. Finally, after fifty years of mystery, the young mother was identified. She hadn't run away, leaving her husband and toddler. She was murdered.

It was important to find the truth about Judith's murder, too, and Gemma had an idea how she might persuade Sister Mary Evangeline to speak to her—though it involved a lie to get her foot in the door.

Her first question was where would a Catholic girl who lives around 78th Street in Cleveland, Ohio have gone to high school?

She did some checking. The nearest Catholic high schools for girls were Saint Marcellin's and Mary Magdalene. She searched for the yearbooks for both schools for 2018 and 2019 graduates because if Sile was born in 2001, she probably graduated in one of those years. That narrowed it down.

Fortunately, for Gemma it was easier than she thought it would be. She went to a yearbook website, put in the state, city, the name of the high school, and graduation year. She paid a small fee and—kabam!—there they were. She got the 2018 yearbooks but saw no one named Sile MacDonald in either one. She tried the 2019 yearbooks. In the Saint Marcellin yearbook, she found the nun's senior photo. Light reddish blonde hair, eyes as green as Judith's emerald ring, peachy skin. She was a flawless beauty.

She became a nun? She could have been a model!

Flipping through the pages, Gemma tried to find out

what activities she was engaged in and looked for photos to see who may have been friends with Sile. Maybe they knew more about this purse theft. And maybe she could say that one of them was a mutual friend who sent her to see her—she really wanted to talk to her.

Sile was on the yearbook committee, and from the photo, it looked like a tight-knit group. She wrote down the names of the other girls on the committee.

****

She spent the rest of the day with customers—and fortunately, people looking for high school graduation gifts and two couples for engagement rings. The first couple decided on a diamond ring from her estate collection. After congratulating them, she performed her mother's 'happy engagement ritual.' She pulled a small champagne bottle from the mini fridge in the workroom, and as they toasted, she clicked photos with both of their cell phones.

The second couple wanted something very modern and trendy—the young lady was looking for a '*Dis Moi Oui*,' a "tell me yes," engagement ring, which had two precious gems in them. Gemma had only one in the store—a pre-owned ring from a store that went out of business.

The ring this girl was looking at was a 1.5 carat pear-shaped, high-quality diamond with a 2.25 blue sapphire, set in 18K white gold. The original price was thirty-nine thousand dollars.

"Because it's pre-owned," she told the couple, "I can give you a good price. Thirty-five thousand."

She fully expected them to raise eyebrows, laugh, or simply bolt. Instead, the young woman placed it on her finger, held it up to the light, turned her hand this way and that, and looked at her fiancé. "This one. This is the one."

Gemma almost tried to talk them out of it. *That's the price of a nice car or a down payment on a house*, she thought. On the other hand, the woman was dripping in diamonds already and he was dressed like a prince. Maybe this purchase wouldn't be a big dent in his budget? The guy whipped out a credit card. Gemma ran it through, and it was approved.

After congratulating them, she performed her mom's little ritual again. The young lady wanted to wear her new ring, so Gemma didn't wrap it up; she just gave them the little red ring box to keep it in. But they wrapped up themselves in each other's arms as they left the store.

"Good luck," she whispered, sincerely meaning it, but also wondering if the groom-to-be had the bucks to keep up with the Mrs.-to-be's champagne taste.

Shaking her head, she thought how incredible it was that people spent that kind of money on jewelry. *I sell it, for crying out loud, but forty grand to say, "Tell me yes?" Whoa.*

But that was her big sale for the month. Now she could feed herself and the cat. And now it was time to do some more digging.

****

She mulled over whether to visit Sile's mother Dervla. She checked her out online and found her listed with people related to her—a daughter, Sile, a woman named Doreen Tobin, and someone, likely a relative, named Toby Tobin. There were several MacDonalds listed as possible relatives, too. She decided that showing up at the pub was best, though she had no idea what shift she worked at the bar.

And she knew Shake would be livid.

When she had showered and changed that morning, she attached the pouch with the ring again. She kept hoping she would get more messages from Judith if she kept the ring close. But her memories and her voice were still MIA.

She closed up shop early to go to the library to read whatever she could find in the newspaper about Judith's attack—maybe if it was on her mind, it would be on Judith's—if spirits had 'minds,' that is.

All of the articles concerning Judith's murder were disturbing. One described her as a twenty-six-year-old nurse who'd been fatally wounded in a knife attack as she walked to her car from church services.

Another quoted the priest who spoke with Judith briefly and prayed with her before she left the church that night. He wouldn't say about what their conversation concerned—the binds of the confessional, after all. One of the other people who were in the church, one of the few churches in the area that stayed open twenty-four seven, found her body, but he didn't witness the attack.

Another article began with *More violence has been reported in the vicinity of St. Aloysius-Xavier Catholic Church. A fatal stabbing of a young woman occurred in the church parking lot.*

It went on to describe several other violent attacks in the area. There were so many incidents that Gemma concluded it wasn't a very safe place for a young woman to be late at night.

At a press conference, a detective admitted, "In this area, this is what we've experienced in the last month. We're dealing with urban terrorists."

The area was also nowhere near her apartment—why was Judith there? What was so urgent that she had to go talk to a priest when it was almost midnight?

As she read Judith's obituary, her brows pinched. She always read them if a spirit contacted her, but she hated them. They were designed to celebrate a person's life, but she didn't think that you could do that in five hundred words or less. These short summaries couldn't reveal all the things that make up a person's life. At most they conveyed a snapshot of the loved one.

Judith's went like this:

This is the story of Judith Marie Walsh. She was twenty-six when she passed, a wonderful young woman who was loved, is missed, and will always be cherished.

The only child of Harry and Josephine Walsh, she attended Mary Magdalene High School and received her BSN and master's degree from Kent State University. She had worked at the clinic for about three years.

In her spare time, Judith loved to cook and bake, and to walk her cairn terrier, "Toto," named for the dog in The Wizard of Oz. *In high school and college, she was active in sports, especially volleyball, and also played cello in the high school orchestra.*

Judith's life was taken in an alleged robbery. The killer is still at large.

In lieu of flowers, please make donations in her name to the charity of your choice . . ..

Heat surged up the back of Gemma's neck in a sudden jab of jealousy. She sounded too perfect, too good to be true. *How do I, with all my weirdness, hope to compete with someone forever preserved in perfection in Luke's mind?*

There was no mention of her engagement to Luke

Bailey. Did her parents not know about him? No, that's not possible. Shake said people at work told him she took her ring off at work. If they knew she was engaged, wouldn't her parents?

When Gemma touched her fingertips to the pouch beneath her shirt, Judith murmured, *"They knew. They knew it was about to end."*

But did Luke know it was about to end? She couldn't ask him—not yet, anyway.

This was going to drive her crazy.

****

Late in the afternoon, Gemma waited on a few more customers—none as profitable as the engaged couples of the morning. She was still thinking of the best way to get the nun to speak with her and what she would say to Dervla MacDonald when her cell rang. It was her mom.

"Hey, you." Her voice has a lilt. She sounded really happy.

"Hey, back. How's the Big Apple?"

"Big!" she laughed. "It will take some getting used to."

"What have you been up to?"

"Mostly getting the apartment the way I want it." She chattered about their apartment at Central Park South. "Postcard worthy, honey. Huge windows with a view of Central Park from every room. Lots of renovations, lots of charm . . . I told you it's actually a pre-war building that's been updated, right? A wood-burning fireplace, soaring ceilings, big rooms. We even have marble countertops. And hardwood floors and Dylan just bought some beautiful Persian rugs. Big kitchen with custom cabinets, high-end appliances. It's, I mean, wow."

Her mother sounded like a giddy kid. "Things are good, Gem. Dylan wants to get to know you better. He asks about you all the time. You must visit soon."

"I will, Mom. Let me get the hang of things here first. And Shake—"

"Has Shake been bugging you again?"

"Not bugging, Mom. But I'm helping with something, yes."

"I thought so. You're being careful, right? Remember, you aren't a detective. Hunting down killers is not your job."

"Mom, it's important. This time especially."

Her mother sighed. "This time especially why?"

Gemma sighed back. "It just is."

There was a long pause. Her mother was surrendering because she knew that Gemma couldn't share any details. Then, "How's your love life? Still crushing on Dr. Luke?"

"We had dinner. It was nice."

"That's almost monosyllabic. Do I get no details?"

"Just dinner, Mom."

"Uh-huh. And what about Antonio? Still giving you grief?"

Like reminding me how sweet and sexy and comforting he could be despite what an adrenaline junkie he was?

"He doesn't do that exactly, Mom. He's just . . . you know, around."

"Take off the earrings. Sell them."

"This from the woman who wore her wedding ring around her neck for nearly five years. And even when you met Dylan and took it off, Dad didn't move on right away."

"You're right. But I'm sure it gave your dad a nudge to back off. Listen, look at your calendar. I want you to come up soon."

"I will, Mom. Now send me photos of the apartment. I'm dying to see it."

"Will do."

As Gemma hung up the phone, it twisted her stomach that she was so far away from her mother. It was a strange flip of circumstances. When she'd been at college and working in Chicago, that had been her choice. Now that her mother lived in New York, and she was the one stuck in a tiny town, it felt different.

She grabbed her car keys and the list of names from Sile's yearbook. With a trench coat and purse over her arm, she headed for the door. But the phone rang again. "Damn!"

But then she looked at who it was.

Luke.

****

She spun around and sat down on the stool behind the counter.

"Hi, Gem," Luke said when she answered the phone.

"Hi."

"About the gift for my mom—"

"Is there something wrong with it? I mean—"

"No, of course not. It's still in the box—which you wrapped beautifully, by the way. I'll be seeing her next Sunday after church. I just wanted to thank you again for choosing it for me."

This reminded her that she had no Mother's Day gift for her mom.

It's just nine days away, and I have to get a gift up to New York. What do you get the woman who has

135

everything or can buy anything she wants now?

"Actually," Luke continued, "I was calling to ask you to come with me to Rockin' Boots because on Friday nights, they give lessons."

"As in line-dancing lessons?"

"Right. Your mom raved about the place when we were talking about her upcoming marriage."

Her mother went to see him before she and Dylan married. She wondered if he thought it was weird that she would be getting married for the second time in that church and she also wanted to know if he'd be offended if she contacted Reverend Ralph Epley, Pastor Emeritus, to officiate.

Luke wasn't of course.

"But what about your . . . you know, your leg? I mean, you have a slight limp and—"

"I do have pins and rods in my ankle, and it still swells if I overdo—that's why my basketball days are over, and I had to give up my career in ballet."

"Well, I am sorry I'll never see you in a tutu." *Or tights*.

"No tutu. Just Speedos, Gem. I swim a lot, you know."

Oh, hurt me. Luke's body in Speedos. I'd probably drool.

"But I still do my exercises every day. I think I could handle a little bit of country. If you're interested."

She thought about her plan to try to talk with Sister Mary Evangeline or to speak with her mother at the pub. These were things she should do. But . . .

She clutched the phone until her knuckles turned white. She felt herself morph from concentrating on the investigation to just wanting to spend time with Luke

Bailey.

Maybe I can kill two birds with one stone.

"Some friends have been urging me to check out an Irish pub, a place called The Old Cork. What if we do a lesson and then grab some pub grub at this Irish place?"

"Sounds right up my alley. I have a meeting and won't be done until around five. I would pick you up, but I also have to run a quick errand right after the meeting. Would you mind heading over to the parish house? Just knock on the door around six? I'll be home by then. Is that okay?"

It sounded rather mysterious, but she quickly said, "Absolutely."

"I'll see you then."

She put down her purse and sat down at the kitchen table.

You're selfish, Gemma Martelli. You're self-centered and self-absorbed. You should be working on the case.

But truth be known, she was blinded by the fear that if she said no to Luke, there wouldn't be a second chance.

She heard laughter—Judith's laughter, for the first time. *"No, you're not selfish. You're falling in love."*

"She's wise beyond her years," Gemma told Fantasma, who was swirling in a figure eight around her legs. Then her mind switched gears. "Judith, tell me more about this nun. Help me find the woman who tried to pawn your ring. Tell me why you were giving it back to Luke. Talk to me."

She tapped a finger on the table, waiting. But there was silence, just silence. She was gone again.

****

She fed Fantasma and changed into blue jeans, a

western shirt, and cowboy boots that Mom left behind to wear when she and Dylan came into town and wanted to rock it at the bar. Lucky for her, she and her mom were the same shoe size.

Then she freshened her makeup and watched the clock tick by way too slowly until it was a few minutes to six. She went to her closet to get a navy-blue jacket in case it was chilly later. It was a knock-off of an iconic vintage Chanel jacket that she always felt very fashionable in. But it wasn't there. She let her fingers trail along her small collection of cardigans and blazers without luck.

Then she heard Antonio laugh.

"Oh, very funny, Antonio. You think I won't go over to Luke's if I can't find the jacket? Well, you know what? My denim jacket will do just fine," she declared as she grabbed it from a hanger.

"You're such a jerk sometimes, Antonio."

He laughed again.

Chapter Nineteen

Standing on the wraparound porch of the parish house, Gemma let out a shaky breath. She took a moment to look around. She had never been inside.

The house was a quintessential Queen Anne, built in the mid-eighteen hundreds. It was white now, but she imagined how it looked in Victorian times—a painted lady with a colorful patchwork of purple and pink, its towers and turrets standing guard over the town. It still had a fairy tale-like, gingerbread house feeling. She loved the front door with its elaborate carved woodwork and beveled glass. It was surrounded by old trees and flower beds; the daffodils, tulips, and irises were in full bloom.

And of course, it wasn't surprising that the house was supposedly haunted.

****

When she knocked on the door, she was surprised to hear a dog barking.

Luke doesn't have a dog.

He opened the door. He wore a T-shirt from a 2013 Rock Hall of Fame induction concert. Rock music blasted from his stereo. He had on tight, faded jeans and brandy-colored boots. The muscles in his biceps were obvious—she was going to have to fight off ladies if they went to the bar or the pub.

A small, growling dog ran up to his side, and Luke

reached out to try to grab his collar, but the dog wagged his tail as it came up to her. He tilted his head side to side as if the wheels in his brain were spinning. It almost looked like he was smiling. He was short legged with a wide head and a wiry, black-and-gray coat and weighed around fifteen pounds.

She bent down, and he kissed her face as if she was his long-lost owner. "Luke, who's this?"

"That was my errand. I had to go pick him up. Some friends—well, he belongs to some people I know, and they're going out of town for a long weekend. They haven't been away in several years, and they called me to see if I'd watch him for a few days. C'mon in."

She entered the living room and crouched into a squat as the little dog practically smothered her with kisses. Instinctively, Gemma knew who this dog belonged to. This was Judith's dog, Toto, the dog mentioned in her obit. And he sensed his Pet Mom—Judith—was nearby, near Gemma.

"Wow," Luke said. "His owners told me he's usually a pit bull when strangers come to the door."

"Don't knock pit bulls." Still petting the dog, she looked up. "We had one named Jacob Marley, and he was great."

Rubbing the top of the dog's head, she whispered, "Hi, Toto."

She looked up again and saw that Luke's face was flushed. "How do you know his name?"

Busted, she thought. She couldn't tell him that she'd read Judith's obituary. She couldn't tell him that Judith had entered her orbit and was whispering in her ear.

"Gem, how do you know his name?" Luke asked again.

She was only able to make a quick recovery because Judith whispered, *"The tag."*

She glanced at the heart on his collar with his name on it. "It's on his tag," she quickly explained. "With his address."

"Oh," he exhaled, in a tone of relief. "C'mon in."

She took a moment to memorize the address. She would add it to her list of places to go, people to see. Continuing to pet Toto, she said, "He's adorable. I haven't had a dog since Jacob Marley died."

"You named him for a ghost in the Ebenezer Scrooge story?"

"Of course. Mom took losing Jake really hard because it was shortly after my dad died. She said she might get one again now that she's got half of Central Park to herself."

He turned down the stereo and asked, "Central Park?"

She told him about talking to her mother and the description of her new apartment in New York.

"She's happy then?"

"She is, Luke. Dad died over five years ago, and she finally felt okay to move on. I think Dylan is a great guy. I think my dad would approve."

She wondered if he was getting her drift—not about her mom, but about him. It had been about five years since Judith's death, too.

She glanced around the living room. It was definitely not a reflection of a young, single guy. She assumed the furniture was left behind by Reverend and Mrs. Epley. There were two love seats upholstered in a floral fabric, two wing chairs, solid wood end tables, and lamps with rather frilly Victorian shades. A complementary rug covered the wood floor.

"I haven't really changed anything since Reverend Epley left. It's not exactly a bachelor pad, is it?"

She feigned a grimace. "Actually, I'm very fond of this shade of floral."

He laughed. "You really are being kind. This whole house is circa several cell phone updates ago."

She grinned. "More like circa Alexander Graham Bell."

Her eyes scanned the books in the built-in shelves that flanked the fireplace. There were sports memoirs, theology books, historical accounts, and tons of poetry—everything from Walt Whitman and Emily Dickinson to T. S. Elliot and Billy Collins. It was like walking into her brother's bedroom.

"You have a lot of books," she said.

"Yes, those are definitely mine. I think no matter where you go, if you take your library with you, it becomes your home."

She nodded.

When Toto started to pace back and forth, she wondered what the dog would do if he were left alone in a strange house. "Do you have a crate for him, Luke?"

He shook his head.

"Hmm. We didn't crate Jake at first, and the first time Mom went out, he demolished several pillows."

She liked the idea of a quiet, face-to-face evening with Luke. Maybe she'd be able to get more information with him in a place that was familiar and comfortable. She decided to use the dog as an excuse to stay in.

"Listen, Luke, Toto isn't used to being left alone, is he? You said that your friends don't go away much. Maybe we should just stay home and order a pizza or something?"

"You'd be okay with that?"

"Sure. Of course. We could watch a movie or a TV show or something."

"Do you like British detective shows? There's this one I started watching about a priest who helps a detective solve crimes."

It was hard not to laugh, given how close to home that felt.

"Two conditions, Luke."

"What?"

"No anchovies on the pizza, thin crust, extra cheese, pepperoni, and sausage. And popcorn during the movie. And not that store crap. Use the corn that Mrs. Wendell gave you from her farm at Christmas time."

"How do you know about that?"

Laughing, she said, "It's not a ghost thing. I pick her up on the Sunday before Christmas and load up my car with boxes and boxes of Mason jars filled with the corn to pass out. I saw her leave you three jars that day. Three—she is clearly in love with you."

Grinning, he quipped, "Well, aren't all the girls?"

One for sure, she thought.

"One for sure," Judith repeated, and Gemma shuddered.

While they waited for the pizza to be delivered, they sat in the living room. Luke refilled his wineglass and poured some in a glass for Gemma. Perched on the arm of one of the love seats, he flipped through some CDs, and then he put on different music. His music tastes and hers were clearly divergent. He liked stuff circa 2009 or so, his mid-teen years. She was more of a nineteenth-century classical music kind of girl; she loved all the great Italian composers that Nonno introduced her to.

He sat down next to her on the love seat and leaned back. They chatted about church politics—specifically Mrs. Ratty—and she told him more about her brother and her dad.

When the pizza guy arrived, Toto went berserk, and Luke jumped up and grabbed the dog's leash. He snapped the leash to Toto's collar and asked Gemma to grab his wallet to pay the pizza guy while he took the dog out back. "It's on the kitchen table."

She followed him to the kitchen, and he went out the back door with Toto.

She quickly looked around the kitchen. It was large, a chef's dream with updated appliances, solid oak cabinets, and a coffered ceiling. There was a large farm table and six chairs, and on the floor were runners in a floral pattern that complemented the wallpaper. Again, it occurred to her that Luke had not done any redecorating in this room since he moved in.

She paid the driver for the pizza. The acidic aroma of the tomato sauce drifted through the house as she walked to the kitchen. When she opened the box, the scent of cheese popped out at her. She set the pizza and the wallet on the kitchen table. But curiosity got the best of her, and she picked up the wallet and flipped through it.

There were three photos. One was of a middle-aged lady, likely Luke's mother. One was a photo of Judith, and the third was Judith and Luke. Judith was truly beautiful, full of life, unlike what Gemma had seen in the vision of the autopsy suite.

She was staring at Judith's photo when Luke and Toto came through the back door.

Chapter Twenty

Luke's gaze settled on the photos in the wallet. He took a deep breath, blew it out, and lifted an eyebrow at Gemma. Then they locked their eyes in a stare.

He took the leash from Toto's collar. The dog sniffed at the pizza, and Luke shooed him into the living room.

She waited, watching him. Tightening her grip on the wallet, she tried to figure out what to say. She was nervous, her stomach heaving. All she could think about was the heavy silence that threatened to spoil the evening, to spoil everything.

Luke took the wallet from her hand and gently closed it. Furrows creased his brow.

Another knot of dread formed in her stomach. She shifted her weight and swallowed hard, watching him. His eyes flashed, but she couldn't read them—if they were mirrors to the soul, the glass was pretty cloudy. But seeing the scowl on his face, tears filled her eyes. The question that fell from her lips was straightforward and clear. "Should I leave?"

Luke shook his head, put the wallet in his back pocket, and said, "Plates are in the far-left cupboard. I'll get the silverware and napkins."

She sucked in a breath and tried to regain her composure as she watched him down the rest of his wine and pour more into his glass. She followed suit and held

145

her glass out for more.

Luke gave a protracted sigh and poured some wine into her glass. The room stayed quiet. Moments like this felt like a lifetime.

"Um, how about we reheat the pizza?" he said. "I think we should talk." He put the silverware on the table.

She took two plates from the cabinet but fumbled them. He quickly took them from her and placed them on the table with the silverware.

Battling the urge to run, she inhaled deeply. "Luke, I'm sorry. I—"

The few seconds that ticked by until he spoke again felt like days.

"No, it's okay. C'mon, let's sit in the living room."

"The pizza—the dog could get it."

"Oh, right," he agreed.

He put the pizza in the oven. At his gentle prompt, she pivoted to follow on his heels to the living room.

They sat on the couch again. She took a long draw of wine and then folded her arms. "Is the woman in the photo . . . who is she? Is she the presence you feel?"

"I think so. But I don't know. I was hoping you'd help me figure that out."

"Is she the reason you left the priesthood?"

He stared into the dark depths of the burgundy liquid left in his glass. Then he nodded. "Her name was Judith. Toto was her dog. I had asked her to marry me, but she died about five years ago."

Though she wasn't happy to be caught red-handed staring at Judith's photos, this had turned out to be an opening for him to talk about all of it. "I'm so sorry, Luke."

The dog came up and nudged Luke for attention. He

bent down to pet him. "I would have taken him, but Father Fowler wouldn't allow it in the parish house. Judith's parents took him. They call me on the anniversary of—on the anniversary. I was stunned when they asked me to look after the dog this weekend."

She thought back to Judith's obit. Luke wasn't mentioned, but it didn't sound like they hated him. She pressed.

"Did her parents like you?"

His face was quizzical. "I think so? They were pretty freaked out about a priest asking their daughter to get married. I hadn't left the priesthood yet. It was all pretty eff . . . screwed up. I asked them not to put anything about it in the funeral announcement or anything because once Judith was gone, I really didn't expect to leave the priesthood."

"I see. But you did leave."

"Yeah."

She sat back and took a sip of wine.

"I was messed up, Gem."

He paused and swallowed some more wine. For a moment, she thought that he wouldn't trust her enough to talk, even if it would do him good to spill his guts.

"I was driving back to the church one night after a bender," he continued. "I went off the road and hit a tree. That's how I screwed up my ankle . . . in that accident."

"And you still drink?"

"I'm not an alcoholic, Gem. Tonight I was having a glass of wine just to—to relax before you came over. I was a little . . . I don't know. Jumpy. I had a great time with you when we went to dinner, and I was afraid that was a one-off."

She fought the urge to throw her arms around him.

147

"It doesn't have to be."

His gaze dropped to his glass. He swirled the liquid, then put the glass on the coffee table. "After Judith died, I was confused, grieving and inconsolable. That's why I started drinking heavily," he continued. "It was a bad time. I got over that, thanks to Reverend Epley. I knew that I had to do something. And Ralph—Reverend Epley—helped me get through the next couple months. More importantly, even though Judith was gone, he helped me understand that my life wasn't over and that it wasn't just losing her that made me self-destruct. I wasn't happy in my vocation."

"Why did you become a priest in the first place?"

He scoffed. "When I was a kid, my parents got divorced, which was a good thing—I hated my father. He's—he's done some bad stuff." He sighed. "I was living with Mom, and she was moving past the divorce. We were doing okay. Then she got breast cancer."

She could not imagine that sort of news. If anything happened to her mother, she wouldn't know how to cope. That would be the last straw.

She shook her head. "How scary. But she didn't die. I mean, you just bought her a gift."

"No, no, but it was a rough time. I was only about twelve, but I was already planning to go to college. I wanted to be a writer, a poet. I dreamed about going to Oxford and studying literature. *Literae humaniores*, the classics. I was very religious then, even though Mom got grief from our parish priest about getting a divorce. That's another whole story, though. Anyway, I prayed. I begged God to make her be okay. I promised if He cured her, I'd be a priest. When she hit her five-year cured date, I kept my promise. I entered the priesthood."

"That wasn't the right reason to do it, Luke," she blurted. "I just mean that's kind of like getting married just because the invitations have gone out, but you really don't want to."

Judith murmured, *"Perceptive."*

Gemma fidgeted with her hair and drank some more wine.

"I was a deacon at Father Fowler's church at the end of my time in seminary. It's almost like an internship. Then I was his parochial vicar—like an assistant. When I was visiting parishioners who had cancer, I met Judith."

"That's how we met," Judith suddenly interjected. *"He was so good with the patients."*

She closed her eyes and took a deep breath.

"She was a nurse on the oncology ward for about a year. But she was much more than that. If one of my parishioners went to hospice when they were released from the hospital for palliative care, I continued to visit them, and if Judith had taken care of them in the hospital, she'd often visit them, too. We got to know each other that way. We'd have coffee, talk. Before I knew it, I was falling in love with her."

Of course he was in love with Judith. And of course his reluctance to connect to a woman was turbocharged. But somehow hearing him say he loved her burned worse than a flame.

"She sounds like a wonderful person." She downed the rest of her wine like a shot. "I'm sure everyone loved her."

"Not everyone," he muttered.

Her ears perked up. Her Spidey-sense anticipated important info was coming.

"Meaning?"

"She was stabbed coming out of church one night. I still don't know why she was there. It wasn't her parish. It was late, after midnight. She went there after her shift. It's a church not far from the hospital, and it's open all hours. I can only guess that she wanted—needed to pray about something right then and there."

It was difficult to sit there and listen to things she already knew, but she just listened.

"Her dad had recently had a heart attack. Maybe that was it. Or maybe it was because we'd had a fight."

Judith's words came back. *He's praying for forgiveness.*

"A fight about what?"

"About me leaving the priesthood. She felt very guilty about that. I was going to meet her after she got off work that night, but I was called to give someone Last Rites. If I had been there—"

This was painful for him and painful for her to hear. She wanted to comfort him, but she really didn't know how.

"Don't do that to yourself. She wouldn't want you to."

"Anyhow, she was killed in the church parking lot. The person who attacked her stole her purse, and they never found him. The police wrote it off as a robbery gone bad."

"But you think it's something else."

"I do. There were people who had threatened her."

"Like?"

"When she was still a student nurse, she stopped to help someone who'd been in a car accident. She did CPR, but the person didn't live. The family sued her. The case was dismissed, but that didn't stop them from harassing her for months. And there was a criminal case against a nurse she worked with."

"Criminal? What happened?"

"Another nurse killed a patient."

"Killed?"

He sipped some wine. "Not as in deliberately or premeditated murder. But, well, here's what Judith told me—and I did read about the case in the papers, too.

"This other nurse went to a medication cabinet to get medication for a patient. This isn't a cabinet or cupboard like we think of—it's an electronic medication cabinet, a computerized device that dispenses a range of drugs. So, this nurse tried to withdraw a drug that's used to help you relax before having surgery or something like that.

"She typed in 'VE' for Versed instead of its generic name, which is . . . I don't remember now. When the cabinet didn't produce that medication, she triggered 'an override.' She searched again, using 'VE,' and the cabinet offered another drug that begins with the letters V and E.

"She ignored several warnings that said she was getting a medication that paralyzes. The even bigger kicker was that before she injected it, she stuck a syringe into the vial, and that means she had to look directly at the bottle cap, which says, 'Warning: Paralyzing Agent.' "

"Jesus, Mary and Joseph," Gemma muttered.

"Yeah. Exactly. The patient died."

She had no words, and she felt her whole body stiffen. He was pouring his heart out, and she couldn't help.

"Her defense was that other nurses do the override, too . . . that it happens all the time. She lost her license.

She was charged with gross neglect and negligent homicide. One defense expert said it's a medication that you should never be able to override."

He tilted his head back and forth. "Maybe that's true, but she could, and she did, and she didn't use caution. She didn't pay attention. Long story short, this nurse went to trial. She was acquitted on the negligent homicide charge but got two years for the gross neglect. Just a few weeks after she was released from prison, Judith was killed."

"What did this have to do with Judith?"

He rubbed his palms on his legs. He rolled his head to stretch his neck. "Judith was a charge nurse."

"What is a charge nurse?"

"They make sure their unit runs smoothly and keep tabs on the day-to-day tasks. Judith was young for that job, but she was a phenomenal nurse, and she had her master's degree.

"When this patient died, the hospital pointed the finger at the nurse—it didn't take any responsibility for any quirks in the machine, and apparently, the prosecutors couldn't counter that. The nurses closed ranks. Except for Judith. In fact, from what I heard, a lot of them thought Judith was a little too—what's the word? Erudite? Academic? That she thought she was better than everybody else. She told me some of them called her Saint Jude."

He scoffed. "He's the patron saint of hopeless cases, you know, and she certainly . . . well, anyway. The other nurses defended this woman who screwed up, but not Judith. When she was interviewed, she said that this woman wasn't just complacent. She was always preoccupied and unfocused, distracted, and sometimes hungover. Judith said this was not her first mistake and that there was no excuse for this kind of error. She had written her up before. Judith was on the witness list, and the nurse expert that the prosecutors put on the stand said the same thing."

"Did this woman threaten Judith?"

"She did. As did her father. Judith was in the courthouse, waiting to be called as a witness. He was there . . . her father. He said he'd get her someday."

"How awful."

"Judith said she felt like chaos followed her or something. The Good Samaritan thing, then this nurse's trial. I have to admit I've wondered if this so-called robbery was just happenstance, or if one of these wackos finally made good on their threats."

"Name," Judith urged. *"Name."*

"What was this nurse's name? The one who went to jail."

"Um, let's see." He shook his head. "Doreen something. Last name was Tobar, Tobis. Something like that."

Gemma's earlier computer searches came to mind. It listed the nun, her mother, Dervla MacDonald, and two Tobins, Doreen and Toby. Was Doreen Tobin the nurse who went to jail? The one who might blame Judith for her conviction? Could Toby be that convicted nurse's father?

"And the police never found the person who killed Judith? No leads?"

"No, the killer stole her purse. They found it later, but her engagement ring, wallet . . . all of it was gone. I just don't know why he had to kill her. The cops said there wasn't any sign of a struggle—she didn't fight him."

His face went dark. She could practically feel the pain churning inside of him. She wondered again if she should leave.

"So, I guess that's pretty much it. I was going to leave the priesthood because it wasn't right for me and because I thought I'd found Miss Right. And it's been difficult to not be angry that Judith got no justice."

Gemma knew how difficult it was to lose someone you loved. But the not knowing—the weeks and months and years of not knowing why Judith was killed or who did it . . . it had to be indescribable, and her heart ached for him.

The flicker of pain that flooded his eyes put a different spin on the situation. He had, perhaps, revealed more than he'd intended, and she couldn't tell him a thing about Shake resurrecting the case to try to get justice for Judith.

Faint furrows denting her brow, she dipped her chin and pressed a hand to her chest. "I can only imagine. Listen, do you want me to go home? Would you rather be alone?"

He grabbed her hand as she began to move away. "No, no, I really don't want that. But if I spoiled your evening—"

She touched the top of his hand. "You haven't. And I'm starving if you still want me to stay and eat pizza with you."

He squeezed her hand but then pulled his hand away. "I do. Should I warm the pizza up in the microwave?"

She wrapped her fingers around her glass, trying not to show how relieved she was.

"Cold is okay with me. Especially for breakfast."

Spirits lifting, he grinned. "Ah, another thing we have in common."

"Another?"

"Believing in an afterlife. Liking cold pizza. And loving Mrs. Wendell's popcorn."

He brought the pizza out to the living room with napkins. She helped herself to a slice. It sagged in the middle, and she struggled to get it into her mouth without smearing her lips with cheese and sauce. Luke laughed, but she pointed at him as he juggled a piece as well and sauce dribbled out of the side of his mouth.

They both slipped little pieces of sausage to Toto, which he devoured. Gemma half expected to hear Judith chastise her for feeding her dog human food, but she went on radio silence again.

After dinner, they settled in on the couch with Toto between them, making small talk. "Can I have another glass of wine?" she asked.

He went to the kitchen and brought back the bottle. He poured some wine into her glass, but he passed.

"I understand loss, Luke. Not exactly like you went through, of course. But I lost my brother and Nonno and then my dad. I adored all of them. And Antonio, too."

"That was your fiancé?"

She nodded. "Losing my brother Peppi was maybe the hardest. He was three and a half years older than me. And, like you, he wanted to write. He wrote poetry, and he'd read it to me before I went to sleep."

"How did he die?"

"He was diagnosed with leukemia when he was three. No one expected him to live past age five or six. But my parents took him everywhere. He'd go into remission; and it would come back and then rinse, dry, repeat. He was in his senior year of college when he died."

Luke took her hand. "I'm so sorry."

Once again, the absence of her brother cut deeply, seeping into her with a mixture of sweetness and grief. She rubbed the back of her neck and looked away. "He was the perfect brother. Handsome, funny, sweet. He never made me feel like a pest."

He said, "I'm sorry," again. Then, "What poets did he like? What did he read to you?"

A few seconds ticked by, and her voice lifted. "Oh, I couldn't name them all. Shelley, Emily Dickinson, Keats, Whitman, E. E. Cummings. He adored Shel Silverstein, and he liked Billy Collins."

He threw his head back and closed his eyes. "Oh, yes. 'Forgetfulness.' The name of the author is the first to go, followed obediently by the title, the plot, the heartbreaking conclusion . . .."

Laughing, she said, "That's the one! Do you have a favorite poet?"

"That's a hard one, but I do like to explore Eastern and Asian religions and their whole philosophies, and there's a poet from India I really like. Rabindranath Tagore."

"I don't remember Peppi ever mentioning him."

Luke closed his eyes again, his face taking a serene expression. " 'I seem to have loved you in numberless forms, numberless times. . . In life after life, in age after age, forever.' That's just part of the first stanza. It's about how you love the same person over and over in different lives."

"That's really beautiful, Luke." She searched his

face for clues before asking, "Do you believe that? Do you believe you keep meeting and loving the same person over and over?"

"I don't believe in reincarnation. Then again, I'm not sure what I believe anymore. What about you?"

"I try to keep an open mind about pretty much everything. I mean, given my . . . my unique—"

She stopped speaking, not quite knowing how to express her openness without sounding like she knew more about life after death than everybody else. "I mean, I have to keep an open mind. Believing that spirits or souls can outlast physical death isn't at all foreign to me. And really, it isn't that foreign to you, is it? Like you said before, even if I cannot see the sun, I know it exists."

"And maybe I'm having a firsthand experience with it?" he asked. He looked down. His confusion and uncertainty and anxiety were palpable.

She realized that this was something of an existential crisis for him, and she felt very protective— he'd already had his inner struggle about the priesthood and deciding to leave it. He didn't deserve yet another one.

"Maybe you are," she said, squeezing his hand. Every cell in her body churned. She wanted to lean forward and hold him and kiss him. Instead, she took another sip of wine, then stood up. "I guess I should get going. Walk me home?"

"No detective show?"

"Next time," she said.

As they approached her door, he said, "I hope my checkered history doesn't—"

She put her forefinger to his lips. "It was a lovely evening. Thanks."

"You're coming to the big quilt raffle Sunday after church, right? I have a lot riding on the competition."

"Gambling?"

"Just a little." Luke winked.

"Yes." She smiled back. "I'll be there."

"Okay."

He planted a quick kiss on her cheek and waited until she was inside. "Good night, Gem!"

She peeked out the window to watch him as he disappeared around the corner. She closed her eyes and saw Judith in her mind again. This time, she was in a low-lit church, with votive candles glowing, her face buried in her hands. Gemma didn't know how she knew that this is where she was and what she was doing minutes before she was killed.

****

Once she was upstairs, Gemma changed into pajamas. She opened her top drawer and took out a small box. It contained precious things, precious memories.

She picked up her brother Peppi's cornicello, the Italian horn he wore all the time. She hated that he was dead. She missed him so much.

She put the horn necklace around her neck and crawled into bed. She closed her eyes. "Read me a story, Peppi. Or recite a poem."

"Should it be one of the preeminent Romantic English poets of the 19th century?" he asked in his smooth, velvety voice. *"Shelley perhaps?"*

"Anything you want."

"Rest awhile, hapless victim! And Heaven will save the spirit that hath faded away with the breath."

"Peppi, are you talking to me or to Judith?"

"She's restless and needs your help."

158

"Fine. You two have a nice chat. I'm going to sleep, perchance to dream."

Chapter Twenty-One

Late Saturday morning, with few customers and pressing things to do, Gemma skipped lunch and poured coffee into a thermos. Then she put the 'Closed' sign on the door.

First, she went online and looked up Sister Mary Evangeline's convent and could hardly believe that an order of cloistered nuns had a website. She had a fake story prepared to get her foot in the door. She needed to figure out what might be the best time to speak with the nun, though she had her doubts—she wouldn't talk to a police officer, for crying out loud.

From what she'd read on the website, Sile was midway through her journey to becoming a full-fledged nun. The first step was to become an aspirant, which meant spending time at the convent deciding if she really wanted to pursue this journey. Then the girl suited up in her white veil and spent a year as a postulant. The novice category was next. There was a ceremony, during which she petitioned for admission to the order. They cut her hair, covered her head with the white veil of a novice, and she started to wear a brown religious habit. Then she became what's called a juniorate, exchanged the white veil for a black one, and took the four vows of obedience, poverty, chastity, and, as a cloistered nun, enclosure. Eventually she took her final vows. All of this took many years.

It seemed to Gemma that Sister Mary Evangline started this process right out of high school, a profound commitment for someone so young.

She looked at the nuns' daily schedule. They rose at five in the morning for prayers, then mass, then work time with a break for midday prayer and lunch. "Free time" occurred for about an hour between noon and one in the afternoon. Then more work, classes, choir practice, saying the rosary at four thirty, then an evening gathering, more work, a little more recreation time, sacraments, night prayer. Bedtime was shortly before nine p.m.; however, the sisters were up again at midnight for a different kind of prayer, then back to bed.

When am I going to catch her when she isn't eating, working, or praying?

Gemma did not want to interrupt the nun's sparse free time, but she seriously doubted that she would interrupt her schedule for her otherwise, if at all. She decided to call the Mother Abbess and try to talk her way into an audience with Mary Evangeline.

Then there was the other MacDonald—Dervla. She would go to the pub late that afternoon. Maybe she'd be there, maybe not, but hopefully Gemma could at least find out from somebody when her shift was.

She called the convent and left a message for the Mother Abbess. Then she got ready to go to the pub and was almost out the door when her mom texted her with photos of her apartment. It was mostly creamy white, like Fantasma's fur, but pops of color brightened it up.

The Persian rugs were large and magnificent, with intricate patterns, and full of vibrant color. Lots of rich burgundy with a dark green border. Gemma bet that they were vintage. The white couches were filled with plump pillows that matched.

I'm going to be terrified to sit in Mom's living room.

She was gathering up her things and checking locks when the phone rang.

It was her mom. "Hi, honey. Did you get the photos?"

"Just now. The apartment looks fabulous, Mom."

They chatted for a few moments, but then Gemma decided to ask her mother for a little help. "Mom, there's this spirit I've been talking to."

"I figured."

Somehow, her mother always knew.

"Well, here's the thing. When she speaks to me, sometimes it's just a word here and there and other times, it's whole sentences, which has never happened before. If she would just make things clear all the time, I could—"

"Solve the case?"

Gemma bit her lip. "Yeah."

"You know, my mother always told me that if I opened my mind, if I truly and totally accepted my gift, I'd be able to actually see spirits. I never did," she admitted. "That really scared me. Perhaps you are more open to this spirit than you've ever been? The way you say you've been with Peppi and Antonio? You've told me they speak to you as if they were sitting on the couch next to you.

"And don't forget, being a medium is more art than science. Who knows if their wires get crossed or if there's some cosmic interference that's an obstacle now and then? Maybe their Wi-Fi goes out?"

Gemma laughed. Only her mother could put it that way.

"Maybe," she said.

"Gemma, be careful. You know I admire this thing you do, but I'm always afraid it could be dangerous."

"There is nothing malevolent about this spirit, Mom."

"Be careful anyway. It's a big responsibility you take on."

Her mother probed about when she might visit, but Gemma hedged. Then she told her she really had to get going, that she had an appointment.

She picked up her purse and headed to the door again, but the phone rang again. It was Jasmine's mom, Lady Laveau.

"Hi, how are you, Lady Laveau?"

"Doing well, Gemma. Are you going to the big quilt fest this weekend?"

"Tomorrow, right? After church? I'm planning to."

"Well, there are a few quilts I made for the competition for the raffle, but I held one back for you."

"For me?"

"Jaz saw something in a dream. She saw a house or an apartment that's mostly furnished in white. But there are beautiful rugs on the floor. Deep red and some green, she said. I made a lap quilt that would match. She said you might need it."

Jaz did it again.

"I'd love to have it for a gift for my mom for Mother's Day. It sounds perfect."

"Well, then you shall. I'll just charge for the materials. Would that be okay?"

"No, no. I know how many hours you put into these. Just give me a price and—"

"We will not be arguing about this, Gemma

Martelli. If you don't agree, I'll submit it to the contest and the raffle. Oh, and I also have a housewarming gift for your mother. That's from me. Can you send it to her for me?"

"Of course. Done deal on both counts. Wow, thank you so much. You're amazing. Jaz is amazing."

The phone rang again. She huffed, but when she saw that it was Shake, she answered. It was time to bring him up to speed.

She told him about the possible connections she'd made between Sister Mary Evangeline and the Tobins. "Did anyone ever interview them, Shake? Doreen Tobin or Toby Tobin? They're somehow related to Dervla MacDonald, the nun's mother. You know, the nun whose purse was stolen."

"Gem, I told you. Judith Walsh's murder was written off as a robbery gone bad. Most of my colleagues think I'm nuts for even looking at it again, even though the ring turned up."

"So the answer is 'no'?"

"Right. I'm not real impressed with the original investigation, to be honest."

She told him what Luke told her about Judith's potential enemies—one of which was Doreen Tobin. "She threatened Judith, and so did her father. I read some articles about Doreen's trial for gross neglect. Her life was pretty much destroyed by this. And she got out of jail not long before Judith was murdered. What if it was revenge? And also, there's the family of the crash victim that Judith tried to revive."

"I knew nothing about any of that," Shake admitted. "There's nothing in the file that indicates anyone talked to Father Bailey about much of anything, either. I mean, he had an alibi, and who would think a priest might know who would murder his fiancée? For that matter, it's unusual for a priest to have a fiancée, isn't it? Anyhow, there are a few notes in the file. The police talked to Judith's parents and a few people at work, and Father Bailey, of course, but what you are telling me never came up."

"Maybe Luke wasn't thinking straight after she was killed. I'm guessing he's thought about these things only recently."

Like since he's felt Judith's presence.

"Shake, I think you should speak to the family of that crash victim who died. And I'm going to follow up with the nun or her mom."

"No. You are not."

There was a controlling tone in his voice. Gruff. But then, as if he was aware of his tone, he softened. "That's not a good idea, Gem. You would not be safe. Let me take it from here."

"But—"

He cut her off. "I'll do some digging into these Tobin people and talk to the nun's mother. Good job, Gem, whether it's from the Great Beyond or info from Luke Bailey. Now let me do my job."

She muttered, "Okay," and hung up the phone.

Then she promptly went to her car and pointed it toward The Old Cork pub.

****

She arrived at the pub around four when it was just opening up. She had never been to Ireland, unfortunately, but she guessed that this was as authentic an Irish pub as there was in the States.

It was frozen in time. Behind the bar and hanging

over it was an array of glasses. On a shelf behind the bar were bottles of liquor, and there were several kegs to draw beer from. The bar, made from a beautiful color wood—she didn't know what kind—gleamed. Stools lined up in front of it, and there were booths and tables throughout the bar that looked like they were made of the same shiny wood.

A few people sat at the bar talking with an older man. He had silver at the temples of a full head of kohl-black hair with sickle-shaped eyebrows to match. He only glanced at her as she entered, but his eyes were joyful, merry as he chatted with a customer. His cheekbones were concave, and his body was thin to the point of waifish. Just above each elbow was a tattoo. There was a harp and a shamrock on his right arm and a 'Fighting Irishman' on the other under which were Gaelic words.

She took a seat at the end of the bar, and he hurried over. "What can I get for you, lass?"

"A white wine? And can I see a menu?"

He shoved a menu toward her, and she pretended to be terribly interested in it. She did find it intriguing. It was filled with things she had never tried, like Guinness cheese dip and pretzel bites, fish tacos, Reuben egg rolls, and St. Pat's boxty. She had skipped lunch, and reading it made her hungry. When he brought her wine, she ordered two pub-style fish tacos.

The only bartender was this man behind the bar, who she gleaned from eavesdropping was the pub owner—the publican, she heard him called. When her food came, she took a few bites and then tried her best to sound professional, to sound like she had every right to be there. "Would you talk to a reporter who is doing a story on Irish pubs in the area?"

He reached across the bar to take her hand. "Fearghal Flanagan at your service. Farry to my friends."

"I'm Gemma."

When he handed her the wine, he said, "*Sláinte*."

She raised her glass. "*Salute*." As she munched on a taco, which was to die for, she asked him a series of general questions. How long have you had the pub? What kind of people come here? Do you have bands come in to play Irish music? Then, "Farry, do you have any female bartenders? I wouldn't mind a lady's point of view."

"I do, and in fact, in she comes."

A woman in her late forties or early fifties sidled up behind the bar. She had dark hair tied back in a tight bun, beryl green eyes, a pert nose, and glowing skin. She was curvaceous and buxom; her tight blouse revealed a more than ample chest.

Farry called her over. "This lass is doing a story on pubs. Why don't you take a minute to tell her how nice it is to work here."

She rolled her eyes. "I'm here to work, Flanagan. Not to kibbitz."

His look was sharp. "Good for business, Dervla."

Realizing she'd struck gold, Gemma's mind reeled with questions.

****

Clearly feeling he had every right to bark orders at Dervla, Farry said, "Go take a table by the back so you can talk."

Dervla lifted her eyebrows and rolled her eyes again.

Gemma grabbed her wineglass and followed her to a high top in the back of the pub. Dervla huffed as she sat down.

Gemma sat across from her and almost slid off because the wooden stool had been so polished. It was like glass. Her toes dangled, too, because it was such a drop from the stool to the floor. "I'm doing this story about pubs and—"

"Don't you take notes? I don't see any notebook." Her eyes narrowed at the empty space in front of Gemma.

Gemma reached into her purse and found a pen and a notebook from the tradeshow. She sat up straight, her pen poised over a blank page.

"So . . . what's your full name?"

"Dervla MacDonald."

"Can you tell me what it's like to work in a pub?"

Dervla told her that she'd always tended bar, that this pub had a lot of regulars who tipped well, and that Farry's bark was worse than his bite. As Dervla spoke, Gemma twirled her hair and tapped the pen on the table. She recognized that she was showing her nervousness and willed herself to stop.

"Is it hard? Working nights with kids? Do you have kids?"

"I do, but they're grown. Grown and gone."

"Sons? Daughters?"

"Two daughters," she answered.

"And you say they're grown up now and out of the house?"

"Right. Working nights isn't a big deal anymore."

"What about your husband? Does it bother him? I mean, are you married? I guess I should ask that first."

A shadow passed over her face. "Does this have anything to do with running a pub?"

Gemma stared at her a moment and flipped through the notebook as if she were looking through prepared questions. She needed to get her to expand on personal things—how to do this?

"Well, it does, Mrs. MacDonald. It's a human-interest story. People will want to read about what doesn't . . . well, the inside story. We know what the menu is, what the drinks are, but what are the people like? The people who come here and the ones who work here. Is there a husband?"

Dervla shrugged. "One long gone. That's my oldest daughter's father. He's a total wanker."

Gemma blinked and scrunched up her face. This term wasn't familiar. "A wanker?"

Dervla's face brightened as she snorted. "A miserable excuse for a human being," she explained. "A criminal. A petty thief and more. When he got into some pretty bad stuff, I kicked him out. Then I found a nice man, but he up and died on me."

"I'm sorry," Gemma said, trying to sound sincere. "That had to be hard on your daughters."

"Doreen was all right for a while. She used to be a nurse."

Gemma had to suppress a gasp.

"She's not around anymore," Dervla added. "She got into some legal troubles of her own and went running back to her father when she got out of jail. She's as bad an egg as he is now. But now, my youngest daughter, she's the complete opposite."

"Opposite? You mean—"

"Devout Catholic. A nun, in fact."

It was not easy at all to keep from showing her enthusiasm, her intense desire to know every single detail. But for now, at least, it had to be enough.

"Wow, a nun." Gemma tried to think of a way to get more without revealing anything about herself. "Does it bother her that you're a barmaid?"

She shrugged again. "I don't think so. She never said. I hardly get to talk to her. She can only see family a couple of times a year."

"That must be hard."

Dervla looked down, fidgeted with the red-and-white checkered tablecloth. "It is, sometimes, yeah."

"Do you see the other daughter?"

"I told you, Doreen isn't around anymore." She stood. "Now, listen, I really have to get to work. Okay?"

Gemma closed her notebook. The interview was clearly over. She mumbled, "Thanks," returned to the bar, finished drinking her wine, and took a few more bites of her taco. She asked for the bill.

"She looks a bit flustered," Farry said as he handed her a bill. "Did you upset her?"

Gemma glanced at the bill. Reaching into her purse to put money down for the food and wine, she realized that she didn't have enough cash and gave him a credit card. "I certainly didn't mean to, but her family situation came up, and I don't think she really wanted to talk about that."

His eyes narrowed, and then he said, "Not surprised." He ran the transaction. "Her first husband Toby was always acting the maggot. Beating the hell out of her and in and out of jail. And then her daughter goes to jail, and the other daughter up and joins a nunnery to hide from him and the world. Would you want to have that conversation?"

She shook her head, then signed the bill and put the

receipt into her purse. "Well, thanks, Farry. Thanks a lot." She grabbed her purse from the bar and walked to the door.

When Farry called out to her, she cast a furtive look over her shoulder. "So when will we be seeing something in the newspaper?" he asked. "And which one?"

A tiny tingle of trepidation prickled through her; her stomach filled with a combination of nerves and excitement. Her gaze landed on the doorknob. She hurried to the door and yelled, "I'll call you!"

On the way back to her car, she dialed Shake as fast as she could.

****

Shake listened to her without interruption as she told him about the conversation with Dervla. He took a deep breath and then tore into her. He was livid.

"What did I tell you? You are not to go near Dervla MacDonald again. Or the nun. Or anyone else! Gem, are you listening? You're not a police officer. You're a—"

"A what?" she yelled back. "A medium? A psychic? A crackpot?" She felt herself shudder. "Shake, Judith is giving me breadcrumbs and—"

"Let me do my job, Gem. Just stop."

He hung up.

She looked at her phone as the dial tone droned on almost as loudly as an explosion. On the previous occasion when Shake enlisted her help, she received enough short messages to lead him where he needed to go to close the case. This time, she got scraps from Judith, scraps from Luke, and she knew she could break the dam, but she needed time.

She took off the earrings Antonio gave her. She took off Peppi's Italian horn. With some hesitation, she

171

removed the emerald ring from the pouch and placed it on her finger. "Talk to me, Judith. Please. Your parents need closure. Luke needs closure. Help me lock up your killer and throw away the key."

But there was no response.

****

After she gave Fantasma her evening meal, she sat at the kitchen table, twirling the ring around her finger. Literally hours ticked by without a single sign of Judith, without so much as a hum or a mumble.

Around nine, she tossed together a salad and ate a few bites as she stared out the window. Here and there, a star winked, like an angel's fiery eyes sending sparks across the heavens. She took in the heavenly silence.

She put the salad on the counter and was about to change for bed when the phone rang. Much to her surprise, it was the Mother Abbess returning her call. She almost blurted, "I read your schedule. Aren't you supposed to be asleep?" Instead, she said, "Mother Abbess, thank you for returning my call."

She was about to launch into her lies, her fabrications to see Sister Mary Evangeline. She planned to say, "I have this friend who went to school with you, a gal named Jenny Ryan, and she told me you could tell me about your calling and what the first years of being a nun are like."

And then what would she say? *Oh, by the way, she said your purse was stolen and someone used your driver's license to pawn a ring. What do you know about that?*

She couldn't do it. "Mother Abbess, I need to speak with Sile MacDonald. She's called Mary Evangeline now. It's important. People have lost someone dear to them, and we're trying to get closure for them. She has information, but the police said she refused to speak with them. Please, Mother, can you talk to her?"

After a very long pause, Mother Abbess said, "I cannot force her to speak with you, Miss Martelli. What I will do is pray on it and ask Sister Mary Evangeline to do the same."

"But—"

"Good night, child."

Click.

Ugh! She forcefully swept her hand through the air and knocked the salad bowl to the floor. The lettuce and tomatoes, covered with salad dressing, spilled out. Fantasma jumped from the kitchen counter to the floor to do 'cleanup on aisle four.' She shooed her away. "Bad cat. Go on, get."

Chapter Twenty-Two

After she cleaned up the mess, she was too restless to think straight. She grabbed a windbreaker and went for a walk. She had started to reacclimate herself to the pace of the village, to its beating heart—its little shops and curiosities, the nearby Amish culture, and the scenic country roads that came alive with color each fall. She felt safe there, even after dark.

Did Judith Walsh feel safe when she went to that church? Did she have any idea that someone with an ax to grind might want to do her harm? It could have been the nurse who landed in jail. Or maybe her father. Or someone in the family of the man she couldn't save.

Or somebody else.

Tired of trying to figure it out, her feet took her to Jasmine's mother's shop, Quilts and Quirks. It was closed, of course, but they lived in an apartment above it. No lights were on, so she figured they must be out. She turned to walk back home. Then lights inside the duplex building next door to the quilt shop, the one that used to be the tire place, caught her eye. The building had been vacant for a long time, but now it was ablaze with lights and a flurry of activity. She was pretty sure she saw Jasmine standing by a second-floor window.

New signs were up on the old tire place. She didn't recall seeing them before. Then she remembered that Jasmine had mentioned her cousins were working inside the building.

The sign over the door on the left said: *Suds, Spuds, and Buds*. The one to the right said *Swap and Shuffle*.

She tried the front door to the *Suds* shop. It was open, and she went inside. This part of the building was dark. She called out, "Hello."

She heard footsteps on the stairway. Jaz emerged from a room at the back and flipped a switch; light flooded the first floor.

"Hey, Jaz." Her eyes swept the room. This building was vacant no more. The room was large, with black-and-white décor and a glossy modern aesthetic. To the left was a counter for serving customers. The back of the store looked like it would house a bakery or deli. On the right were more shelves and displays and a sign that said, "Herbs and Spices, Oils and Minerals."

In the center of the room were several tables with small, flowering plants on each one.

"Hi, what are you doing out and about?" Jaz asked.

"Just taking a walk. Is this one of the new shops you mentioned?"

"Yep. My mother finally talked my aunt into moving up here from Louisiana. She's been through enough. Her family lost everything in Katrina but stayed and rebuilt. But then came Harvey, Barry, Marco—it just never stops. She gave up. She's upstairs right now, unpacking boxes. Me and Mom are helping. They've been working on the new shops for days."

"No announcements in Next Door?"

This was an online message board, usually filled with nastygrams about somebody's dog or somebody's political sign.

"And nothing in the church bulletin?"

"Well, they want a quiet entrance into River Styx life."

As Gemma followed Jaz to the steps, Jaz explained the shops. She pointed to the left. "Beyond the counter is a partition, and behind that is an area for doing laundry. People can drop off laundry or ironing and get it back the same day. One of my cousins will do repairs and tailoring, too. The 'spuds' area in the back will be take-out—they'll offer fresh potato flour donuts in the morning and various kinds of baked potatoes at lunch time. On the other side, they'll sell herbs and such."

"This is a really, really neat idea, Jaz."

Once in the apartment, she introduced Gemma to her Aunt Ambrette and her four daughters, who all looked to be in their twenties. Angelique, Adelle, Albertine, and Allida. Last name Aguillard.

"There'll be a quiz, later," Jaz quipped. "Everybody, this is Gemma Martelli, my best friend."

The girls rushed forward to hug Gemma, all saying, "We've heard so much about you."

Younger versions of their mother Ambrette, they were exquisite. Their skin was the color of black anatase, a dark, shimmering, prismatic crystal. Their raven-black hair was long and tightly waved, their cheeks like mountain tops. Angelique's hair was a little lighter than the others', and she had kohl-rimmed, electric blue eyes. Her sisters' eyes were brown with a golden glint.

"When do you open, Mrs. Aguillard?"

"Brette, please. Just Brette, Gemma. On Monday, if all goes well."

"Well, this is exciting. Nothing has been in this building since the tire place shut down."

Gemma turned back to Jaz. "Is there a Mr.

Aguillard?"

She shook her head. "Not a good subject," she whispered.

"Gotcha." Turning back to Brette, she asked, "And the other half of the building? With the sign *Swap and Shuffle*?"

"My oldest, Angelique will run that—it will be a bookstore and coffee shop. Used books. If you bring one in, you get one for a dollar with a cookie, and there will be all kinds of pastries and some comfortable seating. We'll do tarot card readings, too."

"Oh, you will find me there a lot!"

She was about to say good night when a large, black cat approached. He stopped in front of her, and his big green eyes practically swallowed her up. "Hey, you, what's your name?"

"He's Milo," Jaz told her.

Milo curled around Gemma's feet and pushed his paws against her toes, purring the whole while. But his large, fiery eyes contradicted this improbable friendliness.

Suddenly, all of her new acquaintances exchanged glances. Brette approached, stooped down to pick up the cat, and placed him in Gemma's arms.

She folded her arms around him, and he purred like crazy. "Whoa."

"He's slipped out the door a couple times," Brett said. "There's too much going on with moving and renovations. He likes you. Take him off our hands for a few days, won't you?"

"I love cats. But I already have one, and I don't think she'd like a newcomer."

Angelique, the daughter with the dreamy blue eyes

and orchid-pink lips, stepped forward. She slid a finger beneath the cat's collar to show Gemma a charm. "This protects him." She pointed a blood-red, lethal fingernail at Gemma. "And he will protect you."

"But I don't need any—"

"You do."

Angelique dug one of her long, stiletto-shaped fingernails along his back, just below his fur. Then she buried her nose in the fur on his head. "Milo, you'll behave, won't you? You'll get along with Fantasma, right?"

Gemma turned to Jasmine. "How does she know her name?"

Jasmine looked at the floor and shrugged. "I must have mentioned it."

I doubt that. I doubt that very much.

Gemma stared at Angelique. She couldn't place what she felt about her—apprehension, admiration, curiosity? She just knew that the young woman was different—different in the same way that she and Jaz were different. She had a gift; Gemma just didn't know what it was.

Brette grabbed a large container and scooped cat food into it. "Come back if you need more."

"How long—I mean, when will you want him back?"

"He'll let you know. And here's a charm to protect you, too."

It was copper, flat, and round, like a penny. It was engraved with arrows in groups of three all the way around. She put it in her pocket.

Jaz led her downstairs, carrying the container of food. "Can you handle both, or should I walk with you?"

"I can handle everything, but walk with me anyway."

As they walked toward Gemma's shop, Milo leapt from her arms and fell into step with Gemma.

"Are you sure he's not a dog?"

Her eyes narrowed. "I'm not even sure he's a cat, Gemma."

"Um, your relatives—"

"A little strange, I know."

"Well, they'll fit right in with you and me."

"My sentiments, exactly."

Jaz stopped at the corner, within view of her store, and asked, "You okay?"

Milo stopped and sat at Gemma's heels. "I guess we are, yeah. But I don't know how this is going to go over with Fan."

"Call me if they get into it, and I'll come right over for him. But if Auntie Brette wants you to have him around, there's a reason."

"Okay."

She continued to walk, but Jaz touched her elbow and stopped her. "Hey, Gem, that rock on your finger. Real?"

She'd actually forgotten she was wearing the haunted ring. "Yes, diamonds and an emerald."

"Not yours." Jaz squinted at it. "A victim's piece of jewelry, right?"

"Yes, that's right." She cursed under her breath because it hadn't helped her get anything more out of Judith. Nothing in the ether. Media blackout. Communications blockade. Dead Zone. And she felt ripped apart by the split screen between the intermittent messages that galvanized her and the watchful, awful

179

silence.

"You're trying to connect with the victim. To help Shake find the killer, right?"

"Jaz—"

"Okay, I get it. But you'll be careful, right? You're all I have."

Gemma scoffed. "Jaz, you have the biggest family on God's green Earth. And a bunch of them are living right next door now. A bunch of girls about our age, too."

"And I'm sure I'll love them once I get to know them better. But they aren't you. You've been there for me since forever."

"Ditto. I'm not going anywhere."

"Just remember, killers are cuckoo for cocoa puffs. It's not like you're playing a game, you know."

Gem gave her a shove. "Okay." They took a few more steps. "Jaz? Any more dreams?"

She nodded. "Yes, same thing over and over, but more intense. Watch your back."

Milo followed Gem into the jewelry store and went up the back stairs as if he had lived there all his life. He came face to face with Fantasma. Growling, hissing, and snarling. Then Milo crept toward Fan, stopped, and licked her face. The next thing she knew, they were drinking from the same bowl.

During the night, she heard a few scuffles. She got up one time in the middle of the night and saw Milo's deep green eyes fixed on Fantasma. As in laser focused. It looked like he was hypnotizing her. Maybe he was, because Fan backed up and curled into a ball in the corner.

Then Milo stood guard at the top of the stairs.

She bent down to pet him and scratched the back of

his neck. "You're not going to turn me into something else, are you?"

She remembered an old movie that her mother loved. The actress Kim Novak played the role of a powerful witch who could cast a spell on a human to make him fall in love with her. She had a cat with powers of its own.

"Angelique isn't some witch with super powers, and you aren't her familiar, are you?"

Laughing at herself, she went back to bed. When she got up the next morning, Milo was still there—her own personal bodyguard in feline form.

Chapter Twenty-Three

It was perfect weather for the Quilt Festival and Raffle after church services on Sunday morning. The sky was a cathedral dome of bright blue, cloudless and unending. Daffodils and tulips and crocuses bloomed wherever one looked. An assortment of irises, mostly black and dark purple, had just begun to push through the dirt in the flower beds behind Gemma's shop and vivid primroses in shades of yellow, pink, white, and red graced the school's lawns. Gemma heard pigeons crooning, and the song and call of a few robins joined the dawn chorus. The sound of sputtering lawn mowers had finally replaced the rumble of snowblowers.

It was a good day for the festivities.

She fed the cats, and after a little huffing and posturing—she decided that Milo was guilty of a lot of 'mansplaining'—they retreated to their respective corners. She put on the yellow sundress she liked so much. Once she was ready for church, she considered putting one of the cats in the shop with the door to the apartment closed because she didn't want to come home to flying fur or worse—an emergency trip to the vet.

"And you know what, Fan? Why do we have no veterinarian in town? The nearest one is Theo Wendell's clinic, and that's more than twenty miles down the road."

She was about to lock the door when she realized that she was still wearing Judith's ring. "Oh, for crying out loud!" She took it off, put it safely in its pouch, then into the safe, and dashed off to church.

After services and the usual coffee hour, she helped set up the last of the long tables where they would sell last-minute raffle tickets and people would cast their votes for the grand prize—usually several hundred dollars which was almost always donated to the church by the winning quilt maker. Three churches competed every year—the Catholic parish, Luke's Episcopalian church, and the Congregational church across the square.

Competition was nothing new in River Styx, of course. Something known as A Battle of the Signs among the churches had been going on for years. Last week, Luke posted C H C H – what's missing? U. R." The Catholic church's sign read, "Just Love Everyone . . . I'll sort them out later—God."

Another one a few weeks ago claimed, "The fact that there's a highway to hell but a stairway to heaven says a lot about anticipated traffic numbers." That was the Congregational sign. Luke countered with "I wish Noah had swatted those two mosquitoes."

****

There were three big tents on the lawn behind Luke's church—one rented by each participating church. Thirty quilts were entered this year, ten from each quilting guild. For as long as she could remember, Lady Lisette Laveau won first place, and often second and third. It was an anonymous vote, thank goodness, because there were a few people who thought of Jaz and her mother as 'different' and probably would never vote for Lady Laveau. Truth be known, it was hard not to tell her quilts from everyone else's. They were perfect, they were intricate and complicated, and they were magnificent.

While voting was in progress, people bought boxed lunches and sat on park benches or blankets on the lawn. There was a stand to buy coffee and soft drinks, too. Gemma paid for a box lunch and a lemonade, then looked around for Jaz. She saw her with her cousins, so she didn't want to intrude. She felt a tap on her shoulder.

"How would you like a preacher to take you to lunch?" Luke asked.

She lifted up her box. "I already bought lunch, but I'd love the company."

They found a space on the far end of the huge lawn and sat cross-legged on the blanket he brought. While they munched on fried chicken, Jaz came over with her four cousins in tow. Gemma felt a pang of jealousy for a moment. They were gorgeous. They were single. And they were standing right there in front of the most eligible bachelor in town.

"Hi, Dr. Luke," Jaz said. "I just wanted to introduce you to my cousins."

Luke rose to shake hands while Gemma sat there, mouth agape. She looked down at her favorite dress, one she felt pretty in. But Jasmine's cousins were like runway models in stature and fashion. They were even lovely the night before in their work clothes. For Pete's sake, they could wear rags and stop traffic. Dressed to the nines for church, there were ridiculously stunning.

Jaz told Luke their names, and each one shook his hand. Then she reached over and coaxed her aunt forward. "And this is my auntie, Brette."

They chatted for a few minutes, and then Brette said, "Pastor Luke—is that what I call you?"

"Luke is fine."

"Luke, then. We'll be attending St. Mary Ascension. I understand you served there."

"In a prior life," Luke said.

"What's Father Dylan like?"

"He's nice. He's a good man."

"But Father Fowler not so much?" Brette asked.

"Let's just say he isn't progressive."

"He may have trouble with us then," she sighed. "There will be gossip about us, Luke. I'm sure you have heard stories about my sister Lisette and her daughter Jasmine."

"No, I—" he protested.

Brette just grinned. "And you may hear rumors that we practice voodoo and have crazy rituals and orgies."

"Well, I—"

"It's all true," she said with a deadpan face.

Then she laughed uproariously, and the girls joined her. "We do have our own private beliefs, and we toss in a little magic, but we aren't going to make little dolls and poke them with pins. Just so you know."

Luke was speechless but just for a moment. "Well, Mrs. Aguillard—"

"Brette, just Brette."

"Brette, if you change your mind, I can think of a few people I'd like to stick a pin or two in."

Everyone laughed, but Gem thought to herself, *That's probably true.*

While people finished voting and eating lunch, Brette settled in with Gemma and Luke. "What are the people like here, really?" she asked. "Is there anyone I should be careful around? Anyone who might be difficult?"

Gemma pointed to Mrs. Wendell. "See that little old,

gray-haired lady there? She owns a farm, and a couple of her grandsons manage it. Well, they think they do. She's not going to let go until she's six feet under, and I think she's going to live to be two hundred. They have a hundred acres, I think. She brings everyone corn for popping at Christmas time and knits things for every new baby—there's a knitting circle, too. And she keeps tabs on everyone. Not in a bad way—she just makes sure that if somebody is in the hospital or needs something, she's on top of it. She and Mrs. Bloom, the lady to her right, who owns the floral shop, are good friends. Mrs. Bloom keeps an eye on everyone, too.

"To Mrs. Wendell's left, the lady in the blue pantsuit? That's Eugenia Harris. She owns the restaurant down by Pine Lake. She thinks she's royalty. She tells everyone she's related to some branch of the royal family. She is not particularly fond of anyone who is not British. Honestly, she's one of the most presumptuous, snobbish people in town. But she does serve a lovely afternoon tea every Friday afternoon—by invitation only—I hear it's quite the feather in your cap if you are on her list of invitees. I am not."

Brette laughed. "I think I'd rather stay off it then."

Luke chimed in. "Trust me, you would. I steer clear of her. She still calls me Pastor Epley even though he retired a couple years ago. She pretends it's a mistake but it's not. She just wants to remind me that I'm not Ralph."

Brette shook her head.

"That little cluster of middle-aged men and women?" Gemma said, waving her hand in their direction. "They all own antique stores. They compare and compete—and it's quite the competition, let me tell you."

Gemma pointed out Mr. Finch, the new funeral home director. "He's the son of the original owner who died recently. The others talking with him are, let's see . . . the owners of the gas station, the drug store, the grocery store, the diner, and Henry Hale, our trusty mailman, who pretty much runs the post office. The lady with the short, brown hair in pink—that's Rosy McCallum, a clerk at the courthouse. She's kinda like Barbie, always dressed in pink. I don't see Judge McCallum anywhere."

"Related?" Brette asks.

Nodding, Gem leaned closer. "Rosy is his daughter. The judge has a son, too. Roland. He's an attorney. And a cousin is the court reporter. Brette, it's a small town. Don't be surprised by a bit of nepotism.

"Oh," Gemma continued, waving to Susie Camp, the only gal in the book club that was her age, "that's Susie. She works at our very small library. She's with Mrs. Harris's daughter Elise, the pretty teen."

Brette's eyebrows shot up. "Mrs. Harris, the snob with her own little inner circle, has a daughter of color?"

"Adopted, I guess. I've never asked because—well, who cares? There's a rumor that her son had a fling with someone, and that little fling produced Elise. Maybe taking her in is the one nice thing Mrs. Harris ever did."

"Really, you'll find people of every stripe here," Luke interjected. "It's like anywhere. Most are nice. A few bad apples, I guess, but mostly just with little dings and dents—none rotten to the core.

"But be warned," he continued. "Everyone knows everyone, and some are more curious about your business than others. We have some very private people who won't let you get close, but that's far outweighed by the ones who wear their hearts on their sleeve and will go out of their way to get the latest scoop of gossip."

****

The winners of the raffle were announced. When two of Lady Laveau's quilts won first and second place, everyone clapped and yelped. Gemma was about to congratulate her when she heard Judith in her head. *"Sister. Sister. Phone."*

Gemma reached into her pocket. It was on 'vibrate,' so she wasn't paying attention. Judith's voice was insistent and bordered on screechy. When Gemma looked down, she recognized the number. It was the convent. She touched Luke's arm. "I have to go inside. I need to take this call."

"Everything okay?"

"Yeah, yeah. I'll be back."

She gulped some air and answered. "Mother Abbess?"

"No, this is Sister Mary Evangeline. Mother Abbess told me you called. I need to talk to you."

****

With her phone at her ear, Gemma entered the small library at the front of the church and sat down. After taking a deep breath, she started to explain her inquiry. "Sister, my name is Gemma Martelli, and I'm trying to help some people get closure after losing a loved one."

"And you want to speak with me about it—it's related to when the police came to talk to me, isn't it?"

"Sort of. I—"

"I wouldn't talk to them. I had my reasons. But I've prayed on it and . . . well, I've had this feeling . . . I can't explain it." After a long moment of silence, she said, "Come tomorrow. We have free time shortly after twelve thirty. When you come, you can wait in the guest lobby. Do not be late."

****

Gemma's legs wobbled as she made her way back to the festival. Deep down, she never expected to speak with this nun. She sure didn't expect her to call. Now that she was going to meet with her, what the heck was she going to say?

She was several yards away from the spot where they ate lunch when she heard shouting. Poor Luke appeared to be in the middle of a Ratty Ruckus. That was the term the locals used for any issue that started with Acantha Ratty, the town troublemaker, bully, gossip spreader, and general all-around pain in the butt. She was currently poking her finger in Lady Laveau's face, who simply stood there with her arms crossed.

Mrs. Ratty's brown-and-gray hair was all askew, and she kept tugging on her suit jacket, which was at least a size too small. Figured. It matched her small brain. Her daughter Alexis was just about as pea-brained and petty. They thought they were important because they had money and were on the church board and some other committees.

Gemma rushed to Luke's side. "What is going on?"

Before he could speak, Mrs. Ratty turned and screamed at her. "Stay out of this! I'm simply pointing out that it's become clear that this competition is rigged. This—" She licked her lips and made a 'grumph' sound. "This woman always wins. My quilts are just as lovely and—"

Gem saw that Jasmine was about to lose it. She heard her friend mutter, "Puke-Face," then wound up her arm and looked ready to send a ninety-mile-an-hour

189

punch into Mrs. Ratty's face. Gemma stepped in front of her just in time. "Narcissistic, old bag!" Gemma spat. "Your quilts can't hold a candle to Lisette's, and you know it. In fact, your quilts aren't as good as the ones that the Junior Quilt Guild at the church across the street makes!"

Gemma took a step closer. "Ya know what, Mrs. Ratty?" She allowed her hands to ball up into fists at her sides. "Your hot air is so toxic that all of us really should be wearing hazmat suits!"

Gasps and muffled laughs sounded.

"How dare you!" Mrs. Ratty shot back, her whole face red. "I suppose I shouldn't be surprised that someone like you would stand up for them. You're as strange as they are. I bet they put some kind of magic potion in everyone's drinks to get their vote."

Alexis, who had a shock of red hair and beady eyes, usually followed her mother around like a baby elephant clinging to its mama's tail. She wobbled a little bit like a baby elephant, too. She stepped beside her mother and opened her mouth to speak, but Gemma stared her down. She was close enough to step on her foot, and it took all her strength not to do just that.

Gemma continued. "You know what, Mrs. Ratty? If you can't learn to control your behavior, there's a very distinct possibility that a magic potion will make its way into your gullet. And then, who knows? You may just end up chum for sharks. I mean, wouldn't that be magical?"

Mrs. Ratty plodded off, her daughter right behind her, but she tripped on something and fell flat on her face. No one offered to help.

She immediately heard Peppi's laughter. *"I never*

did like her, Gem."

Peppi, you and your practical jokes.

Alexis Ratty ran over to her mother and did a face plant right into her mother's back. Then Gemma heard Antonio laughing his head off.

All she could do was suppress a smile and shake her head.

She didn't realize that in addition to Lady Laveau, Jasmine, and Luke, a crowd had gathered around. Suddenly, Jasmine's cousins and her aunt and half the congregation erupted in applause.

And Gemma turned beet red.

Chapter Twenty-Four

The clapping and hooting finally stopped, and the crowd dispersed. But Lady Laveau touched Gemma's elbow. "You know you've made her an enemy now."

"It's okay. We never have been anything but. She harassed my mother. She whispers behind my back. I've just had enough."

Luke touched Gemma's arm. She turned to face him. He put his hands on both of her shoulders. "You have a little bit of a temper, I see. Are you sure you aren't Irish?" he laughed.

"One hundred percent Italian—we have Berserk Buttons, too. My Antonio used to—" She stopped and bit her lip. "Well, anyway, I'm sorry, but—"

"Don't be sorry. Acantha Ratty was way, way out of line, as usual. I don't think she's ever read the Beatitudes. How about taking a walk with me?"

"Now? Where?"

"In the Cuyahoga Valley." He swept his hand through the air. "As soon as all this is cleaned up. And you're on the cleanup committee, right?"

She nodded.

"Good, I think you might have some more hostile energy to burn off, and I don't want to be the recipient of an Italian meltdown."

"No—you really don't."

Once all the tables were put away, the coffee urns

cleaned, and the garbage put into trash bins, Luke changed into an old sweatshirt featuring a popular Irish rock group and jeans. He walked her home so that she could change out of her sundress into jeans.

When she opened the door and put her keys and purse on the kitchen table, Fantasma greeted Luke like he was an old friend. Milo was not quite so sociable. He hung back on the counter and slid into a Sphinx position beside the coffee pot.

"Two cats?"

"The white one is mine. The black cat belongs to Jasmine's aunt, Ambrette. I'm cat-sitting while they finish moving in and setting up their new shops."

"New shops?"

"Yeah, where the old tire place used to be."

Luke's lips formed a tight line. "That voodoo stuff she was teasing about. What's up with that?"

She put a cup of coffee from that morning in the microwave to warm it up. "Hold that thought. I'm going to change. I'll be right back."

She changed into jeans, tennis shoes, and her favorite T-shirt, purchased on a previous trip to Spain. The front had a bull on it with glittery eyes. She liked to pretend that the bull was an expression of her 'inner self'—stubborn, a little unpredictable. Jaz said that she bought it for her because, like bulls, her temperament required special handling.

After entering the kitchen, Gemma nuked a cup of coffee for Luke. Then she nuked another cup of coffee for herself and placed milk, sugar, and a spoon on the table. To let in some fresh air, she opened the door that led down the steps to a small parking lot and a little patio behind the shop. Then she sat down across from him, her hands around the mug.

"I never realized there was an apartment over the jewelry store," he said. "Do you mind living right where you work?"

She grinned. "Do you?"

"Oh, yeah—the parish house. Hadn't thought of that."

"No, it's great. Very short commute," she quipped. "Seriously, I like it here. There are two bedrooms, a big bathroom, some storage. The kitchen is not great, but it's okay. The patio down below is surrounded by Rose of Sharon bushes so there's a little privacy. It works for me."

"The school kids next door don't make you nuts?"

"No. I like kids. They make happy sounds."

He smiled and nodded.

"Now, about Jasmine's aunt," she said. "I just met Ambrette and her daughters last night." She told him about the shops they planned to open. "And as to voodoo, look, I think—well, I don't know a lot about it, but they go to the Catholic church, so can they really be stitching up dolls to hurt people or do human sacrifices or any of that nonsense?"

"It's like anything else, Gem. People resist change, and they don't like anything that's different, unusual. It frightens them. Especially around here."

"I guess. But it's ridiculous."

"I suppose. When I studied theology, I tried to learn about all sorts of religions, but voodoo wasn't on the curriculum."

"Well, I talked to Jaz a little this morning about her relatives. She assures me that people who profess to practice voodoo don't put evil hexes on people or worship Satan or any of that. In fact, they pray to saints."

They chatted a little about the quilt competition—he was proud that he placed bets on Lady Laveau—and then she heard some kind of argument on the sidewalk below. She rose to look out the window. Mrs. Ratty was being obnoxious again to some poor woman Gemma didn't know well. She just knew that she was from the Congregational church and that she'd taken third place in the quilt competition.

Suddenly, a low, deep growl came from Milo. His green eyes flashed like jagged bolts of lightning. He jumped from the kitchen counter to the top of the refrigerator and then flew to the screen door. Claws clinging to the screen, he let out a blood-curdling scream.

Luke looked at her. "Okay, that was weird. He didn't just leap. It looked like he had wings."

She thought so, too, but she wasn't going to admit it. Then again, it had to be at least ten feet from the refrigerator to that screen.

"Milo," she yelled. "Get down."

He let out a few more creepy screeches and finally let Gemma pull him from the screen. When she put him on the floor, he lifted a paw to give a playful bat at Fantasma and then walked away in a huff to a corner of the kitchen floor.

"That was different," Luke remarked.

"Um, yeah. Maybe instead of a voodoo cat, he has angel wings," she joked. "Look, I think he's just pretty athletic. As opposed to Fantasma, who exerts as little energy as possible. Food is her sun around which all things revolve.

"But here's the good news," Gemma added, glancing out the window. "Milo scared the daylights out of Mrs. Ratty just now. She must have jumped on her broomstick to fly home."

He smiled, and they sank into a comfortable silence for a few minutes.

"Luke, what you were saying before," she sighed. "It's hard being different. It's even harder when people don't even try to understand you."

He reached across the table, took her hand in his, and rubbed the top of her hand with his thumb. "I'm trying to understand you, Gem. You know that, right?"

"I do."

She withdrew her hand. If he found out her part in the investigation into Judith's death, he might not be so eager to understand. What seemed to be just beginning could well come to a screeching halt.

****

They drove to the valley to a spot where the blue herons made their huge nests every year. He parked the car, and they got out and walked a little way.

"There's a lot of people here, Luke."

"I think that's because in this restless, crazy, unpredictable world, we all like to come back to something that's steady and constant and expected and beautiful and fun.

"I for one have something of a love affair with these guys," he said, pointing to a large nest in progress that was up high in the trees.

She lifted her eyes to the trees where several great blue herons were perched. They must have been four feet tall. When they took flight, the wingspan was six feet or more. Their feathers were blue-gray with blue streaks on the head and wings. The neck and head were white, and above their eyes were black stripes.

"Mom brought me here whenever we visited my uncle Tommy. Look," he said, pointing to a nest in progress. "The herons start building their nests in late April or early May," he explained, "and the nests can be as much as three feet across."

"I can see that. Nonno—my grandfather—used to bring me here. He loved all birds. Mom said that once he taught her how to run the store, he and my grandmother traveled a lot, and he dragged his big, expensive cameras with him everywhere. He took photos and catalogued all the birds he saw all over the States and Canada and parts of Europe. They even went to Africa and Australia. Until Nana died, that is. Then he kind of retreated. He was sort of lost without her, I guess."

She drew in a quick breath. "Somewhere—maybe with Mom—there are four thousand photos of birds that he put in albums and indexed."

Luke shifted his gaze from the birds to her face.

He bent down, picked up a small stick, and handed it to her. "Here, now we're engaged."

She felt the warmth in her cheeks. "What?"

"Herons don't do diamonds. The male gets a stick and presents it to the female. She takes it and starts building the nest. And that's it. They're monogamous. They build the nest and start having babies. Lots of babies. Must be Catholic."

Her heartbeat quickened. She murmured, "Thanks," and put the stick in her back pocket.

From him? She would take a stick over a diamond—or an emerald—any day.

Chapter Twenty-Five

Staring at the ceiling the next morning, as the soft sunlight crept through her bedroom window, Gemma refused to get up. Next to twilight, this was her favorite time of day.

She was thinking about the day before.

After their walk, they drove through the valley, admiring the beautiful flowers and foliage that spring brings. Then they stopped for coffee and pastry and held hands on the way home.

Luke didn't kiss her good night, but she was convinced he wanted to. She fiddled with her keys and planted a peck on his cheek. She let herself in as she mumbled, "This was nice. Good night, Luke."

He's scared, I'm scared. That's the problem.

She conceded that she was terrified she couldn't live up to Judith, or even Judith's memory. She was even more terrified of what the truth of Judith's murder might be and what that truth would do to Luke. She was afraid if he learned she'd been communicating with Judith and keeping things from him while she tried to solve the case, he might run as fast as he could in the other direction. The bottom line was, she feared that they would become more involved, become closer and closer, and then it would blow up in her face and she'd be as hurt as she was when she lost Antonio—perhaps even more wounded.

****

There were no customers in the shop, and it was just as well. Every half an hour, she ran upstairs to try on dresses to determine which was the most prim and proper for visiting a convent. She settled for a black dress with a white Peter Pan collar and then found the one pair of luxury designer shoes in the closet. They were classic black patent leather with red soles and sky-high heels. Her mother bought them for her to wear to prom. She'd rarely had an occasion to wear them since.

But no, today called for stylish but not flashy. She settled on sensible black pumps, then paced back and forth, rehearsing over and over what she would tell Sister Mary Evangeline.

If she will even listen to me.

Finally, it was time for her to leave. She put the pouch with the ring into her purse, checked how she looked one more time, grabbed an umbrella because of the nasty weather forecast, and drove to the convent.

****

Traffic was light but an early afternoon downpour which also featured hail threw everyone for a loop. She saw at least three fender benders before reaching the convent. The accidents bothered her, but the feeling that she was being followed unnerved her even more.

The sign for the convent came into view, and she turned into the parking lot, turned off the ignition, flipped up the mirror to check her makeup, and combed through her hair one more time. She turned off her cell phone and tucked it in her purse. The last thing she needed was the theme from one of the Ghostbusters movies reverberating through a convent filled with mostly silent, cloistered nuns.

****

She'd only visited one convent-type place, and Sister Mary Evangeline's was nothing like the one that she and Jaz toured in Barcelona. They were only seventeen and about to be separated before each went off to different colleges. Spain was their big adventure. They stuffed their faces on a tapas tour, browsed food markets, and explored museums and palaces.

But Jaz had been particularly keen to visit the Montserrat Monastery—the one she'd mentioned to Luke. It was thirty miles northwest of Barcelona. They reached it by cable car that went up the mountain where the air was fresh and cool. She and Jaz stood in line for hours with pilgrims who came to see the twelfth-century Black Madonna statue that was discovered in a nearby grotto. Jaz wanted to touch the sphere that the Black Madonna held in her hand, and it was worth the wait when Gemma saw the tears streaming down her friend's face.

The monastery was impressive. It was ancient and dusty and awe inspiring. The atrium of the basilica was an open-roofed courtyard, and five arches led to the main area. She loved the marbled black-and-white floor of the atrium and the ornate hanging candles around the edge of the church. On the central pillars of the nave were sculptures of prophets, all carved in wood.

****

This home to the Poor Clare nuns was very, very different.

It was an old brick building in the middle of the city, surrounded by an expanse of green lawn and a profusion of flowers. As Gemma entered the main entrance, guilt from several directions needled her. She was hiding things from Luke. She was defying Shake's express orders. But she couldn't worry about that. Her top priority was to get more information from Judith and whatever other sources she could tap.

She saw the sign telling visitors to push the button on the intercom to announce themselves. She did this and sat in a chair across from a grate—a great black gate that made her recall Jasmine's dream. It ran the width of the lobby, which was austere and empty but for a statue here and there. Nothing like the ornate, Gothic eleventh-century abbey in Spain.

She was the only soul in the waiting area. She shed her trench coat and waited. She rose and started to pace. What if the nun changed her mind? Gemma considered that she was about to get stonewalled.

But at precisely twelve thirty by her watch, an older nun and a young nun, the latter wearing a brown habit with a white veil, entered the area on the other side of the grate. Gemma recognized the young nun from her high school senior portrait. She was pretty with a rosy complexion; she needed no makeup to improve her looks.

The two nuns exchanged a few words, and then the young nun took a seat on her side of the grate that separated them. She gestured for Gemma to sit in a chair across from her, and she did.

"You're Sister Mary Evangeline?"

"I am. And you must be Miss Martelli."

Gemma nodded. For a moment, her throat closed. She couldn't seem to utter a word—or think of one thing to say.

The nun helped her out. "The police wanted to know all about when my purse was stolen. They told Mother

Abbess that my old driver's license was used to try to pawn a piece of jewelry. They obviously discovered fairly quickly that it was irrational and absurd that it could have been me. I've been in here for a while."

"Right. But there is more to it than that," Gemma said. Her tone must have sounded urgent because the nun's eyebrows lifted. "That piece of jewelry is a ring that was in a murder victim's purse. She was killed by the thief."

Sister Mary Evangeline sucked in a breath. Then she frowned and shook her head. "When I entered the order, I gave everything to my sister. She was in prison at that time." She paused for a moment, then continued without prompting. "Before that, she was a nurse and made a terrible mistake. I didn't have much, but I told her there was a box waiting for her at our mother's place. Some money, a small sum that I inherited from my grandfather when he died. And some jewelry, but nothing of value. My purse wasn't stolen, Miss Martelli. I think that Doreen must have taken the license from my wallet."

"Okay and—"

"I love my sister, Miss Martelli. Do you have siblings?"

"I did. My older brother died."

Sister looked surprised by her answer. "I am so sorry." She paused again. "I was . . . I mean, when the police inquired, I knew that Doreen probably took it and used it. But I just didn't want to get her into more trouble. I know nothing about any ring. But her father—my mother's first husband—he is not a good man. I pray for him every day. After Doreen got out of prison, she went to live with him."

"Do you know where, Sister? Where he lives, I

mean?"

She shook her head. "I truly do not. I do not like to remember anything of it, anything that came before this. I do not dwell on it."

"Do you and your sibling look alike?"

She nodded. "Very much. I mean, she's twenty-nine now, I think. Quite a bit older than me. But yes, our hair, our eyes. Yes."

"And she would do what her father asks?"

Her green eyes glistened. "Unfortunately, it would seem so. I understand that, I guess. When she was arrested, when she was on trial, he was the only one who showed up. Mom didn't go. I didn't, either. I regret that. I very much regret giving her no support. I pray for her now."

Gemma took a deep breath. It was clear that this conversation was difficult for the nun. "Has she visited you since she got out of prison?"

"Once. Right after."

"She didn't tell you anything about a ring or where she and your father—"

Clearly annoyed, she stared down at Gemma. "Her father, not mine," she corrected.

Gemma looked at the nun's hands as she fiddled with the sleeves of her brown habit. "No, I told you," she said. "Doreen had access to my purse, to my license, that's all I know. But . . . .." She stopped for a moment and closed her eyes. When she opened them, she continued. "But my sister's father, Toby Tobin . . . he worked for a man who ran criminal enterprises. Or at least that's what my mother thought. I don't know who or exactly what, but I do know my stepfather did a lot of things on behalf of that man. My mother may know more.

"What *I* know is that he's dangerous. He's controlling and manipulative, and he has my sister under his spell."

"Don't you want to help your sister then? She may be in danger. I mean, if she's involved—"

Sister Mary Evangeline's face reddened. She looked down at her lap and gave Gemma the definite impression that she was making an effort to tamp down her temper. "She's made choices. Bad choices, Miss Martelli. I have encouraged her to straighten herself out. I've told her to get her house in order."

Gemma felt a pang of sympathy. She had a great family, what was left of it. Not everyone was as lucky. Lots of families straight out sucked. Luke's. This nun's.

The nun took a deep breath and looked down at her hands again. She played with her unknotted cord. She looked up. "I aspire to be the perfect nun, Miss Martelli. I am far from it. I *don't* expect my sister to be perfect, but she lost her way a long time ago. She killed a man because she was distracted and wasn't paying attention. It was unforgiveable, but I try every day to forgive her and pray that she seeks that for herself. This is my principal family now, this community. We rarely see old friends and relatives. The bond inside this community is my source of strength to continue my journey. Even at this moment, I am not complying with the rules."

"But you had permission from the Mother Abbess to speak to me, right?"

"But not permission from a higher place."

Gemma breathed deeply. "Don't you get lonely, Sister?"

The nun smiled. "I see my mother twice a year. I

have my sisters here. And we have a cat."

Gemma smiled. "I do, too. Right now I have two. One is visiting."

The nun stood. "Is there anything else?"

Gemma thought a moment, but she didn't want to put the young woman through anything else. She stood up as well. "I appreciate your help, Sister. I really do. It means a lot. Just one last question. Why did you agree to see me?"

Sister Mary Evangeline lowered her head and then summoned up a brief smile. "Do you know *Walden*?"

Baffled, Gemma asked, "Who?"

The nun smiled again. "*Walden*, written by Henry David Thoreau. Have you read it?"

"No, I've heard of it, but no, I haven't read it."

"I was drawn to that book. I've been reading portions of it over and over since you called Mother Abbess."

"You read books like that?"

She laughed, a deep, sincere sound. "We read and watch movies and play board games and play with the cat." She laughed again, clearly amused by Gemma's perception of the convent. "Thoreau wrote, 'Rather than love, than money, than fame, give me truth.' "

"Uh-huh."

"Miss Martelli, ever since the police came to talk to me, and even more so since you phoned, that line from the book is all I could think of. It's like a song stuck in your head—an earworm—only worse. I can't sleep. I can't pray or work as I should. I hear that in my head over and over and over again. I believe I was being led to tell the truth."

"I think you were led to it, too."

Sister put her palm up against the grate and spread her fingers. Gemma mirrored her gesture on her side of it as if to touch her hand. Then Sister Mary Evangeline stuffed her hands into the pockets of her habit and walked to the door without another word. She turned to Gemma.

"Please don't come again, Miss Martelli. I'll add you to my prayer list."

****

Only one other vehicle, a large tan car, was in the parking lot when Gemma left the convent. She turned her head to look at it. She didn't see the driver. She didn't think anything of it until she pulled out of the parking lot and about a block later, realized that it was a couple of cars behind her and had switched lanes and took the same turns she did. As the feeling of being followed grew, she constantly glanced in her rearview mirror.

The vehicle—she didn't know the make—always seemed to be a car length or two behind her. When she turned, it turned. When she slowed, it slowed. She turned down streets that took her out of her way, and it did the same. If she buzzed through an intersection, it went around cars to keep up.

Her stupid, old car punked out at a red light, and she couldn't get it started again. She was in no mood for this, and she was scared. "Well, Sister, add my car to your prayer list, too, will you?"

She took a deep breath and turned the ignition again. No dice. What if someone tampered with her car when she was inside the convent? Worried that the car that she'd seen was still following her, she glanced in the rearview mirror yet again, watching for it. She let out a breath. This time, it was nowhere in sight, so she tamped down the frustration and fear. Mostly.

"Stop it, Gemma," she said, smacking the wheel. "Who would do that? You're imagining things."

I really have to get my life in order. Get a new car, make repairs at the apartment, buy new windows, fix it up so it doesn't feel like I'm living in a third-world country.

Antonio warned her, *"Do not flood it."* And then Peppi said, *"Take a beat, Gem. It'll start. Just stop revving it. Try—"*

"Stop being so condescending! I do not need advice from either of you!" she yelled though she knew that they were right.

"But caro—"

"Stop, both of you! You know I don't know a lug nut from a walnut, but—"

"Well, maybe get the battery checked?" Peppi taunted.

"Right," she grunted.

And what she would have given to call her dad to rescue her right now. He might have cussed like a sailor while he fixed it, but he was so darn handy that this car would have been running like a top in a heartbeat if he were still around.

She exhaled, counted to ten, and tried again. It started. Finally!

She didn't notice that the light had changed to green, and the car behind her honked. It was only because of the person and place she'd just left that she didn't flip him the bird. But several not-so-acceptable curse words did trip off her tongue.

The nun told her so much. She would call Shake when she got home. He'd be angry that she went to the convent, but maybe she could give him something more to go on.

****

When she got home, she went straight to the cubbyhole where she kept suitcases, stuff for travel, and the few boxes she hadn't opened after the move. She still had several boxes of Peppi's books. Most had been collecting dust. She saw the box marked 'Memoirs.' Was *Walden* a memoir? She huffed as she dragged it out. She had never opened it. But all the tape was off. She lifted the lid, and there, right on top, was Thoreau's *Walden*.

Okay, Antonio, you're off my you-know-what list. For now.

She flipped through the book until she found the quote that Sister Mary Evangeline recited. 'Rather than love, than money, than fame, give me truth.' In the margin, Peppi wrote: 'Thoreau is saying that he would rather have truth in his life than any of those other things. Truth = more important than material things.'

She leafed through the book, pondering the author's deep reflections. Another one that Peppi highlighted was: 'Be yourself, not your idea of what you think somebody else's idea of yourself should be.'

He used to tell her that, in slightly different words, all the time.

She whispered, "I miss you, Peppi." She longed to take a nap and just let him fill her head with pleasant thoughts.

But right now she needed to call Luke. Sister Mary Evangeline had made her very curious. She was convinced that Judith had influenced her, that her spirit had prodded her to look up that specific quote.

She was about to turn her cell phone back on to call

Shake and then Luke. She had a stupid line to feed Luke. She'd say, "So I went to this new bookstore today. Um, I was wondering. There were some books on sale here. You know, stuff I didn't read in high school or college, like Walt Whitman and . . . well, I haven't ever read *Walden* by Thoreau. Just wondering, did Judith like Thoreau?"

Stupid, stupid, she thought. Then Judith intruded her thoughts again.

"It was one of my favorite books. I knew a lot of it by heart."

Hearing Judith voice, she swallowed hard.

I knew it. So, you and the nun have some kind of ESP-superpower link going on.

She said, "We're going to solve this, Judith. We're going to find a way to give you peace. No matter the consequences."

Chapter Twenty-Six

Luke paced around his office as he spoke with his mother about plans for Mother's Day. "So how about brunch, Mom?"

"That would be great, Luke. But no presents."

He looked out the window. "I already bought you something, Mom."

"That's not necessary, honey. Don't spend your money on me."

He rolled his eyes. "Who should I spend it on then?"

"Well, dinner and a movie with a nice girl comes to mind."

He popped an aspirin into his mouth and swished it down with a glass of water. His head throbbed again. Not enough sleep. Too many dreams. And too much looking over his shoulder every time he felt . . . whatever it was that was watching him, following him. That morning, he thought he'd seen a hand in the mirror when he was shaving and about had a heart attack. He blamed it on overactive imagination.

"You aren't dating at all, Luke?"

He laughed. "I'm doing just fine."

"Like hell you are. I know what you want out of life, Luke, but you can't get it if you don't go after it."

"Yeah, I know," he said to appease her. "I'll pick you up after church on Mother's Day, okay? Put on your Sunday best."

"For you, always. But Luke, really, no present was necessary. Giving someone gifts has nothing to do with showing your love. You know that, right?"

Of course he did. His father was long on gifts, short on love.

When they hung up, he sat down at his desk to work on a sermon but was interrupted minutes later by the shrill of his cell phone. "Luke Bailey," he answered.

"Luke, it's Ralph Epley."

"To what do I owe the pleasure?"

"I'm trying to reach Gemma Martelli but she isn't answering her phone. It's urgent."

"I can run over and see if she's home, Ralph. But what's going on?"

"Look at your phone. There's an Amber Alert, and it's my granddaughter. She's missing."

****

When Reverend Epley told him that he had tried to reach Gemma, Luke shook his head, wondering what the old man thought Gemma could do about it. But he promised he'd keep trying to contact her.

Luke tried to reach her by phone several times. Finally, finally she picked up. She sounded breathless, as if she'd just run up the steps. "Luke? I just—"

"I've been trying to reach you. So has Reverend Epley."

"Why? What is it? What's wrong?"

"Have you heard the Amber Alert? Or did anyone else call you?"

"My phone was off," she told him. "I was in a place where I didn't want . . . Never mind. Hang on a sec." A moment later, she said, "Okay, so who is—"

"It's his granddaughter Amelia. She's missing."

"Amelia Randall is Reverend Epley's granddaughter?"

"You probably wouldn't recognize the name. She's Ralph's daughter's little girl. Their family doesn't go to our church."

He heard her suck in a breath. "Oh, my . . . What are they doing? Who is looking for her? How long has Amelia been missing?"

Instead of answering, he asked, "Can you come to the church? Ralph is on his way here. He wants to talk to you."

"I'll be right there."

****

Luke paced the office as he started making calls to congregants to act as volunteers, either to help search for Amelia or to set up coffee and food stations—whatever they felt comfortable with. He also wondered what it was that Ralph Epley thought Gemma could accomplish. Was he convinced that Amelia was dead and Gemma could contact her spirit? Did Gemma have some other hidden talent, some other unusual gift he didn't know about—and perhaps didn't want to know about?

After he had called everyone he could think of, he decided he needed a moment to collect his thoughts. He went to the sanctuary and sat in the front pew.

"Please," he whispered. "Please help us find this little girl. I'm not asking for me—but a miracle or two right now would go a long way to boosting my faith. And if You work through Gemma, maybe that would help me understand her better, too. I'm trying, really I am."

He heard footsteps and felt the hitch in his breath. Almost afraid to turn around, he slowly shifted his gaze to the doorway leading to the sanctuary. Relieved it wasn't a spirit, he nodded and said, "Ralph, I reached Gemma. She's on her way. But I don't understand what you think—"

Ralph Epley hurried over to where Luke was seated and joined him. He patted Luke's shoulder. "We don't have to understand, Luke. We just have to believe."

Chapter Twenty-Seven

Gemma didn't take time to change out of her dress. She kicked off her heels and slipped on tennis shoes. She tossed on a windbreaker, took Judith's ring from the safe, slipped it into one pocket, and zipped it. Then she took the earrings from Antonio and her brother's Italian horn and slipped them into the other pocket.

"Every tool in the toolbox. All hands on deck. Antonio, Peppi, I need your help. And you, too, Judith."

She ran down the steps and out the door in less than two minutes and raced across the square, huffing, and puffing. She hadn't run that fast since she'd failed miserably to try to get on the high school track team with Jaz.

When she arrived at the church, people were everywhere. They were in the front hall, in the church library, on the lawn behind the church. Jaz and her mom were there, as were Ambrette and all of her daughters. She recognized lots of people from her congregation as well as many from Luke's prior parish who had been at the quilt contest.

She saw Luke at the far end of the front hall. He was huddled with three other young men.

She recognized Danny Givens, a paramedic from one town over. He was tall and lean, with broad shoulders. He was probably about thirty now, but he was a brand new paramedic when he'd arrived to give her

214

grandfather CPR. It didn't work.

She took a deep breath and pushed the memory away because it still stung.

She didn't know the African American man next to Luke, but he reminded her of an actor from one of the Marvel movies. He wore a police uniform. The third guy had his back to her, but she was pretty sure she knew who it was just by seeing the lion's mane that spilled over his collar. It was Theo Wendell whom she dated briefly in high school. He was now the local veterinarian.

Under very different circumstances, and if she weren't crazy about Luke Bailey, she would have considered this a target-rich environment.

She ran up to Luke. "What's happening? How long has Amelia been missing? Who's looking for her?"

He put his hand on her shoulder. "Slow down. Ralph's daughter and her husband, and their two kids, and another couple with their kids, rented a cabin at Beaver Hills for a long weekend. The other family had already left, and Amelia's parents were packing up the car. Amelia was riding her bike. All of a sudden, she was gone. They looked for hours and then called the police, and Ralph. He called me and we started gathering people. We're trying to organize a volunteer group."

"Here's the problem with a rural area," said the Black Panther clone, "It's a big area, wooded, desolate. Park rangers are searching, but response time from other agencies is slow. We're still waiting to hear back on getting a canine search and rescue team. I trained in doing searches for missing kids before I moved up north. Truth is, statistics aren't great—of the two thousand kids who are reported missing every day, some come home, and some don't."

So, she thought, *Cute guy, sexy Southern drawl, very, very bad attitude. Skeptical, cynical.* She supposed that was SOP for cops, but she didn't like his pessimism. Not one bit.

"Gemma, sorry," Luke said. "This is Officer Delphin Durand. He was a neighbor to the Laveau family in New Orleans. He and his family just moved here recently. Earlier this year, he joined the force in Hagersfield, just up the road. But he was off duty today."

Del gave her a nod.

"And this is—" Luke gestured to the paramedic.

"Danny." She smiled. "I remember you. You tried to save my grandfather."

"Oh, yeah." Tousled brown hair and deep brown eyes went downward as he looked at his feet. He looked up, and his sad eyes met hers. "He didn't make it. I'm sorry."

"You tried."

"And what was your name again?" Luke asked, turning to Theo Wendell. "Theo—"

Twirling a strand of her hair, she cut Luke off. "Hi, Theo," she said, nodding to the guy with the strawberry hair who looked like a young Robert Redford. He smiled at her.

"Oh, you know him, too?" Luke asked.

"Oh, Gemma and I go way back, right, Gem?"

Her cheeks warmed. "Luke, this is Mrs. Wendell's grandson, Theo. He's a veterinarian. And we went to school together."

"And to prom," Theo interjected.

She saw Luke lift his eyebrows. He started to say something but pulled back.

A bit of jealousy? She could hope.

Then Antonio decided to barge in . . . again. *"You went to a dance with this guy? This guy? C'mon!"*

She cleared her throat—loudly as if to drown him out.

Theo's eyes met hers. "Hey, Gemma. Good to see you. It's been a while."

Theo was three years ahead of her in high school, a dear friend of her brother. He took her to his senior prom. They were a 'thing' for a while, but he went off to college, and by the time she left for college, he was in his senior year at Ohio State and then went on to study veterinary medicine. She'd heard he recently moved back to the area after doing vet work of some kind in some exotic place. Their high school 'thing' was pretty short lived, though it felt intense at the time.

Her brother decided to pop in. *"He didn't come to my funeral. We were really good friends. I didn't even beat the living crap out of him when he came on to you and took you to prom. He didn't show up for my funeral, Gem."*

Right on cue, as though Theo had somehow heard Peppi, he apologized. "I'm sorry I missed Peppi's funeral, Gemma. I had just left for Kenya."

"Right, right. I heard that you were in Africa doing a senior year thing at a wildlife preserve."

"I was just there again," he said. "I just got back to Ohio a few weeks ago."

"I'm sure Peppi would have understood."

Hint, hint, Peppi. Even if you're floating around on Earth 2, you gotta keep up with Earth 1.

Theo turned to Luke. "I'm a veterinarian, but I'll help however I can."

She turned back to Luke and touched his shoulder.

"Reverend Epley, where is he?"

"In my office. But why—"

She didn't answer. Instead, she dashed to the office and found the retired minister sitting behind the desk, twirling a piece of jewelry in his hands.

"Pastor Epley."

He looked up. "Gemma, thank you for coming."

She went over and touched his hand. "What can I do? Why did you want to talk to me? I'll do anything but—"

"Before your mother left for New York, she told me about your gift."

"What?" Her heart skittered at the thought of her mother talking to Ralph Epley about her ability to communicate with ghosts. What was Mom thinking?

"She wanted me to keep an eye on you," he explained. "She said that it's hard for you. That sometimes people think you're . . . I don't know, odd or something. And that you take the weight of the world on your shoulders."

"Pastor, I—"

"We all know that He works in mysterious ways, don't we? Will you help?"

"Of course, but—"

"Amelia is my only granddaughter. She was born on the day that my wife died, you know."

"I didn't know that."

"She's named after her." He handed her a little bracelet with Amelia's name on it. "This was on the ground near her bike. She was wearing it."

She took it from him and clasped her hand around it.

Amelia is not dead.

She knew it in her bones. With this bracelet in her hand, if she were gone, she'd know it. That was the other half of her 'sixth sense'—on one hand, knowing a person was gone, on the other hand, knowing they were still breathing. It was something that had always proved accurate.

"And this," he said, "was her grandmother's. It's a ring with my birthstone, my wife's, our daughter's, and her husband's, and the two kids' birthstones."

"A Family of Joy ring." She held out her hand. "Yes, I've seen these."

"I don't know if what your mother told me about you is true. And I haven't done a very good job of looking after you, child. But if you can help—"

"I'll do what I can."

She put the jewelry in her pocket and zipped it up again. Hand on the door, she turned to him. She gave a wobbly smile. "Pastor Epley, we'll find her. I promise you that we will find her."

She made another silent plea to the spirits. Peppi, Antonio, and Judith. Now she added Mrs. Epley, the pastor's late wife. *Help me find your granddaughter, Mrs. Epley. I know you can.*

As she headed to Luke's car, she overheard Acantha Ratty in the hallway, speaking to some other women. "You know what happens when these young girls get abducted."

Gemma marched over to her. "Shut. Up."

She turned to Gemma. "I beg your pardon?"

"I said, stop it. Or I swear I'll find a voodoo queen who really *does* stab dolls and make their human counterparts bleed."

Chapter Twenty-Eight

She rode with Luke to the state park. "Gem," he said, "I need to keep you away from Mrs. Ratty. She definitely brings out your dark side."

"She brings out everybody's dark side. If I really could use the Force and find a light saber, I'd—"

He chuckled, and she turned her head and stared out the window.

Instead of his usual rock music, Luke turned on a soft radio station. It was soothing, but it didn't stop her head from pounding or her heart from thrumming.

When they arrived, the area swarmed with people. It came to her that if this was a crime scene, they might be destroying evidence.

Luke jogged toward a long table where volunteers had gathered. Gemma stood there, thinking, *Okay, step up. Help me. Tell me where she is.*

There was muffled noise in her head, followed by an eruption of discordant voices, a collective dissonance so intrusive that she felt like her head was going to explode. Trying to sort it out was like trying to pick out each instrument in a symphony. They were all there, but who was playing what?

She sat on the ground and crossed her legs. Then she brought up her knees, hugged them to her chest, and covered her ears with the palms of her hands. *I can't do this! There's too many, too many voices.*

Then she clasped her hands for a moment, slapped her knees and bounced to her feet. *No. I have to do this.*

She ran behind the cabin where the two families had vacationed. It sat at the top of a hill, and there was a path to a gully behind it.

I need quiet, Gemma thought. She walked along the rough path toward the gully, where they found Amelia's bicycle. She looked up the hill to the back of the cabin. It was steep. If Amelia had biked down here, surely she fell.

Why didn't she just run back to her parents? And if she was knocked unconscious, they would have found her. But if she were abducted—

Gemma crossed a stream and several minutes later, found a log to sit on.

"Vacant. Off. Abandoned. Shed."

The disembodied voices were loud and distorted, but each of the ghosts said the same words over and over. She repeated them out loud. Then Peppi said, *"Abandoned shed, sis."*

"Okay, Peppi. I'll find it."

She was about to get up when she saw Luke walking toward her.

"Gem, what are you doing? Who are you talking to?"

She shook her head and told him to follow her.

"Wait," he said, reaching out. "Gem, what did Ralph Epley want?"

"He wanted me to help."

"Help how?"

"How do you think? The only way I know how."

She traveled the path back from the gully, up the hill, and around to the front of the cabin. She wasn't sure who to talk to, so she approached Del Durand, the young police officer. She didn't like his attitude, but he was the only cop around whose name she knew.

"Del?"

He turned to face her. "Yes?"

"Try looking for a vacant cabin."

"These are all basically vacation and holiday cabins."

"Not just vacant. Abandoned."

As Luke came up behind her, she heard Judith's voice loud and clear. *"Dilapidated."*

"One that's in bad shape," Gemma said. "Like ready to fall down. Maybe with a shed? Something off trail?"

"Where did you get this idea from?" Del asked, his eyebrows lifted, his lips pursed.

"Books. I read a lot of books."

He shook his head and gave her a blank stare. "Right."

Jasmine's cousin Angelique came out of nowhere and touched Del's shoulder. "Del, if Miss Martelli is giving you advice, you should listen."

He pinched his forehead. "Angelique."

"You should listen. You understand me, right?"

As if he'd been placed under a spell, he nodded.

Or maybe he would walk barefoot on hot coals or jump off a cliff for Angelique? Gemma thought.

"It's worth a try, right?" Angelique added.

He nodded again and touched Angelique's hand.

Gemma retreated.

****

Minutes, then hours ticked by as the volunteers searched the woods. There were many dangerous places for a child—ravines, cliffs, rugged trails. Not to mention the animals that were about.

Every once in a while, a choir of the voices sounded inside her head, and they weren't whispers by any stretch. It was more like a convention of cawing crows. There would be a lull, and then all at once, all of them—Peppi, Mrs. Epley, Antonio, Judith—started again. Rattling, growling, squalling.

Her head pounded.

A short while later, Officer Del found her sitting on the back porch of the cabin the couples had rented. He handed her a cup of coffee. "Here, you look worn slap out. You could use this, I imagine."

"Thanks."

"Mind if I sit? They're laying out a new grid. They'll call when they need us."

"Okay," she sighed.

He sat to her left on a wicker rocker. "This would have been a good day for sweet tea and pecan pie." He turned to face her. "Those are the two things I miss most about home and my mama."

"Is she—"

"Died a while back."

"I'm sorry."

Staring out into the woods, he asked, "So what do you think of Ambrette's new tater store?"

"The new Spuds place? I think it's brilliant."

"She talked about it for a long time," he said.

Her head was splitting, and he'd really rankled her earlier with his statistics about lost children, but she tried to be civil. "Did the hurricanes make you move, too?"

"Partly. But I also knew Angelique—well, Ambrette and her daughters were going to be here. At least I'll know some people here."

"What is it like, being in a hurricane?"

"Scariest thing ever. It wasn't just Katrina that drove me out. There were tropical storms, too. Rita hit and then Ida. Then we had Harvey in 2017, Barry in 2019, then Delta, Zeta—they just keep coming."

As he spoke about the storms, she noticed a large ring on his left hand. It featured a blue stone in the center. The stone was surrounded by gold and engraved with the rank Petty Officer Third Class and his name, Lavelle Durand.

She felt compelled to touch it. "Were you in the Navy?" she asked, pointing to the ring.

"Oh, that's my dad's Navy ring."

When she touched the ring, unfamiliar emotions washed over her. They ranged from fear to an adrenaline high, from relief to severe depression. Images and sounds bombarded her. The light drained from the sky. The wind moaned and shrieked. Rain banged against a metal roof. Gutters, fences, tires, you name it, flew through the air. Waves of water swept the houses with a whooshing sound. She saw people on rooftops; she saw cars floating down streets.

As her heart began to hammer, she realized she was seeing and hearing and feeling what Del's father felt during a hurricane. She jerked her hand away. "Del, your dad, was he . . . what was he doing during Katrina?"

"He was a cop also. He tried his best to help people who had nowhere to go. And afterward, those who had nothing to drink or eat and no home to go back to."

"It must have been horrible."

"He never really got over it. I think he had PTSD. He was depressed every day until he died."

She closed her eyes. *Lavelle, be at peace. Your son*

is okay.

Del cocked his head as if he'd just heard something—a whisper on the wind, an animal in the bushes. Then he turned and smiled at her. "But you know what? I feel like he's with me, and we'll find this little girl. I think he'd be happy about that."

"I think he would, too."

"But he wouldn't be happy about me sitting around. I'd better get moving."

"You said they'll call us. Too many cooks spoil the soup. As in too many volunteers who don't have a clue what they are doing, and they may get in the way of what they're doing right now."

He nodded. "Right."

She sipped some coffee and said, "Earlier, when I met you, Luke said you and your family moved up here. Are you married? Kids?"

"Nope. But I have two younger brothers, and I brought them up here with me. We leased a little place between River Styx and Hagersfield. It's an awfully small police force, and I want to get on a larger one someday. Cleveland, Akron, maybe. But this job was open."

"Mmm."

Antonio's voice sharply came out of the chaos. *"Oh, my Gemma. He lies to you. He's chasing his love. The one with the lighter hair and the blue eyes."*

Angelique, she thought.

"What we will do for love, eh?"

She gazed out at the forest. This was a beautiful area, one she had always meant to visit but never got around to doing it. The forest was lush with rugged cliffs and serene waterfalls. But when it got dark, it would be even harder to find little Amelia.

She had read about this place. In the stories, the serenity was clouded with evil. Ghosts and goblins and more came out of the fog. There was an abandoned railway tunnel, where the ghost of a brakeman who died working on the tracks, walked, swinging his lantern. In the late nineteenth century, a young couple tried to cross Aidan's Creek, and their wagon slipped into the "Death Hole," a fifteen-foot pool with undertow. They drowned, and people still heard them speaking to each other along the shores of the creek, always followed by a horse screaming.

It was also said that a man who actually lived with his dog in one of the caves had haunted the area for two hundred years. His dog could be heard baying at the moon. According to legend, Joseph Mitchell and his brother roamed with their father along the Ohio River and opened a trading post. He lived along the river and became a loner after the 1812 war. He liked to visit the gorge and trapped in the area. One wintry, arctic day, he stopped at a stream for water and used the butt of his musket to crack the ice. But the musket fired and hit him under the chin. The story went that trappers found him a few days later and buried him in the forest near the cabin that he built before he decided to live in the cave.

As all these ghost stories swirled in her head, without warning, Jaz ran toward her. "Gem, c'mere."

Gemma rose and walked over to a corner of the deck where Jaz was shifting her feet and pacing. The look in her eyes made Gemma's stomach turn. "What is it? What is wrong? Did they find Amelia? Is she—"

"No, it's not about Amelia. Gemma, I just closed my eyes for a couple of minutes, just a couple minutes, and what I saw . . . images came out of nowhere. A jet of blood surging in the air, and blood dripping from your mouth. I could taste it. I heard bones breaking and popping and snapping and crunching. A bat or some kind of wooden pole splintering. I'm scared for you, Gem."

It didn't seem to have anything to do with Amelia or this place. It was something else, and it was deeply disconcerting. "Be careful, Gem, okay?"

Before Gemma could respond, Jaz turned. Shaking her head, she went back inside the house. Her actions had Gemma ready to jump out of her skin. She rushed over to the porch railing and gripped it tightly; her fingers turned white.

"Hey, you okay?" Del and Luke asked at the same time.

She turned to see Luke. She fell apart, and he took her in his arms.

"Hey. Hey, hey, hey." He rubbed her back. "Gemma, it's okay. We'll find her."

She pulled back and saw him looking at Del. She stepped back and walked back to the railing. She held on to it and leaned forward, looking down at the gully. "Del, do they usually catch people who abduct kids?"

"I don't know any statistics on that." He rubbed his face. "I do know that after the first few hours . . .."

She turned away. *It's been way more than a few hours.* She turned her face skyward. *The sun will set in an hour or so. Then what?*

She heard Theo Wendell's voice. "Del, we're going back out. They have a map of the next grid area to search."

She stepped off the porch.

They went back inside to 'suit up' for another

search. She was about to join them because the voices
had hushed. Then she heard her brother's voice loud and
clear. *"Just listen to the voice that speaks inside."*

She heard a dog baying, howling. Could that be the
best friend of Old Man Mitchell who lived in the cave?
Was that story even real?

Got it, Peppi. The cave. Amelia is near the cave.

****

She rushed inside to look for Del again. Brette and
her daughters and some of the women from all the River
Styx churches had set up a coffee station with
sandwiches and pastries. It was nice to see people come
together.

It just stinks that it happens only when it's a tragedy.

She saw a derelict cabin in her mind—and it was
near the cave. Del was about to go out again with some
kind of backpack and a flashlight in his hand. She ran up
to him.

"The cave. I think she's near the cave."

Del shook his head and frowned. "With all due
respect, Miss Martelli, we've been through that cave
several times. Evey inch and—"

"No, *near* the cave. An old cabin that's falling
down. And some kind of shed that's behind the cave, off
the road. Because of thistle and briar, you can't see it."

She turned when she heard a woman say, "Amelia
was fascinated with that cave. We were just there
yesterday." It was Amelia's mother. A toddler,
apparently Amelia's brother, held tight to her hand. The
woman's eyes were red and swollen.

"I'm going," Gemma yelled and took off. Del
reached out to stop her, but she yanked away. She heard
him scream her name and "What the—" followed by an

expletive.

She ran, her breath whistling with excitement, anticipation dancing in her blood. She raced toward the cave that she saw earlier on a map in the cabin. That had to be it. It was maybe a mile and a half away. Up hills, through thicket, over tree stumps and roots. Something caught her dress and ripped half the hem away. She didn't care.

She shivered even though it wasn't cold. Her throat was dry, and she was wheezing. She opened her mouth to breathe, to grab the air, even as her head was violently drubbing. Not daring to look back, racing toward the cave, she heard Luke and the voices of other men who were hot on her trail. Her lungs were puffing, she was gasping for air, but she kept running.

It still hurt when people didn't believe her. She could still remember the sarcasm and laughter and snide remarks the first time she directed the police to a body in Chicago. But what did she expect? Especially in this situation, a situation in which she had zero experience— why would anyone follow her directions? She knew that the guys were only running after her to keep her from falling over the ledge next to the cave or getting tangled in the overgrowth.

Though she knew that the sun was still shining, everything around her turned dark and ominous, primeval, as she made her way around the cave and down a rugged off-the-path trail. The trees seemed grimy; the air smelled decayed, stifling every breath of air she took. Spiders clutched to puzzled webs, and the yowling of coyotes didn't seem as distant as she would have liked. In the dark, she saw eyes aflame, frenzied mouths eager to dine on prey.

Me.

The hair on the back of her neck rippled like the hackles of a dog. A mad dog. Everything hurt. Her bones shuddered, her blood simmered, her brain stewed.

And the voices in her head had gone silent.

But real voices, human voices came from behind her. Luke's and Danny's, Del's and Theo's, and others.

Just ahead were thickets and coppices; they were sooty, like some ancient, rampant fire had torched the bark and the leaves. She pushed through the undergrowth, and there it was. The neglected—no, abandoned, ramshackle cabin. It didn't look safe. A good gust of wind would have blown it over. But the shed seemed intact.

She heard the baying of a bloodhound, and up ahead, to her right, stood a man. An old man with a pipe hanging from his lips. He had a musket in one hand and a makeshift cane made of a light-colored branch of wood in the other.

Is the cave that I just passed the rock shelter where Joseph Mitchell spent years as a hermit? The cave where some people believe he is buried under a cave ledge? Am I seeing Joseph Mitchell, and hearing his old bloodhound? It cannot be—I've never seen a ghost. Never.

It's just the adrenaline, she told herself. *You're too spiked, too wired. You're imagining things.*

Again, she heard a whine, a bark, and a howl. Gemma pushed her way through the thicket and brush until she reached the small clearing in front of the cabin. Foolishly giving no thought to what might be lurking in there, she scurried inside. And there was Amelia.

Chapter Twenty-Nine

The child was curled up, sound asleep. Her arm was in the air as if it was draped over something. But for a fraction of a second, for the briefest instant, Gemma swore she saw a large dog beneath the little girl's arm.

She was dumbfounded. She didn't understand. "It can't be," she whispered. "I don't see ghosts. Let alone a ghost dog."

Theo sounded breathless as he appeared at Gemma's side. He ran to Amelia. He touched her shoulder. "Amelia?"

She woke with a start. She rubbed her eyes with her little hands. "Where's my mommy?"

Danny, the paramedic, caught up and checked the child. "Scraped knees and a cut on her lip. That's it. I think she's okay."

Del and several other people who were right behind, gathered around. Luke was still a few paces behind.

Del ordered, "Give them room."

Gemma bent over, hands on her knees, catching her breath and trying not to fall over when her knees buckled.

Theo steadied her and whispered, "Who were you talking to, Gem?"

"What?"

Was I talking out loud? What did he hear?

"I . . . I thought I heard a dog howling."

He took her aside, out of the earshot of the others. "Me, too. I thought I was the only animal whisperer around here, Gem. You weren't imagining it."

Absorbing his words, she said, "You heard the dog? You hear animals?"

"Sort of. I have since I was a kid."

"You never told me, Theo. Why?"

Before he could answer, Luke caught up to them and put his arm around Gemma's waist. She looked over her shoulder and saw Theo shrug.

As they started to make their way back to the cabin, she heard a lot of murmuring and whispering by volunteers behind her. *Heaven only knows what they're saying.*

Luke, visibly shaken, draped an arm across her shoulders. "How did you know, Gem? How?"

She shrugged him away, and she didn't answer. If he didn't already know, what could she possibly say that he'd believe?

****

When Danny handed Amelia to her parents, they checked every inch of her to be sure she was okay. As Gemma passed by them in order to go inside to a first aid station to have her own scrapes and cuts looked after, she heard Amelia's dad ask the girl what happened. Gemma stopped to listen.

"I rode my bike down behind the house, and I fell and broke it. I broke my bike, Daddy," she cried. "And I thought you would be mad, so I followed the dog. He took me to the cave, and then I found the little house. The dog stayed with me, and I guess I fell asleep."

Luke turned his head sharply to look at Gemma but said nothing.

"What did this dog look like, honey?" her mother asked.

Sniffling, in a little voice, "He was big. He had wrinkles on his face like Grandpa. And big, long ears. He was sad, Daddy. His eyes were sad, and he cried a lot. He cries real loud." She gave a little shrug. "I wanted to stay with him because he was sad."

Someone muttered, "That sounds like Old Man Mitchell's dog." Someone else laughed.

But Luke looked from the little girl to Gemma and back again.

At the first aid station, with Jaz and her mom putting peroxide on her cuts, Gemma didn't notice the sheriff coming her way. Then, he was in her face. His brown hair was buzz cut, and he had a hawkish nose. His sunglasses hid his eyes which made her immediately distrustful. It didn't take long to figure out he had a fragile ego.

"I understand you knew where the little girl was."

"Good guess."

The sheriff snorted. "Yeah, right. Like you're psychic or something, right?"

She winced, hoping he was just being a sarcastic jerk.

"Where were you earlier today, Miss . . .?"

"Martelli. I came here to help when I heard about Amelia."

"But before that. Say around one or so?"

Bristling, she protested. "I don't understand. I—"

It hit her. *Does this idiot really think I kidnapped a kid and then did everything I could to 'find' her? He thinks I could be a suspect?*

Shake came out of nowhere. "She was at a convent,

Sheriff."

Oh, for crying out loud, was Shake the one who was following me in the tan car? He does drive a tan car.

Gemma looked down at her feet, feeling the warmth fill her face.

Turning to Shake, the sheriff asked, "Who are you?"

"Detective Shakespeare Williams. I work cold cases."

The sheriff flashed his badge. "Yeah? Then why are you here?"

Shake ignored him and went over to Gemma. He leaned and whispered, "I reckon he could eat corn through a picket fence."

She suppressed a giggle.

The sheriff's smirk turned to a scowl. "I think you're interfering with my investigation."

She saw Shake's eyebrows go up as his jaw set just a tad harder. "I think maybe you're interfering with mine."

"Where were you?" the sheriff asked Gemma.

"She was at a convent," Shake answered.

Gemma's eyes fluttered in surprise, but she jumped in. "Sheriff, he's correct," she said. "I was visiting a friend at the Poor Clares convent. You know, in downtown Cleveland?"

"She visited a convent, huh, Mr.—"

"Detective Williams."

"And you would know that how?"

Shake was in plain clothes. Easy enough for the sheriff to make a mistake at first, but not a wise error, given Shake made his rank and affiliation clear—twice in less than five minutes.

"I'm saying she was at a convent visiting a friend,"

he repeated, "and I happened to be there myself, following up on a lead in a cold case. A purse was stolen from one of the nuns, and her driver's license was used recently to try to pawn a very valuable ring. This may lead us to a break in a cold case . . . an ongoing investigation into the murder of a nurse several years ago, Sheriff."

Gemma glanced at Luke. He had plastic cups filled with hot coffee in his hands. He dropped both and swore.

The sheriff pressed. "So, Miss Martelli, is that about the size of it? You were at a convent earlier?"

Speechless, she nodded. Shake was bailing her out, but now the cat was out of the bag as far as Luke was concerned. Luke knew that someone had killed Judith and had stolen her purse, and that the murder remained unsolved. Shake had just told the sheriff that the victim was a nurse.

Luke was a smart man. He'd put two plus two together and figure out the cold case had reopened.

Luke busied himself cleaning up the coffee spill. When his eyes met hers, he looked away.

"Yeah, that's about it," Gemma said quietly. "I visited a friend around twelve thirty. Sister Mary Evangline. Ask her. Or the Mother Abbess."

"I think I'll do just that," the sheriff grunted, jiggling his keys in his hand.

Gemma felt her face flame all over again. After blowing out a breath, she shot the lawman a dirty look.

Shake glared at the sheriff. "I don't think you will, Sheriff. Like I said, it's an ongoing investigation, *my* investigation. Your assistance is not required. Nor warranted. Y'all should stay in your lane. Besides, these nuns covet their privacy. We clear?"

The sheriff spit on the ground, grunted, and stomped off with his deputies storming after him.

Shake put his hand on her arm. "I'll take you home, Gem."

"But I came with Luke and I—"

"Not a request, Gem. We need to talk."

****

Gemma had a hard time keeping up with Shake as he marched back to his car. By the time she caught up to him, her nerves were at a razor's edge. Her seat belt wasn't even fastened before Shake ripped into her.

"What in the Sam Hill were you thinking?"

"I was going to call you, but then Pastor Epley called and—"

"I don't care!" he shrieked. "I told you not to go near Dervla MacDonald or the nun. Didn't I? Didn't I tell you not to get any further involved in this?"

"But you need to know what Sister Mary Evangeline told me. And what gives you the right to follow me?"

"What are you talking about?"

"You followed me to the convent. Just because you weren't driving some kind of black sedan like the FBI or something doesn't mean I didn't notice."

"This car isn't tan, Gemma. It's blue. It's my wife's. She took mine in to have the tires rotated this morning. I didn't follow you. But I saw you pulling out of the convent when I pulled in. I wanted to talk to Sister Mary Evangeline myself."

A shiver went through her as his explanation sank in. If it wasn't Shake tailing her, who was it?

"The nun wouldn't talk to me," he admitted. "But she spoke with you?"

Gemma nodded.

He inhaled deeply, exhaled slowly. "Shoot."

She gave him a summary of what Sister Mary Evangeline had said, and he listened intently.

"Okay," Shake said. "Then it's clear her sister, this Doreen Tobin, is the one who tried to pawn the ring. And it sounds like her father may be involved. We don't know how she got the ring. We don't know if Judith was a specific target. We don't know a lot, but I'll admit I know more than I knew a few days ago.

"But Gem, you absolutely must promise me that you're done. I'll talk to Ms. MacDonald, and I'll track down the Tobins. You. Are. Out. Got it?"

Shaking, trembling, she nodded weakly.

Then she just stared out the window, because honestly, she didn't know what else to say.

****

Shake pulled up in front of her shop and silently waited for her to exit. Before she closed the door, he said, "I heard that Pastor Epley and Luke are having a little service at the church—a thank-you thing for Amelia being found. I'm going to go, and then I'm going to talk to Luke and bring him up to speed."

She whipped to look at him. "What are you going to tell him?"

"I'm going to tell him about the ring turning up in a pawnshop and that we now know who took the nun's driver's license to use there."

"I think he's already figured that out."

"Well, I'll try to assure him that we're going to follow up—talk to Dervla MacDonald and try to find the Tobins and see where that leads.

"Gem, you do understand, right? I'll take it from here."

Again, she simply nodded. "Shake, Judith led me to the nun. I think there's more that I can glean from her spirit."

Shake frowned. "Go get cleaned up. Have something to eat. Have a glass of wine. From what I hear, you had a rough day."

"Yeah, kind of."

"It isn't that I don't appreciate your help, but you have to stop now. Okay?"

"Yeah."

She went upstairs, took off her ruined dress, and stuffed it into a trash bag. She checked the pockets of her jacket; all the jewelry was still there. She placed Antonio's earrings and Peppi's necklace back in her little box of precious things.

The look on Luke's face—she couldn't get it out of her head. She was trespassing in his area of expertise, into his core beliefs—just as surely as she'd trespassed on the farm to find Marjorie's body.

She was pretty sure he'd never get what she did or who she was.

Chapter Thirty

Luke's hands shook as he tried to jot down notes to give a little speech to those who were gathering in the church. He wanted to thank everyone who had shown up to look for Amelia Randall. He wanted to choose the right words. But he'd spoken with Detective Williams, and all he could think about was the investigation into Judith's murder being reopened and wondering just how much Gemma Martelli was involved.

He rose when Pastor Epley came into the office. "Are you okay?"

"Yeah, yeah, sure. Very thankful that Amelia is okay."

"Yes, of course. But what about you, given all that the detective told you?"

"It's a shock. But I'm glad he's looking into Judith's case. It's Gemma's involvement I can't wrap my head around. And you asking for her help—I really can't conceive of that."

"Desperate men, desperate measures. And who was the one who found Amelia? It worked, didn't it? If spirits spoke to her—if angels—"

"Angels? C'mon, Ralph, what are you talking about?"

Pastor Epley inhaled deeply and sat down in one of the wing chairs. He ran a hand through his tuft of silver hair and fixed his eyes on Luke's face. "Have a seat."

"They're gathering in the sanctuary, Ralph and—"

"Sit."

With a sigh, Luke sat down in the other wing chair.

"Read your Bible, Luke. Angels are mentioned at least twenty times. They visited people, brought messages. Take the time that Mary Magdalene and the other Mary went to see the sepulcher; the angel rolled back the stone and told them Jesus wasn't there. Or when the Angel Gabriel met with the Virgin Mary and told her she would bear a son and call him Jesus."

"Those weren't dead people communing with a ghost whisperer, Ralph. And even those stories—"

"How about when the Egyptians were pursuing the people of Israel after the Pharaoh let them go, and an angel went to the Israeli's camp and spoke to them? What I'm saying is who knows if Gemma is receiving text messages from angels?"

Luke shook his head. "She claims ghosts talk to her. Dead people."

"And you find that difficult to buy into?" Ralph replied.

Luke chortled. "Yeah, yeah, I sure do. And by the way, angels and humans aren't the same. Angels are their own species."

"Have you ever studied Jewish texts?"

"A bit," Luke said, placing the papers he'd held on his desk. "But—"

"Think back then to what you may have studied about ancient texts. In the book of 2 Baruch, it says that righteous believers will be transformed 'into the splendor of angels,' and that 'the excellence of the righteous will then be greater than that of the angels.'

"It goes on to say that those who are righteous

become angels who are greater than other angels, greater even than the stars . . . they were believed by many ancient people to be fantastically great angels."

His lips turned into a wry smile. "I have no trouble believing that my lovely wife is an angel who guides me. Is it so hard to believe that your Judith is an angel, Luke?"

****

Exhausted, confused, and irritated, after his short thank you speech, Luke went back to his office and sat. Detective Williams hadn't kept him abreast of the investigation; Gemma was clearly involved in the same investigation and keeping things from him. And this thing she'd just done—the way she'd found the little girl
. . ..

Once the church cleared, he went back to the sanctuary, sat, and looked skyward. "I can't handle this."

He inhaled deeply. He wasn't sure if he believed in angels. He certainly had never believed in mediums who could speak with spirits.

And yet . . ..

He started to get up. But then he closed his eyes. He could still see her—Judith. He could still see her silky hair that fell in waves over her shoulders. The blue light that was in her periwinkle eyes. The smile that fell on him. He still remembered being unable to take his eyes off her rosy, velvet cheeks. He would think of her long after they parted, and he believed that she thought of him after their long talks.

He had loved her, and he had lost her—lost the sun that she brought to him, even if that had always been threatened by a cloud. After all this time, he still felt that sun, beating down with all its strength, leaving him always with a sort of grave sweetness amid the grief.

Despite his efforts, he could not forget her. It wasn't *right* to forget her. His mind of its own accord would recall the smell of her hair, the pleasure of holding her hand, the glimmer of a different life he'd not managed to discover before he met her.

Sometimes at night, he would lie in bed, motionless, looking, breathing, trying let go of the images of Judith. Lately, he would concentrate on Gemma, on the totally logical way she suggested that he look at things, at his life. He sensed she was ready for him, open to yield to him everything she was.

But wouldn't that be betraying the woman he'd been willing to break his vows for?

He buried his face in his hands.

For a moment, he felt it again. That uneasy, unreasonable feeling of being watched. He thought he recognized the scent of Judith, that he felt a hand on his shoulder. He thought he heard a voice whisper, but without words.

For a second, he pressed his own hand against his shoulder, expecting to feel flesh. He suddenly felt perfectly relieved, permitted, allowed to catch sight of something else—allowed to hurl himself joyfully into a new love, leaving the hollow sadness behind. To go to Gemma, to be happy, to be fulfilled. She had filled him with a new light, like morning rays to the gardener. Reaching out to her was like the bright funnel-shaped flowers that climbed up the walls of the parish house to reach the sun. They could trail through trellises, fences, stakes, arbors, their long vines twisting around canes or whatever it took to reach the warmth. Like the nasturtiums, he yearned to reach for that light and warmth that Gemma offered.

But could he really let Judith go? Could he really accept Gemma's gift?

He shook his head. "I don't see how, God help me, I don't see how."

Chapter Thirty-One

After a quick shower, Gemma tossed on a shirt and slacks, slipped the ring back into the pouch, and put that in the safe. Then she walked over to the church.

When she walked up to the front entrance of the church, Pastor Epley hugged her. She slipped Amelia's bracelet and his wife's ring into the pocket of his blazer. He whispered, "Thank you, Gemma. Thank you."

Once inside, she saw Luke shuffling papers at the pulpit. She immediately left the main sanctuary and went straight to the small chapel, part of the original church where mostly elderly parishioners enjoyed an early morning traditional service with familiar hymns in a hymnal with large print. No one was in the chapel now. It was quiet, which was what she needed. Quiet with a capital Q.

And solitude.

She sat in the back pew. No voices. No whispers. But that was fine with her. More than fine.

She thought back over the day's events. The nun's admissions. The search for Amelia. She chalked up seeing the ghost of Old Man Mitchell near the cave to a hallucination, based upon her recollections of all the ghost stories she'd heard over the years and the crazy fugue state her brain was in at the time.

But the dog—what about seeing and hearing the dog? And what about Theo hearing him?

Amelia saw him, too. And didn't it seem like the old bloodhound was protecting her? Watching over her?

So what now? Can I see animal ghosts?

She thought of Milo, the cat who could fly across the room. Truly flew, like he has wings. But people could *see* him—not just Gemma. *He's just a cat, Gemma Martelli. Interesting, intriguing, unusual, yes, but just a big, black cat.*

For the first time ever, she was really struggling with her gift. It was always odd and strange, and it always made her different. She really didn't want it anymore.

She pondered what Shake would tell Luke. *And what will I tell him?*

She lost track of time. She wasn't sure how long she sat there. A long time. She was finally thinking about going home when she heard the doors to the chapel creak. She looked over her shoulder and saw Theo.

****

"Hi, Theo," she said in a faint voice.

"Hey. How are you doing? You okay?"

She looked down. Her hands were quaking, and she folded them together in her lap. "I think so. Scary day, though, wasn't it?"

"Yeah, for sure. I thought you might be here," Theo said. "My grandmother sneaks in here when she needs peace and quiet."

"It's a good place for that, I agree."

"Listen, Gem, I just took a little walk. I was down by your place because I didn't see you in church. There's a big black cat guarding your back door. I mean, truly guarding."

"Yes. He belongs to Jaz's cousin, but he's been hanging out with me while they finish renovations of the new shops."

"Well, you keep him close, Gem. He's a . . . he's unique. Special. He is all about protecting you."

She squinted at him. "You're serious. About talking to animals?"

"I shouldn't say that I talk to them or that they talk to me. I just get feelings, vibes. I kind of know what's going on with them, more than the average person."

"That must make you a good vet."

"Maybe. I don't know. Sometimes it makes it harder. You know, like if they're suffering, dying. Or if they're suffering emotionally. Like if they need something and I have to try to figure out what."

"Boy, do I ever understand that," she blurted.

"You do?"

She took a deep breath. There weren't many people who understood people like her. She was really tempted to just admit, "I see dead people," like the kid in the movie—only she didn't see them.

Until today.

But they certainly bombarded her brain with thoughts and images, like body snatchers.

"I do get it, Theo. I hear things that other people don't, too."

"When we were younger, like when we went to prom, I sort of figured that."

"You did?"

"This town is a rumor mill, Gemma. And now pretty much everyone thinks that you found the remains of Marjorie What's-Her-Name, and rumor has it that you found some bodies in Chicago, too, which was why Detective Williams hired you."

Shake's words bounced back. "You know where the

all the bodies are buried."

She did. But she wished she didn't.

"Well, that's just great. Just what I need is everyone blathering about me and—"

"It's a gift, Gemma, without a doubt. Don't worry about gossips or some shit-show that people would make of it. And you can talk to me about it, you know."

He stretched his arms toward the ceiling and rolled his head to loosen his neck. "Anyhow, you keep that cat that I saw close by. I think he's better than a guard dog. Okay?"

"Sure. Okay."

He rubbed her shoulder and then got up. "I guess I should get going. It's great seeing you, Gem. I have been meaning to stop by for ages."

"Good to see you too, Theo." She was about to let go when the door opened again. She was still holding Theo's hand when Luke entered the chapel.

So much for trying to recapture the quiet.

Theo pulled his hand away and said, "Hello, Dr. Luke. I was just . . . I was just leaving."

Luke just nodded, and when Theo left the chapel, he sat down next to her, but not too close. "You two catching up on old times?"

As she was not in the mood for snide remarks, she said, "Just talking if that's okay with you."

"Mm-hmm. Are you okay, Gemma?"

She shrugged. "I guess. You?"

He sighed heavily. "Yes, very relieved for Amelia and her parents. And for Ralph. But tell me about you and this Theo guy—"

"We've known each other forever. He and Peppi were close."

He moved closer, but she scooted away to put some distance between them.

"I was just talking with Ralph Epley." He paused. "He asked me if I believe in angels."

Her face scrunched up. "What?"

"Angels. Do you believe in them?"

"I have an open mind. I mean, given my own experiences, I'm open to pretty much any supernatural phenomenon."

"Hmm."

She turned to look at him. She could not read his expression at all. "So, did Shake—"

"Talk to me? Yes. He told me about what the nun said—that it was her sister, the nurse who hated Judith, who took the driver's license and tried to pawn the ring. He said now that they know who tried to do that, they are looking for her. He said he'd be interviewing her mother."

"Right. Yes. Luke, I—"

"Just exactly how involved were you in all of this? How much did you learn from . . . you know, supernatural sources?" As if he just couldn't hold back, venom spilled out next. "Just how much did you pry out of me? How much did you lie to me or lead me on to get information?"

His voice dripped with the double Ds: disdain and doubt.

"Isn't it enough that Shake is making progress? I mean, if it weren't for him opening up the cold case, none of this would have come out. Now, there's a chance that he will catch Judith's killer."

"And I want that. You know how much I want that. But this? I don't know that I can handle it if these leads have come mostly from you."

She didn't know what to say. She was speechless, and hurting, and she just couldn't find any words.

Finally, his own words echoed in her head. "You told me the other night that even a priest you read about acknowledges that spirits may linger, that they may have a need. Remember? That Saint Thomas Aquinas wrote of ghosts? And that other guy . . . Collins."

"Yes, the theologian, but I don't know Thomas Aquinas or Peter Collins. I'm not *involved* with them. I want to move forward, Gemma. But I just don't know if—"

Certain this conversation was going nowhere, at least not right then, she basically announced that she was done with it. "If you can? I guess then, maybe that's something you have to pray on."

As she rose, he reached out to touch her elbow. "What's next?"

"Next with what exactly? With the investigation? You'd have to ask Shake about that." She yanked her elbow away from him. "I'm going home."

****

She started to walk home, thinking only about how fast she could get out of River Styx. She needed a break from pretty much everything. As she crossed the square, she saw a tan car parked in front of her store. She halted, trying to see the driver, but the driver's seat was empty. She took a few more steps, then paused for a moment in front of the drug store, pretending to stretch her arms and legs. As she got closer to the car, she still saw no driver.

She reflected on the tan car that she saw before—the one she thought was following her. Was this the same one?

Glancing over her shoulder the whole time, and anxious to get inside, Gemma ran the rest of the way. She sprinted up the back stairs to her apartment two at a time. When she got to the top step, she found a dead fish at the top of the back stairway to her apartment.

It had a cork in its mouth.

****

"What the—?"

The pungent smell of the fish made her sick to her stomach. Panicked by the implications, she twisted away from it at first. Her heart hammering, she ran down the steps and around to the front of the building. There were no cars there now. But someone was watching her. She could feel it. And the fish taco she had at the pub suddenly popped into her head.

She gripped her keys and tried to control her trembling fingers as she opened the door. She stepped over the fish, went inside, and punched in the numbers to disarm her security system. She got paper towels to pick up the fish and was about to toss it in the trash when she thought better of it. Wouldn't this be evidence if—if what? Of what?

Using paper towels to pick it up, she lifted the fish and set it aside on the landing and went back inside. She set the alarm again. Hands quaking, she dialed Shake's cell phone number.

As the phone rang, she paced the kitchen. "Answer, answer. Shake, please pick up."

She let out a long breath when she heard his voice, then blurted, "Shake, somebody left a dead fish on my back doorstep. With a cork in its mouth."

There was a long pause, and her chest tightened. She continued to pace and looked out the kitchen window. It was dark now, and for the first time since she'd moved back to River Styx, she was afraid to be alone.

"A cork," Shake said finally.

"Yes, a cork. Shake, what does it mean?"

"No note? Nothing else?"

"No. That was it."

Which in her opinion was enough.

"I'd say that someone is sending you a warning, to put a cork in it. Be silent."

Her heart throbbed, and her stomach knotted.

"Gemma, I don't know exactly what we are dealing with here, but . . . listen, can you get away for a bit? I'll pick up the fish in the morning and try to follow up on this. I'll ask a patrol car to go to your place and stick around tonight, too."

Nodding, she said, "Okay, yeah. Yeah, I'll get out of town for a few days. But what if he comes back?"

Her chest heaved now, and her breaths were short. She couldn't remember ever being quite this frightened.

"Just get away for a bit and stop poking around. Y'all need to let them think you've backed off."

"Okay. Okay, Shake." She hung up and immediately called her mother.

****

After relating only some of what had happened in the last few days, leaving out any reference to the little gift at her back door, Gemma asked if she could visit. "I paid Lady Laveau for a quilt for you as a Mother's Day gift," she said, "and I'm going to pick that up, pack it and a few clothes, and get on a plane, if that's okay. Maybe the Big Apple is just what the doctor ordered."

"I'll go online right now and order you a ticket," her mother said. "I'll text the details."

"Mom, I can pay—"

"Oh, don't. Watch for my text. And one of us will pick you up at JFK. Is tomorrow too soon?"

Tomorrow was not soon enough.

****

An hour later, she received a text from her mom about her flights. She'd leave on Tuesday afternoon, fly nonstop to New York, and land at JFK. Her mom and Dylan would meet her at the baggage carousel. She ended her text with a heart emoji.

Gemma knew that she should be excited about visiting New York City for the first time and about seeing her mother. There were many places she wanted to see, and who hadn't seen *Sleepless in Seattle* and pictured themselves meeting the love of their life up there?

There were other things she wanted to see and do, too. The 9/11 memorial at Ground Zero, the museums, Broadway shows. What tainted the trip was that she was running from River Styx, running from all that was going on there, and running from herself.

Early the next morning, she gave Jaz a call.

"I was just about to call you to come over for breakfast," Jaz said. "This morning I am enjoying Italian coffee with some lovely dried-fruit-and-almond scones with Irish butter. My cousins are great cooks."

"Well, I'm leaving for New York, Jaz." She didn't tell her about the fish. She just said her mother had arranged the trip and she needed to get away. "Can you take Milo back and look after Fantasma?"

"Things are still a little upside down and sideways in the new shops, and Auntie Brette is really, really insisting that Milo stay with you a little longer. But I'll come over and feed them both."

"But Jaz, I won't be here. Won't Milo want to be with Ambrette and Angelique and—?"

"Gem, you have no idea what an argument with Ambrette Aguillard is like. Think of a two-headed mule with a kick that can send you three weeks from Sunday. It's really not wise to butt heads with her. How long will you be gone?"

"I'll come home next Monday, the day after Mother's Day. I really need to get away, Jaz."

"I'll drive you to the airport. When does your plane leave?"

"Two-ish. I should be at the airport by noon at the latest. But I can take an Uber."

"Give me a break. Are you all packed?"

"Everything except the quilt your mom made for my mom."

"Oh, yeah, forgot about that. Look, I'll pick you up in half an hour. You can snag some coffee and a scone, and we'll get the quilt into your suitcase. Brette and the cousins want to hear more about how you helped find Amelia."

"Jaz, I—"

"Gemma, we all—all of the people in our family have a little magic in our veins. Even Shake, though he just won't accept or admit it. They're interested in your particular kind of magic. They admire it. And you'll admire theirs when you get to know them.

"So get your act together, have some breakfast with us, and then I'll drive you to the airport."

"You're the best, Jaz."

"I know," she teased.

****

Because it was a nonstop flight, Gemma didn't feel queasy about checking a bag that might go astray. She decided to check the one with her clothes and toiletries but put the lap quilt into her carry-on. Nobody was getting their hands on that quilt. Jaz gave her a smaller package, her mom's housewarming gift to Gemma's mother. "It's a quilted table runner that complements the lap quilt. It will look beautiful on the table in their dining room."

With the car loaded, she followed Jaz into the new bookstore. Angelique was almost done pulling it all together. She placed a latté and scones on a table, but first Gemma had to wander.

At the front of the store were shelves and shelves of used books. The building was renovated and chopped up into several small rooms, most of which contained a variety of books on African American magic, witchcraft, vampires, ghost stories, magical realism, and the most haunted spots in Ohio. There were bookmarks and earrings depicting skeletons, witch's hats and brooms, haunted houses, ghosts, and goblins. The wallpaper in each room was spiders or black cats or some other creepy image, except for the small children's room, where unicorns and rainbows reigned supreme. It was an adorable room to cuddle up with a toddler and read.

After her tour, she settled down with her scone and coffee. Angelique and Jaz joined her. She was dying to ask Angelique if she had something going with Officer Del, but she didn't want to pry.

She was frazzled and unable to slough off the questioning looks she got sometimes, but there seemed to be chinks and dents in her armor. Hence, the escape to New York and she was anxious to get going.

Angelique was willowy, sylph-like, and her head-to-toe black attire only accentuated her slim figure and mystery. Her long eyelashes were velvety, and her eyes were magnetic and flickered as if they were made of pixie dust. Her bony shoulders drooped, though. She rubbed her abused fingers and palms. It was obvious she had been working day and night on the place. It showed in the charm of the store and in her battered appendages.

"Tell me . . . what's the deal with Father Fowler at St. Mary Ascension?" she asked. "We went to church yesterday morning, and when the Amber Alert went off, he seemed annoyed."

"According to Luke, he's a fossil. I mean, like an insect preserved in amber fossil. Just not interested in twenty-first century anything. But I hear the younger priest is okay."

"It's not like I think we'll fit in here," Angelique said with a sigh. "Because we won't. But someone who isn't living in the sixteenth century would be nice. He strikes me as someone who would believe that we turn into Mumba-Black zombies and serve children on a platter to each other."

Jaz's eyes flashed in amusement. Turning to Angelique, she said, "You don't? How disappointing. I like them rare, you know. Very pink."

Angelique tossed a wet dish towel at her.

They asked a few questions about the Amelia hunt. Much as she tried to skirt the issue, her gift was right out there, and not one of them batted so much as an eyelash. Eyes sparkling, Allida, the youngest of the sisters who had snagged a coffee and stood nearby, even asked, "Are you sure there's no Laveau blood pumping through your veins? Sure seems like there might be."

Jaz rolled her eyes. "She's Italian, not Creole, Al."

Allida shrugged. "Just sayin'."

****

Her scone now where it belonged, in her belly, she told Jaz they should get going.

Angelique stopped her from getting up by putting both hands on her arms at the elbow. "While you're away, I'm going to make a bundle of some sprigs and branches of white spruce to take to your place and light a smudge stick. I'll open the windows to get good ventilation."

"But the cats could get out."

"Fantasma isn't going anywhere," Angelique said, "and Milo likes to roam, but he'd come back. While you're gone, I might form a Goofer Dust Protection Ring around your shop, too, if that's okay."

"A what ring?"

"Goofer dust is a hexing material," Angelique said.

"The word *goofer* comes from the Kongo, Gem," Jasmine chimed in. "It means 'to die.' "

"It protects the home from malicious intruders. In theory," Angelique said.

Gemma breathed in and gave a slight nod. "Okay. And when you say it means 'to die' . . .."

Angelique's mouth turned up. "It can be any powder we use to cast a spell—it's always a concoction to cause trouble or kill an enemy, or to protect yourself from one. But graveyard dirt really is best."

"I guess I have a lot to learn about your . . . talents. But back to Milo, what if he comes back here? You're nervous about him being here while you guys are working here. Isn't that why you asked me to watch him?"

"He won't come back here, Gemma," Angelique said. "The noise and clutter and chaos were messing with his inner peace. He doesn't like turmoil, and he knows where he's supposed to be right now."

Jaz disagreed about the turmoil. "I think he's a walking trainwreck of turmoil, Ange."

"No, no. He has his particular form of feng shui. Milo's rules. Anyway, we're nearly done."

"Listen, Angelique," Gemma said. "A girls night out when I get back is clearly in order. I'm clueless about this stuff."

"Sounds good."

"And why do I need this smudge stick ritual?"

"Because you are about to face danger, and I'd like to protect you from that."

Gemma looked at Jaz, who simply shrugged. Taking a deep breath, she said, "We really gotta get going."

"Okay."

"Here," Angelique said, as she slipped another small charm into Gemma's pocket. "Keep this with you."

That scared her a bit. She was already spooked by the car, the fish—all of it. This was not the peaceful send-off she wanted.

****

As Jaz pulled up to the curb at the airport and popped the trunk, Gemma handed her a key to the apartment. "Thanks for looking after the cats, Jaz. I appreciate this."

"Text me when you get there, okay? And Gem, to be honest, I think Milo was meant to look after you."

Chapter Thirty-Two

The flight was short, but it gave her little time to reflect quietly on the events of the past few days. *What is it I'm missing? Why can't I get something from Judith that might actually lead me to her killer? Is it Sister Mary Evangeline's sister?*

She remembered the coroner's report specifically said that the attack appeared to be intentional, that whoever wielded the weapon knew what he—or she—was doing. When they thrust the knife, there was enough precision to be certain Judith wouldn't survive.

She supposed it could be Doreen. From what Doreen's sister said, her father wasn't exactly Johnny Angel, and who knows what he'd taught her?

She didn't remember Shake saying he was going to interview the family of the person who died when Judith tried to revive him when she was a student nurse. She opened her laptop and did additional research on that crash and the lawsuit that followed.

She could not imagine how that made Judith feel—to be sued because she was trying to save someone's life. But she also couldn't imagine how the family felt when she wasn't successful. Shake needed to talk to them. Yes, he said to stay out of it, but it couldn't hurt to shoot him a text to remind him, which she did.

****

She looked out the window as the fluffy, white

clouds billowed by. She thought back to when she was a kid and she and her brother lay in the grass, looking up at the clouds, and deciding what animal each one looked like. They identified cats, dogs, rabbits, horses, and one day he said, "That one is your favorite TV character. The one with a head like a hairy mammoth or something. The one with no ears."

"That is definitely not him, Peppi," she scoffed. "His hair looks like brown feathers. That cloud is white."

At six, she considered herself fully informed, an expert, in fact, about all things on children's TV, particularly the giant anteater.

"No, no, Gemma, you're wrong. See, look—it's a mammoth, and there are no tusks or ears, and look at the long, pointed tail. He's like a sauropod."

"A sour pod? He is not sour. He's nice."

He affectionately ruffled her hair. "And it's okay to have pretend friends, Gummy Bear. You know that, right?"

Peppi understood. Mom understood. Jaz understood. Even Shake got it. Why couldn't everybody else?

****

When she saw Mom and Dylan waiting at the baggage carousel, she practically went butt over elbows on the down escalator to get to them as fast as she could. She ran into her mother's arms.

"Hey, there. It's okay, Gem. Whatever is going on, it's gonna be okay, and you're here to have a good time. Relax."

Dylan was, as usual, wearing his ten-gallon hat. He was a big guy—really tall and even taller in his ten-gallon Western boots. He towered over Gemma and her mother, and pretty much everyone else in the airport. He was built like an offensive tackle with super broad shoulders and really big feet. He had brown-and-silver hair, though he was beginning to have a rather shiny circle at the top of his head. At sixty, he'd been a widower for almost thirty years before he married her mom.

Gina Martelli-Brooks was as beautiful as ever. She was so well preserved that sometimes Gemma wondered if she was hiding a picture in the attic to keep from aging, like Dorian Gray. She looked very slim and athletic in her designer jeans and navy-and-white striped sweater. Her brown hair was heavily highlighted with a honey tint, and she still wore it in a sleek, chin-length bob.

When Gemma finally let go of her, she smoothed her bouncy bob and slipped one side behind her ear. The diamond in her earlobe caught the light. "Your earrings are even bigger than that rock on your hand, Mom. Don't you, like, wobble when you walk? I mean, it must feel like vertigo all the time."

Gina laughed and slipped her arm through Gemma's as Dylan picked up her suitcase, and they made their way to their car.

****

The photos Gina had sent of the apartment didn't do it justice. Lots of white and cream, pops of color in just the right places, a kitchen that a chef would die for. Gemma opened the suitcase that contained the quilt. Gina was thrilled and carefully placed it on a love seat that faced the incredibly large window that overlooked Central Park. Gemma handed her the housewarming gift from Lady Laveau and urged her to open it.

At first, she wasn't sure what it was.

"It's a small table runner, or it can be used as a quilted wall hanging, Mom."

"And these tokens around the edges?" she asked.

"Those were added by Lady Laveau's sister Ambrette," Gemma explained. "Some charms protect, some are spells for love—which you don't need. Some are for money—which you also don't need."

Gina laughed.

"I have the protection charm," Gemma said, reaching into her pocket and pulling it out to show her. "Ambrette gave me this one, and her daughter gave me another one just before I left."

Her mother's eyes clouded over and narrowed on her daughter's face. "She thinks you need protection? That's worrisome, honey."

"They're just charms, Mom. It doesn't mean anything."

"If it came from Lisette Laveau or any member of her family, it means something. Something important. You ignore her at your peril."

****

That first night, they ate at home, and Dylan's culinary prowess surprised the heck out of Gemma. When he brought out a sheet cake for dessert, Gemma could only manage one bite.

She turned to her mother. "I'm gonna need a bigger plane, Mom. I won't fit in the seat."

"Not to worry. Dylan has to work most days this week, and we'll go back to normal—you know, our usual witchcraft fare . . . root veggies, deviled eggs, Pagan hummus. The ordinary stuff."

Dylan's mouth was agape until he realized she was teasing. "Honeybun," he said, "you stay out of my kitchen."

Because Dylan did have things to do at work, Gemma and her mom spent most of the week taking long walks in the park, visiting museums, attending matinees, and going to landmarks. They went on mega-shopping sprees, too. Even though Gemma had the empty suitcase that she brought the quilt in, she actually needed a new one to take home the new clothes Gina bought for her.

All of this took Gemma's mind off what had been going on at home—at least a little bit.

One evening after dinner out, while Dylan watched a baseball game in the den, Gina and Gemma sat in the living room, drinking wine, and talking. Gina peered over her wineglass and asked, "Honey, where are things at with you and Luke Bailey?"

She brought her up to speed. "It's pretty plain to me that things aren't going to work. But I don't know what I expect, Mom. Antonio was different. He just was."

Her mind drifted, and she closed her eyes.
****

Antonio had discovered Gemma's 'talent' in an unusual way. She was nineteen and had met Antonio about six months before. The first night they were together—as in 'together-together'—they were in his dorm room. She rose up early in order to go back to her room to get ready for class. She didn't want to wake him. She dressed in the dark and took what she thought was her brother's Italian horn from the dresser and put it on. It was actually Antonio's necklace which he always wore. It had belonged to his grandfather. All of a sudden, she heard a melodious male voice in her head. It washed over her, and she had to sit down in the desk chair across from the bed.

The spirit spoke Italian, and she only understood bits and pieces. She made some kind of sound, a little shriek that woke Antonio. He got out of bed and knelt down in front of her. She took off the necklace and handed it to him.

"I thought it was mine—my brother's."

"That was my grandfather's. I heard you speaking Italian. Can you say it again?"

She fumbled through the words in her head as best she could. Antonio sat back on his heels.

"Caro, what did the voice sound like?"

"Like a crooner. Almost like he was singing."

"Say the words again."

She did, and he swept his hand through her hair and stroked her cheek.

"He approves, caro."

"Of what?"

"Of you. He is saying, 'Do not let this one go. Do not let her down. She is yours.' "

She never really thought Antonio would settle down. Much as she adored him, she knew that he was an adrenaline freak. Skydiving, driving fast cars and motorcycles at Mach II, skiing—eventually off a darn mountain.

But from that day on, though he continued his scary, dangerous, crazy lifestyle, he was hers. He made it clear that when they finished college, they would get married.

So much for that.

****

Her mom's voice interrupted the memories.

"You care deeply for Luke, honey. I can tell. Maybe if you give it time, he'll come around. If not, then—"

"Mom, don't give me that 'there are plenty other

fish in the sea' talk, okay? That doesn't apply to me. Truth is, I don't want my gift anymore."

"Don't say that. You're just tired and disappointed, honey. In fact, I believe that if you'd really let go, really accepted it, you'd find that your gift would expand. Maybe you'd actually see ghosts one day."

Gemma thought of the old man and the dog near the cave. She wasn't thinking about anything except finding Amelia. She wasn't trying too hard; she was just giving in. And when she witnessed Judith's attack and then the scene in the autopsy room, she wasn't really trying to see that. It just happened. What if her mom was right? Maybe if she just surrendered, she could—

No. Why would I want that? What I hear and feel is bad enough.

"I thought I did, Mom, when we were searching for Amelia. You know, the little girl I told you about?"

"Reverend Epley's granddaughter."

"It scared the wits out of me, Mom. The last thing I want is to have more ghost access."

"Gem—"

Gemma touched her hand and interrupted her. She wasn't ever going to tell her about being followed, or about the fish with the cork that was left on her doorstep. But both were just more reasons to want to be relieved of this so-called gift she had.

"Really, Mom, I'm just tired of it. I don't want it anymore. Don't you ever feel that way?"

"No, never. I wish I could be useful."

"She'd totally freak if she saw me," Peppi whispered.

Gina stared into space for a moment. "Like now. Peppi is here, but I can't see him or hear him."

"He is, Mom."

"Remember I just see a gray, misty apparition. I get bits and pieces of the spirit's thoughts. I don't really try to use it. I know when the spirit needs something. That's about it. Your gift is actually useful, Gemma. You advocate for justice."

"Be glad that's all you have to contend with, Mom. It's overwhelming, this so-called gift."

With a sigh, Gina fidgeted with her wineglass, swirling the red liquid. "You know, I wish your nana Martelli had lived to see you grow into such a beautiful young woman. It devastated your grandfather when she died."

"Cancer, right?"

She nodded. "And then Nonno really let himself go. Ate too much, drank too much. No surprise he had a heart attack. And Gemma, I'm sorry that I'm not around."

"Don't you dare feel guilty. Dylan is good man, and you're happy here. And that makes me happy."

She smiled. "You know, my mother, your nana Marie, understood me and helped me. Your papa Joe, too. I'm sorry they died when you were so little. What a waste—a stupid car crash."

She wiped away a tear.

"From what you've told me, I could have learned a lot from Nana."

"Absolutely. We come from a long line of stregas, Gem. Ya know, we should go to Italy. You have relatives there on both sides."

"I'd love that, Mom. Maybe next year?"

"If you aren't planning a wedding or something."

Fat chance, she thought. "There's, like, zero chance

of that, Mom, but even if a wedding was looming. I'd leave that up to you."

Gina laughed. "You say that now." She patted Gemma's hand. "I'm gonna get a quick shower and change for bed. Pour yourself some more wine."

****

Gemma poured more wine into her glass and went out onto the balcony. She felt the power of nature at that moment. The sun was setting, and Central Park was just breathtaking. People were walking and skateboarding and sitting on benches, deep in conversation. The park was the beating, green heart of the city. Even though it was close to a frantic, busy city, it felt a million miles away. The lakes and the woods were a sanctuary, one that Gemma could easily lose herself in every day.

Maybe I should move up here to be close to Mom, leave River Styx and all of that behind.

She heard the glass doors slide open, and Dylan popped his head out. "May I join you?"

"Sure."

He poured wine into his glass from a fresh bottle, topped off hers, and placed the bottle on the round glass table.

"I hope you're having a good time, honey."

"I am having a great time, Dylan. It's been wonderful. And it's really good to see Mom. She's just, well, I haven't seen her this happy in years."

"I aim to please. And Gemma, you are welcome anytime, you know. My first wife Marti and I never had kids. Always wanted them. And then she died so young."

"What happened—if I might ask?"

"Ovarian cancer. Back then, thirty years ago, it did a lot more women in, I reckon."

"I'm sorry, Dylan."

"Yeah, well."

A few minutes later, after a very comfortable silence as they admired the view of the park, he asked, "Gemma, will you do something for me?"

He took a gold wedding ring from his breast pocket. "Your mom told me about your power."

Oh, God. Is there anyone Mom hasn't told about me? I swear, I'm going to put her in a corner and duct tape her mouth.

"Not a power, Dylan."

More like a curse.

"Your gift. Talent. Well, here's the thing. Gina— your mother—is the best thing that's happened to me in thirty years. And I have to tell you, I felt compelled to go to that convention and then that country music place. It was like something, someone was making me go there to meet Gina. I really think it was Marti. But I would like to know that she's resting in peace. That she's okay with this."

"Dylan—"

"It doesn't matter." Dylan waved a hand. "I love your mother more than I can say, and I'm fixin' to make her as happy and comfortable as I can for as long as I can, come hell or high water. Truth is, every woman I met after Marti was all hat, no cattle—until your mom."

She laughed.

"But my feelings for Gina—they're bigger than Dallas. I'm just wondering—could you see if maybe Marti is at peace with all this, and then I'd be too?"

Someone else may have been angry that he needed to be sure his late wife was in peace, but not Gemma. She understood. Her father's spirit was a relentless pest until

267

she found Dylan. Antonio was certainly not at rest and might never be, given his reckless, careless, wild nature.

"Give me the ring." She held out her hand, and he dropped it in her palm.

She placed her wineglass on the table, closed her hand around the ring, and held on to the railing with the other hand. She closed her eyes.

It only took a few seconds for her to hear a slightly gravelly female voice. *"Y'all tell him when you find the right filly, you rope her, brand her, and go straight to the Blue Ribbon Circle."*

She repeated this to Dylan, and his eyes widened. He took a long draw of wine and swallowed hard. "That's what she told me when she proposed."

"She proposed to you?"

He laughed. "I reckon she was tired of waiting on me. She said, 'Dylan Brooks, when you find the right filly, you rope her, brand her, and go straight to the Blue Ribbon Circle. What in tarnation are you waiting on?' "

He came over to Gemma and gave her a hug. She handed him the ring, and he put it back in his pocket. "Thank you, Gemma. I can rest easier now and put things where they belong."

"You'll always have her in there," Gemma said, touching his chest. "And that's okay. You have a big Texan heart and lots of room to love."

His eyes were wet, and he wiped away a tear. "Must have been that last popper I just ate. Darn hot, weren't they?"

He retreated to the den and his baseball game while she stayed on the balcony, watching the sunset.

Sometimes her gift was worth having, nurturing. She just wished she could make Luke really understand that.

Chapter Thirty-Three

Luke opened the door to his mother's apartment and followed her in.

"Tea?" she asked.

"Sure."

He sat down on the couch in the living room and put his head in his hands. He was still in that position when his mother returned with a tray filled with a teapot, cups, sugar, and lemon.

"Headache?"

He quickly sat up and leaned back into the sofa cushion. "Nope. Just thinking."

She put the tray on the coffee table and sat down. She touched his hand. "Luke, talk to me."

He smiled. "Did you enjoy brunch? And do you like your gift?"

"Yes and yes. Of course, but that's not what's on your mind. C'mon. Spill."

He frowned this time.

"Luke?"

His heart jackhammered as he thought about everything that had happened in the last few weeks. Every time he replayed a moment when he was with Gemma, his stomach did a flip-flop. Navigating the whole thing with Judith—if in fact that was the presence he felt—was one thing. Dealing with the investigation being reopened, that was another. But he felt confident he could handle both. Eventually.

Gemma—that was a whole other universe.

She made him tremble. She made him want to slow the world down so that every precious moment with her lasted just a little longer. He dreamed about tracing her face with the tip of his finger, bending down to let his mouth trail down her neck, and then kissing her, and gently placing his tongue in her mouth.

He shivered, just thinking those thoughts in daylight. But this thing she could do. This supernatural highway she was on. How to handle that?

Over tea, he finally confided a bit more of what had been going on, and his mom listened without interruption.

"Do you know what's much worse than having your dreams dashed, Luke?" she said. "Failing to even try to fulfill those dreams. If they're just dreams and you don't act on them, what's the point?

"What are you going to do—live on and on, hoping that the day comes that you no longer think about Judith? It won't come, Luke. Look, Judith had a gift—compassion for people, helping people, and for recognizing the richness of your soul, and she wouldn't want you to waste your life. You are separated by shadows now. Perhaps Gemma can explore those thick and unknown spaces in time that other people can't, and that's a gift, too. And it sounds like she is compassionate and wants to help people as well. Her gift must be very, very hard to deal with, yet she did deal with it to try to help you. If you have found love again, let it encircle you; let it envelop you. For God's sake, don't withdraw from its sweetness."

He was speechless. He'd felt shriveled, small since

Gemma left town . . . no, since he'd belittled her gift. But his mother's words lifted him out of a darkness. A darkness that he hoped he could bury so that he could seize on the link to his future instead.

"Luke, have you called Gemma since the whole Amelia thing?"

"She's out of town. Her friend Jasmine said she went to New York to visit her mother."

Her face turned stern. "Have you called her? New York is not the space station, Luke."

"Jaz said she comes home tomorrow."

His mother picked up her teacup, leaned back, and said, "Well, then."

Driving home, he thought about what his mother said. He ejected his rock 'n' roll CD and put one in that his mother liked when he took her places. She loved soundtracks from her favorite movies, and this was one of them. The words of the king who was trying to figure out what to do about his queen struck home. "How to handle a woman" the king wondered. His answer? "Just love her."

So fine, Luke, he said to himself. *What do you do now? She'll be home tomorrow. Buy flowers? A nice wine? A book of poetry?*

Just fricking fall on your sword?

He didn't think prayer was going to answer this one.

He stopped at the grocery store to pick up a few things, and when he'd finished shopping, he impatiently stood in the long line. He checked his phone again for recent calls and messages. There were none from Gemma.

Well, what do you expect, you idiot? He tucked the phone into the back pocket of his jeans.

When he felt the thrum of the phone vibrating, he grabbed it and looked at the text message.

His heart sank when he saw that Jaz had texted him, not Gemma.

—*What are you planning to do, Dr. Luke? Gem comes home tomorrow, you know.*—

Yeah, I know, he thought. *You told me.*

Before he could text back, she texted Gemma's favorite flower—carnations. Especially red ones. Then she texted her favorite wines, and finally, she wrote, "If you don't know this already, her brother was a poet. She's really into that. Just sayin'."

He smiled to himself. It couldn't hurt that Jaz was on his side.

But his throat went dry. *What if I do all this romantic stuff—about which I know very little—and she still rejects me?*

He watched the cursor blinking.

What time does she get home? he wrote.

She texted the time and added, She's pretty okay with surprises, by the way.

He texted Okay, thanks.

Then he spun around, pushed past the people who had been in line behind him, and dashed over to the mini florist shop. He turned to a woman who was perusing the variety of bouquets. "What do you think I should get for a special person and a special occasion?"

"This one is nice," she said, handing him a somewhat meager bouquet with carnations, baby's breath, and leafy stems. He looked at the price. $12.99. "Sheesh," he muttered. *But she's worth it*, he thought. He grabbed three bouquets, went to the aisle with wine, and put one red and one white in his basket.

"Next stop bookstore," he said as he walked back to his car.

He loaded the trunk and then slid behind the wheel. He watched a family approach the car next to him. Dad, Mom, and two kids. All of them were smiling and laughing, and after the kids were seated and belted, the man turned to his wife, smiled, and planted a kiss on her cheek. She gave him a playful push.

Can I have that, he wondered. *Or have I scared her away for good?*

He could have sworn he heard a quiet voice whisper in his ear.

"Not a chance."

Chapter Thirty-Four

Gemma didn't hear from Luke all week. She hadn't heard from Judith either for that matter. She'd gone incognito. As for Luke, she wasn't sure if he even knew that she went to New York, but with the way tongues wagged in that town, someone probably told him. She wasn't surprised at the silent treatment. They didn't exactly leave it on "I'll call you in the morning, love" terms.

She packed all her new clothes and a new pair of high heels that Gina insisting on buying in a new suitcase. They were vintage and bright red and totally impractical. *I'd feel like clicking my heels and saying, "There's no place like home," whenever I wore them.*

All the same, her mother said she had to have them.

She packed old stuff in the old suitcase, and gifts and souvenirs went in her carry-on. Lady Laveau got perfume; Jaz got a fabulous and ridiculously expensive purse that looked like a gold fan. She knew that Jaz would flip out when she saw it.

She bought bookmarks for the women in her book club. She also had one for Luke, but it seemed like such a small thing to give someone who owned such a sizable portion of her heart.

She hadn't stopped thinking about him. Just the opposite. She hated admitting it, but she really was falling in love with him, and the thought of never being able to sort things out tore her apart.

Gina came into the guest room to help her pack. "How's it going?"

"Close to finished. But I'm leaving room for a few more things after our last, quick shopping spree."

"What did you buy Luke?"

"A bookmark."

She shook her head. "A bookmark for the love of your life?"

"I told you, we didn't part on the best of terms, Mom. It may be hopeless."

"Do you remember your brother's Emily Dickinson poetry phase?"

"Huh? Was that between Shelley and Poe or Collins and Maya Angelou?"

"His favorite was Emily Dickinson—well, I only know a bit of it. 'Hope is the thing with feathers that perches in the soul. And sings the tune without the words and never stops at all.' So where did our hopeful, optimistic self go, Gemma?"

"Mom, the only thing that perches in my soul is a big, fat, evil raven that calls out 'Nevermore.' "

"Do you really feel that way?"

"I didn't used to, but this murder investigation—"

"Which you've told me very little about," her mother reminded her with a little frown.

"Because I can't, Mom." She thought again about the little doorstep present. "And it's taken me to a very dark place." *A hollow place with invisible tentacles that are choking me.*

Her mother leaned forward. "Then use that."

"What?"

"Use that negative energy and flip it to something

positive. You want to solve this case, Gemma. Get to work and solve it."

"Mom, Shake—the detective—"

"Shakespeare Williams? He's on the case?"

Gemma nodded.

"He's a good man."

"Yes. He is. He told me to butt out."

With a sigh, she continued rolling socks and sticking them into corners of the suitcase.

"The killer," Gina said. "You think you know who it is?"

"Did I tell you it was a homicide?"

"Honey, Shake opens old homicide cases."

"Oh, yeah," Gemma mumbled. "Right."

"So, the killer—have you been getting clues?"

"Yeah, little bits and pieces. Breadcrumbs. I have an idea or two."

"Then figure out a way to lead Shake where he needs to go."

"Yeah. Sure," Gemma said, her voice as uncertain as ever.

She rubbed her shoulder. "Taxi will be here in ten. I'll go get my credit cards."

Lead Shake where he wants to go, Gemma repeated in her mind, *yes. Right. But how?*

****

The vacation over, Gemma closed up her suitcase. Gina came into the guest room and tapped her watch. "We have to leave for the airport soon. And you're sure Jasmine is picking you up?"

Gemma nodded. Before she zipped up the case, she reached out to touch the tie and pocket square that she purchased at the last minute for Luke. The swirl of blues and silver would match the color of his eyes and the ice-cold gaze she saw the last time they were together.

"It's nice. He'll love it. And I love my Mother's Day gift."

"Well, I didn't make it. It was all Lisette."

"It's beautiful. And having you here for Mother's Day was really, really special, Gem."

****

The flight home was similar to the one to New York. Short but enough time to curl up under a thin, cheesy blanket and think.

Her thoughts turned to Antonio. She'd never know if they would have had a marriage like her mom and dad, but with every fiber she knew that he loved her. She knew there would be ups and downs, and some obstacles.

Would she have worried every time he went out the door that he wouldn't come back? Of course, she would have. He was incapable of resisting danger, and he wanted to take down the bad guys, to clean up what was left of the Mafia.

Suddenly, she heard the word *Mafia* over and over in her head. The word *Mafia* and the word *green*. Over and over.

What on earth did this have to do with Judith Walsh's murder?

****

Jaz was waiting for her at the baggage carousel at Cleveland Hopkins Airport. She shook her head and laughed. "How did I know that you would come home with more than you left with?"

"Mom went a little crazy. Well, I sort of did, too. How are the cats? Do I have to plan a funeral for one or for two?"

"They're fine. Both of them. No casualties of war. Angelique did her smudge thing, too. It kind of stunk, but she opened up a window. It should be fresh when you get home."

Jaz hoisted up the largest suitcase. "So, are you hungry? Just tired?"

"Actually, Jaz, there's someplace I'd like to stop before I go home."

"Where's that?"

"It's not far out of the way. There's a family I need to see."

"This is about the case?"

"Right."

"Okay, just give me an address, and I'll pop it into Google Maps."

Gemma had not heard back from Shake, and she was going to see the family of the man Judith tried to save. They were royally ticked off; they sued her; they threatened and harassed her. They were still suspects in her mind.

She texted her mom that she had landed in Cleveland, and then she pulled out her laptop. There was an address on the court website for the people who had sued Judith and lost.

Then she wondered what the heck she was going to say to them.

****

The Leonards' house was in a run-down neighborhood and wasn't in very good shape. The lawn and flower beds were overgrown with weeds, and the gutters on the house were dented and slumping. An elderly woman answered the door. She was on the heavy side and wore wine-colored knit pants and a big, white sweater that wasn't the slightest bit flattering.

"May I help you?" she asked.

Gemma cleared her throat. "Hello, I'm writing an article about so-called Good Samaritan attempts to save people . . . you know, like after car crashes. I read about the crash your brother was in. There's been a recent change in the law in some states about the Good Samaritan thing."

Gemma waited, jiggling her hand until the pen she held fell to the ground. She picked it up.

"What kind of change?" she asked, her face brightening.

She sort of shimmied her foot in between the woman and the screen door. "Well, the new law doesn't throw all Good Samaritan cases out. Like your case was thrown out. And I'm writing a story about cases like yours."

What she was telling her wasn't exactly true, but it wasn't a lie either. Usually a person giving aid out of the goodness of their hearts could not be sued. The change in the law wasn't new, and it was only in a few states, but some courts had decided that a person giving nonmedical aid in an emergency could be sued and held liable for damages under the state's 'Good Samaritan' law.

On the other hand, Judith had attempted to give medical assistance. She'd tried to save his life.

When Gemma read about the Good Samaritan law to see why the family's lawsuit against Judith had failed, she zeroed in on a particular case about some kids who had been doing drugs and drinking. When their car crashed into a light pole, Mary, a passenger, got out. She dragged her friend Sue from the car. She said she did it because she believed that the car would catch fire or explode.

As a result of her injuries, Sue was permanently paralyzed. She sued Mary, the 'Good Samaritan,' because she said she was 'dragged like a rag doll' from the car and that made her already injured back worse. The judge dismissed the case because Good Samaritan laws made it impossible to collect money from someone who tried to save a person in an emergency. But a state Supreme Court reversed the trial judge's decision. They said that the law referred to emergency medical care only, but not to all emergency care, like the care Mary gave to her friend by removing her from the car.

Long story short, Gemma felt she was sort of lying to this woman—but sort of not.

When Marion let her in, she signaled to Jaz to wait. Marion offered tea, but Gemma declined.

Gemma asked her how she felt when the lawsuit she filed against Miss Walsh, the student nurse who stopped to help, was thrown out of court. Before she could answer, an elderly man entered the room. He stood in front of Gemma and leaned in, scrutinizing her face.

Lionel Leonard said, "We were angry; that's how we felt."

"Well, wasn't your—was it your brother?" Gemma asked.

"Marion's."

"Wasn't he in cardiac arrest?" Gemma asked.

"Joseph went off the road and hit a light pole," Marion explained. "I guess he had a heart attack."

"I think that the crash caused the heart attack," Lionel insisted.

"Lionel, that isn't what the doctors said."

"Don't matter," he spat.

Gemma looked straight at Marion. "From what I've read, it isn't unusual for someone whom a person tries to revive doesn't make it."

"Who says?" Lionel asked.

"Well, science says. When someone does CPR on a person who has had a heart attack, the victim only survives about ten percent of the time."

Gemma groped for all the information she'd scanned. "I mean, what I've read . . . what I'm saying is, fewer than one in ten people survives an out-of-hospital cardiac arrest, and only seven or eight percent survive even after they've been in the hospital."

Marion looked down at her feet, and Gemma saw her wiggle her toes inside her ratty slippers. Gemma looked around again—the house was old and worn out, too. It was badly in need of repairs.

I guess I can't blame them for trying to get some money but not if they didn't deserve it.

"Were you very angry when Miss Walsh couldn't save your brother?"

Marion didn't answer. But Lionel let loose with a few expletives. "She should have had to pay." He puffed out his chest and added, "I read somebody stabbed her, so I guess she got what she deserved. I'm glad somebody had more guts than I did."

"I read that you threatened her. Did you threaten her, Mr. Leonard?"

Marion jumped in. "Just nonsense crazy talk. He was just PO'd that we lost that court case. His bark is worse than his bite."

He grunted and left the room.

"So you don't think Lionel took things into his own hands?" Gemma asked her.

She laughed. "Lionel? He's all talk. Like I said, just bark. He didn't think it was fair, but it was just talk. Besides, when that nurse got killed, we were down in Tennessee visiting family."

If that was true, then Lionel Leonard was, as Dylan might have put it, 'all hat, no cattle.'

****

Feeling deflated, Gemma didn't really think the couple had anything to do with Judith's death, which meant she was no closer to figuring out who killed her.

She ticked off the suspects. The Leonards, though she pretty much ruled them out. Doreen Tobin? Her father? They were still in the mix.

Or was it what the police always thought—some complete stranger who lost it when he thought she was going to fight or scream?

And now there were these new words—*Mafia* and *green*. What on earth did they mean?

Gemma stared out the side window, her mind racing. Exasperated, she thought, *Judith, why can't you just tell me what you know instead of playing this word game?*

Jaz wanted to stop at her place before she took Gemma home. "Mom made supper for you; she wants to hear about New York. Okay?"

Normally, she would never say no to Lady Laveau. But she did.

"Not tonight, Jaz. I promise I'll stop by tomorrow, but I need to get home. It's late, and I need to make up for lost time in the shop this past week."

Jaz shrugged. "Okay but be prepared for my mom's wrath when you do show up."

Gemma frowned, but Jaz just laughed. "Kidding,

hon. She'll understand."

She was about to pull up behind the shop when Gemma turned to her and asked, "Hey, can you stop at the parish house? I want to drop off a little gift I bought for Luke."

"I thought you were, you know, kind of not speaking."

"Well, it's a peace offering. Or something," she mumbled.

Jaz smiled. "Good thinking." She turned around and drove to the parish house. She pulled into the drive, handed Gemma a flashlight, and popped the trunk. Gemma opened the suitcase, took out Luke's gifts, walked up to the front door, and put them on his doorstep.

As they backed out of the driveway, the light over his front door went on. Jaz stopped the car.

"No, don't, Jaz. He'll find the gifts, and if he wants to call me, he will."

"Okay," Jaz said. "Up to you."

She dropped her off behind the shop and offered to help with her suitcases, but Gemma waved her off and gave her a hug. "I'll see you tomorrow. Thanks, Jaz."

****

She dragged two of her suitcases up the stairs but left the heaviest on the patio. It was pitch black, and she just wanted to get inside and collapse. She opened the back door to the kitchen. It dawned on her immediately that the door wasn't locked.

It also occurred to her that the security alarm siren wasn't screaming. Jaz had been there to feed the cats. Angelique had done her magic smudge thing. Didn't they think to check the lock on the door and set the alarm?

Gemma stepped inside and put her carry-on and one suitcase on the floor next to the table. One of two kitchen windows was wide open, and the screen was up. Clearly, Angelique had done her protection ritual and forgot to close them.

She glanced around the kitchen but saw no cats. She wasn't worried about Milo, but Fantasma wasn't used to being out.

They're probably just hiding.

Then, for the first time in days, she heard Judith's voice. *"Watch out!"*

Chapter Thirty-Five

"Don't scream," the woman warned as she put Gemma in a choke hold. Then the woman grabbed her arms and twisted them behind her.

Gemma struggled to get away, but the woman was strong and tightened her grip. She forced Gemma into a kitchen chair and turned on the light. She wore a hoodie and jeans. She held a gun.

She flipped the hood back, and Gemma saw short, curly red hair and desperate green eyes. She had seen those eyes before—the nun's eyes—only hers were kind and had a soul behind them. These eyes were green ice, cold and hard.

Gemma knew instantly that she was Doreen Tobin, Sister Mary Evangeline's half-sister. The woman who tried to pawn the emerald ring. And perhaps, Judith's killer.

"You're Doreen Tobin."

"Do you live in some fantasy world? The back door is unlocked. And no security system for a jewelry store?"

Her eyes darted around. Gemma could tell that despite her tone, she was nervous, scared. "You've been poking around where you shouldn't. I need to know what you know and who you've talked to."

Gemma's eyes narrowed. "I know that you tried to pawn a ring that was stolen from a girl who's dead. Did you kill her?"

"Wouldn't you like to know?"

Tired, frustrated, and sick of stupid word games from Judith or anyone else, Gemma crossed her arms. "Yeah. Yeah, actually, I would."

"Careful," Judith warned.

"If you took the purse, why did you have to kill her? And the ring. Why did you wait five years to try to pawn it?"

Doreen's hand was shaking. Gemma suspected she was not used to handling a gun. Plus, she didn't think she'd killed Judith. But this was hardly the time to tempt fate. "Why? Why did you kill her?"

Doreen let out a long breath. "You sell jewelry. You can give me stuff. This time I'll find a pawnshop that will take it."

"You can have anything you want. Just—"

Gemma heard footsteps. Paw steps, actually, on the back steps. A moment later, Fantasma leaped onto the windowsill, then into the house. She landed with a thump on the floor, and Doreen pointed the gun toward her.

Gemma's heart skipped a beat. "Please, please don't hurt her. You can take anything you want."

Doreen swiveled the gun back toward Gemma. Creases scored her brow; beads of sweat spread across her forehead and slipped down her cheek. Her face was white. Her lips quivered.

Gemma knew she was scared. Maybe not as scared as Gemma, but it was clear she did not want to do this.

"Doreen, listen—"

"No, shut up. I'm not listening."

She jiggled the gun in front of Gemma's face. The animosity in her face made Gemma shiver. "I hated Judith Walsh. She ruined my life."

Gemma wanted to yell, "No, *you* ruined your life, and if you didn't kill Judith, then who did?" but Judith cautioned her again. *"Careful."*

She summoned a calm voice. "I don't believe you killed her."

Doreen paced the room, tapping the butt of the gun against her forehead. "Are you stupid or something? I was still in jail at the time of her death."

Gemma tried to stay focused. "I thought you were out. I thought—how did you find me? Did your sister call you and tell me I went to see her?"

With a tilt of her head, Doreen looked puzzled. "My sister? No. No, she didn't give me a heads-up." She snorted. "Figures. She and my mother didn't help me when I was going to jail either. The only one who was around was my father. It was my mother's boss who told my dad that you were poking your nose where it didn't belong."

The credit card.

She'd signed the credit card—with her real name. It didn't take a Mensa candidate to find her. These days, it was easy to find someone.

"Farry? The bartender? That's how you found me?"

And the tan car—that had to be Farry or Doreen following me, not Shake.

"My father and Farry go way back. They both work for Bailey. He sent my dad to get the ring and to scare Judith."

Bailey?

Gemma's mind reeled back to what little Luke had told her about his father—that his father was a mob guy. "You said Bailey? Luke Bailey's father? Did you say that your father works for Luke's father?"

"Luke . . . oh, yeah, the priest. Dad and I had a lot of laughs about him. Yeah, it was Michael J. Bailey, the priest's father who sent my dad to get his ring back."

"But why?" Gemma asked. "He got the insurance money for it. Why would he do that?"

She wrinkled her nose. "You did do your homework, didn't you? Because he wanted the ring back anyway. My dad told me the old man was pissed that his ex-wife gave it to Luke, and even more pissed that his son was leaving the priesthood. Dad said he wanted to scare Judith—to steal the ring and scare the daylights out of her. His precious priest son was going to break his vows and leave the priesthood for her. That didn't sit well with his father."

She laughed. Her fingers clamped around the handle of the pistol, but her hands were still shaky. "Makes no sense to me," Doreen continued. "But here's the kicker. Dad ditched her purse, but he kept her wallet. There was a letter in her purse addressed to the good Father Bailey. She was breaking the engagement. Dad and I thought that was pretty rich. His father didn't need to scare her off at all."

"You're lying."

"No. I'm not."

It was hard to breathe. She couldn't think of what to say to convince Doreen to drop her gun, to leave, to stop the insanity of her life. "Luke doesn't speak to his father, hasn't spoken to him in years," Gemma said. "How would he even know that Luke was engaged?"

"Because he has eyes everywhere. Nothing gets by him. But St. Jude Walsh didn't want Luke to leave the priesthood either. Isn't that a hoot? She wasn't going to marry him whether he left or not. In her letter, she told him that all those little talks they had about religion made her realize how important it was to her. She'd decided she was going to become a nun. A nun! Just like my stupid sister. St. Jude, we used to call her at the hospital. Boy, was that ever spot on."

Gemma's head was spinning. "Are you saying that Luke's father sent your—Toby?"

"Right. But—"

"She saw his face, and she knew him," Gemma whispered.

"Because he'd been in court to be with me. He saw Judith there, and she recognized him the night she was killed." She shrugged again. "It left him no choice."

"And the ring?"

Doreen's lips twitched. "Yeah, my dad found the ring, but he never told Bailey it was in her purse. He said she wasn't wearing it, didn't have it on her. Then he waited, and when he really needed it, he asked me to pawn it with Sully. But Sully wasn't there anymore."

Gemma understood the importance of keeping Doreen talking. If she could buy some time, she could figure out what to do next. But she was terrified. Images of her mom flooded her mind. And Jaz at that abbey . . . Jaz touching the Black Madonna, hoping to be blessed. And memories of her dad, her brother, Antonio.

And Luke.

"Why did he suddenly need the ring? Why did your father make you pawn it?"

Doreen's face contorted in raw fear. "Dad fell out with Bailey. He screwed up a job, and Bailey was out to get him."

Doreen paced back and forth, touching the barrel of the gun to her forehead. "Dad was supposed to grab the dope from some tires that people in a chop shop stashed in them before they sold them to anyone. Bailey owns the chop shop, I guess." She shrugged. "But some guy bought them to take them to a garage to have them put on his car, and, well, Dad missed the drop. The tire was leaking. The way the packages were packed in there, it wasn't a tight fit. When they pulled it off, they found the drugs.

"They couldn't trace the tire directly back to Bailey. The customer wouldn't give up the chop shop, or he'd get in trouble. I guess he told the cops he just found the tires somewhere. Dad became a target because what if he told the cops about Bailey? He had to get lost because Bailey got all pissed off about the missed drug drop and never getting his ring back. My dad was not a rat, but Bailey was still worried he'd squeal. Dad needed money."

"Because he's hiding," Gemma said softly. "And he's putting you through hell to try to get out of it." She remembered the nun's words. Toby Tobin was manipulative. "Doreen, he's using you. Don't do this. You can just walk away."

Doreen's eyes glistened with unshed tears.

She's unraveling. It's going to end badly.

"What did your father do for Mr. Bailey? What does Farry do?"

"Farry is one of his spies, I guess. Bailey makes a fortune running drugs. The Bailey family goes way back with the Mob. Your priest's grandfather, Mickey Bailey, was in the Irish Mafia. He ran with Danny Greene."

Judith's recent murmurs flew to the forefront.

Mafia.

Green.

Gemma bit her lip, desperate to find the right words—words that would make Doreen listen. Words that would keep her breathing.

"Doreen, please listen to me. You don't have to do this. Right now all you're guilty of is trying to pawn stolen property. You want jewelry; I'll give it to you. And you can just leave."

"No, no," she whispered. Tears ran down her cheeks. "It's too late for that."

Gemma inhaled deeply.

She's slipping gears. She's been sucked into a world of crime, one that would take more grit than she can muster to stop herself from finding a taste for it.

Frightened as Gemma was of what may happen next, she couldn't help feeling sorry for her as she looked into her eyes—eyes filled with unknowable sorrow.

But I'm not going to go down without a fight, Gemma thought. *I'm way too young to transition to haunting other people.*

"Take a beat, Gummy Bear," Peppi urged. *"Look around. Think! Remember Jasmine's warning."*

Her eyes drifted to the wooden pole that was on the floor below the closed window. The one that held the broken window up. She remembered how heavy the poles were. *If I can grab one . . ..*

Chapter Thirty-Six

Gemma stood, then took a step forward. "It's not too late, Doreen."

When Fantasma hissed, Doreen's focus darted around the room before she trained the gun on the cat, then turned it back on Gemma. "Okay, now let's go downstairs. Get a trash bag."

"Okay, okay," Gemma said, holding her hands in front of her. "Just, you know, just wait. The trash bags are over there in the cupboard."

As Gemma turned to walk to the cupboard, something caught her eye. Though she heard no footsteps or paws stomping up the stairs, suddenly there were two large green eyes just outside the window staring at her. Body tensed, fur rippling, Milo's eyes went to slits.

As he hopped over the sill and into the kitchen, he bared his teeth. Hearing his chattering and strange clicking noises, Gemma was pretty sure if cats could swear, Milo was using some pretty colorful language. She suddenly recalled what her grandfather told her . . . that when you hear a cat chattering, they are getting ready for the kill bite. "It's instinct, Gemma," he said. "They position their bite to sever the spinal cord of their prey."

At the time, she had cringed. But now she had zero doubt that Milo was getting ready to attack. If Doreen were anyone else, she would have shouted at her to run.

He was a black panther in the body of a domestic cat, swishing his tail side to side. He leaped—though it was more like flying through the air like a bird. Defying gravity, he landed softly on the table. Then he shot up to the top of the refrigerator, swooped down onto Doreen's head, and dug his claws into her scalp.

All of it happened in the blink of an eye.

Blood streamed down Doreen's forehead as she screamed and swirled, unable to free herself from the flying cat.

This is my chance.

Gemma whirled around. She picked up the wooden pole, squeezed her eyes shut, and took a swing.

When she opened her eyes, she realized the pole had connected with Doreen's shoulder. The force of the blow sent her into the chair. That damn, wonderful, accident-waiting-to-happen chair. The chair broke, and Doreen sprawled across the floor. The gun flew across the room and stopped near the top of the steps.

Doreen was crying and holding her limp arm close to her chest. As Gemma saw her jaw twitch, and her mouth open as if she was about to scream, she brought the pole back up and to the side for additional power. This time, as she swung the pole, it struck the brick wall next to the window. She watched it splinter.

It made no sense at the time, but Jasmine had predicted it . . . *bones breaking and popping and snapping and crunching. A bat or some kind of wooden pole . . . splintering.*

It was just like Jasmine's vision of the black grate— that was precisely what she'd seen when she visited the nun. And now what she'd said about breaking bones and a bat . . . no one should ever question Jasmine's dreams.

When she saw Doreen scramble toward the gun and pick it up, Gemma lunged forward to push her down, but Doreen whacked the side of her head with the butt of the gun and punched her in the face. Ignoring her cracked and bleeding lip and the bump rising on the side of her head, Gemma tried to pitch herself forward. She pushed Doreen as hard as she could. Doreen slammed back against the refrigerator and the gun flew out of her hand again. All the while, Milo growled and clawed at Doreen's scalp, screeching like he was in a fight for his life.

"Gemma?"

She heard Luke say her name and did a double take. He couldn't be here. But he was. She tried to shout a warning, but her throat closed.

He rushed toward Doreen as she reached for the gun.

Panic squeezed the air out of Gemma's lungs. She closed her eyes, then blinked them open—just in time to see Luke plow his fist into Doreen's face. She was out cold.

A moment later, he was at Gemma's side, running his hands over her hair and face. "Are you okay? Are you all right?"

She glanced toward Doreen. She pulled back and gazed up at him, resting her hand against his chest. "Yeah, Luke. Yeah, I'm okay."

His eyes softened as he leaned toward her. He kissed her, just a soft brush against her lips, but heat rippled through her.

He stepped back, picked up the gun, and pressed the magazine release button. He pulled the clip from the magazine and tossed the clip on the kitchen table. He did this effortlessly, without batting an eye, as if he were a trained marksman who had done it a thousand times. He reached behind his back and stuck the gun in the waistband of his jeans.

They stared at each other for a moment.

She was stunned by what she'd witnessed with her own eyes. But given what Doreen had revealed about Luke's father, perhaps there was a time that this was just part of his life. Maybe, once upon a time, violence and guns were second nature to the gentle minister.

Luke calmly took the splintered pole from her grip, pulled his cell phone from his back pocket, and dialed the police.

When she slumped back to the floor, Fantasma hopped into her lap and Milo licked her face with his rough, nubby tongue. After a moment, he jumped to the table, then from the table to the windowsill. He slithered over the sill like a cobra and disappeared.

Luke moved to Doreen's side and brought her arms to her back, then pulled her wrists together. "Rope? Something to keep her like this until the police arrive?"

Rope. I don't have any . . . but wait!

She spied Fantasma's favorite toy. The one with the feather tied to six or seven inches of rope. She pulled it from under the kitchen table and tossed it to Luke.

"That'll do," he said, grunting as he tied it tightly around Doreen's wrists.

Again, Luke asked Gemma if she was okay. She nodded as she scrambled to her feet. She straightened her shoulders and mumbled, "I'm okay, really." He slid his arms around her and pulled her close.

She let her head rest against his chest and listened to his heart, drinking in that warmth she'd been craving.

****

Though as small as Mayberry, River Styx didn't even have a jovial sheriff or a goofy deputy. But within minutes of Luke's call, her place was surrounded by police officers from nearby jurisdictions.

Del Durand was among the first to arrive. He was the one who cuffed Doreen and dragged her out of the kitchen. When Jaz and her mother, and the entire Aguillard entourage, showed up, Luke momentarily faded into the background.

Jaz made her sit down. She gave her an ice pack for her head and ointment for the cut on her lip. "We heard the sirens, Gem. Wow." She looked at the splintered poor excuse for a bat on the floor. "And when did you learn to swing a bat and actually hit something? You sucked at T-ball."

Gemma made a face. "I was six. And I did hit the ball sometimes."

Lady Laveau turned to Luke and laughed. "Like Jasmine said, the girls were in T-ball as kids, and one day Gemma was at bat, and the coach told her to 'go left,' because the girls out in left field sucked at catching. What did Gem do? She did actually hit the ball, but instead of running to first base, she ran to third . . . to the left, like Coach said."

Luke shook his head and laughed. "Remind me not to tap you for the church softball team."

Gemma gave him a fake punch.

Shake showed up a few minutes later. At first, Gemma had no idea who had called him, but Jasmine gave her a shrug. "I figured Uncle Shake was involved somehow."

He leaned down and patted Gemma on the shoulder.

"You okay?"

She nodded and stared into his eyes. For the first time, she understood why he had such hard lines in his face and eyes that had seen too much grief and tragedy.

"I'll need a statement. And we have to figure out—"

"Yeah, how you're going to write up your report. Shake," she said with a hitch in her breath. "Listen, her father—"

She proceeded to spill everything that Doreen told her, including about the letter Judith wrote and what Doreen said about Luke's father. Luke went pale and excused himself.

"We'll put an APB out for Toby Tobin," Shake said. "We'll find him. My God, Gem, you could have been killed."

"I know. I mean, I guess so. But she isn't her father, Shake. She's just really messed up and scared and lonely and—oh, I don't know. She never had anyone who cared about her except him."

"He doesn't care about her either. He just uses her."

"Maybe, but that isn't how she saw it," Gemma said.

Finally, Jaz broke in. "This cop-show crap can wait until tomorrow. I'm taking her to our place for the night, okay, Uncle Shake?"

Shake agreed.

Jaz grabbed Gemma's carry-on bag on the way out, and Luke stood at the bottom of the back steps, arms crossed over his chest.

"Gem," he said as he reached out to her. "C'mere."

Jaz let go of her elbow, and she walked over to Luke. He took her in his arms. "We have a lot to talk about."

"Yeah, I have some questions, too. Like some things

need to be clarified."

"Agreed."

"You can talk to her tomorrow," Jaz insisted as she whisked Gemma away to her place. Her mom, Auntie Brette, and her daughters fussed over her for the next half an hour until she finally collapsed.

Chapter Thirty-Seven

The next morning, Shake showed up again, this time at Lady Laveau's home. Gem wasn't quite sure if it was to talk to her or for the fabulous coffee and pastries.

Shake took her outside. "So, here's the deal. I received anonymous tips. I followed up with the Leonards and a confidential informant—you—did some legwork with the nun and Mrs. MacDonald. And it all fell into place."

"I really am a CI? That's cool."

"Don't get any ideas. I just have to cover my backside, so I don't get fired and lose my pension."

"But what if I have to testify at her trial?"

"Maybe there won't be a trial for Doreen. She may take a deal. The only problem is that her father is on the run, and I don't know how long it will take us to find him."

"What if you don't? He'll come looking for me, won't he? And—?"

"We'll find him, Gem. I promise."

"Okay, but what about the fact that she showed up at my apartment? If I'm asked about that then—"

"She showed up there because Farry told her you were nosing around—on my behalf. The whole point of confidential informants is that they can get information out of people that we can't. Speaking of Farry, we picked him up this morning. I doubt it will take him long to spill, but we'll see. Drug Enforcement has been alerted about what Doreen said about Father Bailey's father. They're involved now. But they'll need hard evidence, not just the word of a criminal's daughter. But it'll work out, Gemma. This time."

She had the distinct feeling that his emphasis on 'this time' meant he didn't want her services in the future. Or at least not anytime soon.

Just as Shake's car pulled away, Luke showed up. She was dying to talk to him, but could she find the words?

Could he?

****

"How about a walk?"

"Where?" Gemma asked.

"Anywhere you want."

"Back to blue heron country?"

"Sure."

"Let me go home and take a shower first, okay?"

"After last night . . . are you sure you want to go home?"

"I do. Jaz is coming over later to help me clean up the place. But I want to check everything and just, you know, be where I belong."

"Okay."

She put coffee on for Luke before she took a shower, then threw on jeans and a black T-shirt with a message in white—one she'd never worn in front of him. It was a Christmas gift from her mom and said, 'Let me see what the spirits have to say.'

They drove to the park in silence. He stopped for coffee, saying, "One cup just didn't cut it this morning."

She stopped a major sneeze—it was pollen time—

301

with a tissue from her purse. But she felt something else in the compartment. She took it out. It was the piece of bridal fabric that Jaz gave her that she'd forgotten all about.

"What's that?"

"Oh, just some fabric from Lady Laveau's shop."

"You aren't going to tell him it's supposed to be for your wedding, Gummy Bear?"

Very funny, Peppi. You're just hilarious.

Finding it certainly started her brain spinning, though.

Luke parked the car, and they walked for a few minutes. They sat on a log that gave a clear view of a couple of large nests. The herons were very, very busy.

She saw one soaring through the sky, gliding high above the treetops with a long branch in its beak. He was huge but graceful and agile. He landed at the top of a tree where his mate was waiting. He handed the branch off to her, and she carefully placed it in the nest they were building. Feng shui was clearly important—it had to be positioned just right.

Luke drank some coffee and said, "They're monogamous, but they like to use nest building as an extended date night."

"Come again?"

"They go through a dating and mating thing each season."

"Well, you gotta maintain the magic, right?"

He grinned. "I guess."

They watched the couple for a little while. The birds stared at each other. The first one opened his beak, and then the other one followed suit. They bowed to each other.

One let out a roaring squawk. "If that's a serenade, I'll pass," she said.

"Can you see the bottom of his feet?" Luke asked as the male flew away from the nest again in search of more nesting material.

She nodded.

"They turn gold during breeding season."

Her eyebrows shot up. "Well, that's . . . different."

"Sometimes different is pretty okay," he said in a low voice. "More than okay."

He leaned over and brushed his lips lightly against hers. "Okay, Gemma, moment of truth. About my father."

"Yes?"

"You said that Doreen mentioned a man named Danny Green. He was a big Irish mob guy back in the day. He got blown up. And that pretty much ended the mob around here. But my grandfather wasn't about to give up and neither was his son, Michael J. Bailey, Jr. My father. They ran drugs and laundered money. At least that's what my mom told me. It's why she left my father. And I'm sure he still does for that matter."

"And you were raised in that environment?"

"Until the divorce. Mom kept him away as much as she could, but she didn't have hard evidence to give to the police. He bought half the town, and he's never been arrested. As part of their divorce decree, the court ordered that he could have access to me. Every time we were together, he taught me about guns."

She lowered her eyes. "I see."

"Obviously, he would have loved to bring me into the business. But, also obviously, I chose a different path."

Gemma blinked back a tear. It was so much to take in. "Doreen said he was furious when you considered leaving the priesthood."

"Yeah, he was. It's weird, I know. I think it's an Irish thing. Now fill in the blanks for me, Gem. Shake told me a lot. I know you were involved but give me the rest."

She gulped. *Does he really want to know?*

She hesitated, but she did as he asked. She started at the beginning. Well, pretty much. She didn't go all the way back to her very first ghost experience, but he got the drift.

"Okay. Well, there it is."

He took it pretty well, considering. She could see he was a little taken aback, a little nervous. But he didn't bolt. He didn't glare. He didn't even wince.

She pointed to her T-shirt. "See this? It says, 'Let me see what the spirits have to say.' That's me, Luke. It's part of me, of who I am. You can't change your DNA."

He nodded and sipped some coffee. "It's a lot to take in, Gem. All of this is a lot to take in, especially that Judith was breaking the engagement to enter the convent. But really, I shouldn't be surprised. She asked me many questions about religion, about my calling. She was in love with what I represented and what she longed to have, not me. I didn't see it because I didn't want to see it. I think that she only said yes when I proposed because her parents wanted to see her get married and settle down." He paused and took a breath. "And I don't think she wanted the guilt she'd feel if I left the priesthood for her. I think that would have been too much to handle. God knows, it's been hard for me to handle."

He finished his coffee and put his cup on the ground.

"But now it's my turn again," she said. "I have more questions about your father and all that."

He let out a long breath. "Like I said, by the time my father came along, the Irish Mob in Cleveland was pretty much wiped out. But that didn't stop him from dealing in drugs and a lot of other stuff. It's how he made his money—not from the businesses he owns. He has laundered money, I guess, through some of them, like that Irish pub that Shake told me you went to. I'm sure my father owns it and the owner.

"I told Shake what I know about it all. But it's been years since I was privy to any of that. I can't prove a thing. It's all second hand."

"But he really is an Irish Mob guy?"

"Yeah. From what I heard, my grandfather went underground for a long, long time after Greene got killed, but he always had his sights set on starting operations up again. He raised his son, my father, that way. And they tried to pull me in, too. I was learning to shoot a pistol when I was eight years old."

She closed her eyes, unable to imagine what such a childhood would have been like.

"I didn't want anything to do with him. He finally left me alone when I entered the seminary, but he showed up for my ordination."

She shook her head. "Luke, I can't even fathom living like that. With that cloud over you all the time. How despicable. Do you think that Shake will arrest your father?"

"On the word of an unreliable informant? Doreen is a criminal and a criminal's daughter. What she says she knows is from her father. Honestly, I doubt it, until

Shake can get a warrant for surveillance or get somebody inside."

Her eyes trailed back to the birds. Watching them was calming, peaceful. She could gladly stay right there forever.

He gave her a sideways grin. "Let's walk a bit," he said in a whisper and pulled her to her feet. She brushed the dirt off her butt, picked up the coffee cups, and tossed them into a trash bin. Then she fell into step with him.

She looked down. Her tennis shoes were covered in mud and dust. She stooped down to brush them off, and her cell phone rang. It was her mother. "Hey, Mom."

"Gemma, what's wrong? I've been climbing the walls all day. I know something is up."

Maybe she sensed my grandmother or something, Gemma thought. Nana was always Johnny-on-the-spot with obscure warnings. But her mother and she had always had this sixth-sense kind of thing between them. They always knew when something was up.

"Hang on a sec, Mom. Luke," she said. "I have to take this call. It's my mom."

He formed 'okay' with his fingers.

She wandered a little way up a trail but kept him in sight. He stuffed his hands into the pockets of his tight jeans and lifted his eyes skyward to watch the spectacle of nest building.

"So, Mom, I can't explain everything. But—"

She gave her enough information that she clearly understood that Gemma had been in danger. She kind of freaked out.

"I don't think you should be working with Shake anymore." Her voice was pretty stern. The last time she sounded like this was when her grandfather died, and

Gemma told her that she was dropping out of college.

"I'll be more careful, Mom. And I don't think Shake wants my assistance in the future either."

"He will. And you'll do it. I know you. But please, Gem, you have to use your head. You have to be careful."

She swallowed her usual 'I'm a grown-up, Mom' retort. "I know. But I'm the one who got enough information from Judith to get the case rolling again."

Gina sighed. "What happened to 'I don't want my gift anymore'?"

She shook her head and hit back. "And what happened to you saying I can use it for good? That I can lead Shake where he needs to go."

Match. Game.

Gemma could just imagine her mom's face. She'd wrinkle her nose, purse her lips, and then muster up a sad smile, a surrender. She'd keep worrying.

And I'll keep doing what I do.

She hung up and stumbled a couple of times over tree stumps as she made her way back to Luke. "Hey, no more dents and dings, okay? And is your mom okay?"

"Yeah, she was just checking on me. She knew something was up."

"This . . . gift really does run in the family?"

"Sort of. But mothers just know when you need them, I think."

"They definitely do, Gem," Peppi whispered.

She recalled her mother, holding Peppi's hand, knowing that he would soon take his last breath. He smiled up at her and quoted Poe's poem about heaven and angels and mothers.

"Luke, why didn't you call me when I was away?"

"I didn't even know that you went to New York at first. I went to your store a couple of times, and then I finally went over to talk to Jasmine. She told me you went to visit your mother in New York. She called me to tell me you were coming home—and she told me what wines and flowers you like."

Gemma hugged him. "Seriously? Well, we're pretty close. Hardly anyone else understands us."

"Us?" Luke asked. "Does Jaz talk to—?"

She cut him off with "No!" and then she shook her head and leaned up against a tree, scratching her back against the bark. "No, she has a different . . . gift. She has dreams that often come true. She warned me about everything that just happened. Not in so many words. She doesn't see every single thing—she sees symbolic things. But that isn't something you can chat about at cocktail parties in River Styx, is it?"

"I guess not. Anyhow, as I was saying, when you were in New York, I picked up the phone to call you a dozen times, but I figured you needed space—I mean, you went all the way to New York to get away from me—"

"No, it was to get away from everything. To just not be in River Styx. To try not to think about ghosts or the case or any of it."

"Did it work?"

"No," she answered quietly. "Not very well. But what about you? Why did you come over last night? If you hadn't showed up—"

"When you dropped off the gift, obviously I knew you were home. I had bought flowers and a card and wine and a poetry book."

Her eyes lit up.

"You did?"

"Yeah, I dropped them all on the landing of your apartment. I took everything home when you went with Jasmine. They're at home. I'll prove it to you when we go back."

He kicked at some dead leaves. "I am worried about this Tobin guy, though. He's still out there. He killed Judith because she recognized him. And for a lousy ring. There's no telling what he'll do."

"Do you know him?"

He shook his head. "He must have been after my time around my father. I don't know. But no, I don't know him." He thought a minute. "What happens to the ring now?"

"It stays in custody until this whole mess is over. And not just the Tobins. I'm thinking your father is guilty of insurance fraud, too. He got the money for the ring after all. But that would have to be proven, too."

"You know, I could kill him myself."

"Don't say that. That's not you, Luke. That isn't who you are."

Scowling, he mumbled, "I guess. But there must be a way for them to search my father's warehouse. Heaven only knows what's in there, what he's pushing out of there. I have to think about that."

"About what?"

"About how to get the goods on my father. Even if I have to do it myself."

"Don't," she whispered. "Don't think like that."

Suddenly he pulled her close. "Right now, I just want to think about you. You know, I felt sparks around you from the start. I love everything about you."

He leaned down to kiss her, but his phone rang. He

ran his hand back and forth over his hair. "I gotta take this. It's Shake."

He walked a few paces away. When he returned, he said, "He wants to talk to me more about my father's business. He's trying to figure out a way to get a warrant. He's still looking for Toby Tobin, of course. But he's in the wind, he's a ghost." He grimaced. "I told him that I might be able to help him."

"Don't do anything rash," she urged.

"Yeah. I know. Oh, he also wanted to let me know that he spoke with Judith's parents and that he had a message for me from them."

"A message?"

"They thought it would be nice if the three of us would visit her. You know, her grave."

"You should. You should go."

He agreed. "Yeah, I'll call them when I get back to the church. And that won't bother you?"

"Of course not."

He put his arms around her and kissed her. A long, deep kiss. Finally.

He pulled her close as they walked back to the car. He looked into her eyes and said, "You know, this isn't the easiest relationship in the world—for either of us. But, well—"

She pulled back slightly to stare at him. "Well?"

"When I'm with you, I think of this one poem," he said.

"Which is?"

"It says that if I have the love I long for, my sad thoughts will be put away forever."

"Yeah?"

"Yeah," he said, and he kissed her.

When they got to the car, there was a surprise waiting for them. Milo was curled up in the back seat, sleeping, purring away to beat the band.

She turned to look at Luke. "Oh, wow, how did he get in here? And how did we not notice him before?"

Luke just shrugged.

Does he do more than fly? she wondered. *Does he have, like, his own portable transporter beam?*

"Luke, I have to call Jaz. The cat is not supposed to be with me anymore. They'll be frantic."

"Somehow, I doubt that. From what you've told me, Milo is a free spirit, Gem."

When Jaz answered the phone, she asked, "Is Milo with you?"

"Yeah, yeah, he's in Luke's car. I was calling so you wouldn't worry."

"Gem, that's just his way. Angelique said this morning that she expects him to go back and forth between our place and yours indefinitely. I think you've got joint custody whether you like it or not."

"But why?"

"Because he knows that you need him. He knew the other night, too. And there's another reason. He's going to be a dad, right?"

"He's what?"

"I'm pretty sure Fan is pregnant. And oh, by the way, I'm so sorry that I didn't lock the door, and, also, by the way, you forgot to tell me how to work the alarm."

"I did?"

"Yeah, you did," she laughed. "And I'm sorry that Ange left the window open. But Doreen would have broken in, and Milo wouldn't have been able to get in to help you otherwise."

I'm not so sure about that. That cat has magic in his veins.

"Well, we're heading home. I'll bring him back."

"Don't bother, Gem. He'll go where he wants to go. And right now, he wants to be with you and his lady."

As she stood there, watching Milo, it occurred to her that Angelique and Milo probably did have a special relationship. All of the Laveau family was—well, interesting to say the least. They had hidden talents that Gemma wanted to explore.

And as for Milo . . . well, all cats … they hunt, they hide in strange places, they seem to know exactly what lies in ambush on a dark and stormy night. They hear and see things most humans can't. But Milo was different. He took flight. He protected her because he seemed to be able to sense danger. Maybe he even communed with invisible beings. His eyes glowed.

She was very, very glad that, for whatever reason, Milo had decided she was a friend, not an enemy.

When she got into Luke's car, she scooped Milo into her arms, and he just snored away.

"Oh, Luke, what about Toto? Did you take him back to Judith's parents?"

"Not yet, but actually, I'm going to ask them if I can keep him or at least share him. I've become accustomed to his face."

As they drove home, she rested her head on Luke's shoulder and every once in a while, he petted the cat or squeezed her hand.

"You smell kinda like chlorine," she said.

"I went swimming this morning before I went to find you at Jasmine's. I coach the high school kids, and there's a meet Sunday. You'll come, won't you? Cheer me on?"

So, I'm finally going to see Luke in Speedos.

"I'll be there, Luke. I'm your biggest fan. Haven't you figured that out yet?"

He put his arm around her and hummed along to a rock tune.

Epilogue

About a month later, Luke asked Gemma to go with him to Judith's grave. She was a little uncomfortable at first, but Judith's parents could not have been more gracious, and she knew it was the closure they had been seeking.

Toby Tobin was still on the run, of course, but even if Shake wasn't exactly Dirty Harry, he was on top of it and he struck Gemma as the "I always get my man type."

She hung back, standing near an old willow tree, as Judith's folks and Luke spoke in soft tones. They put two bouquets of yellow roses—Judith's favorite—on the headstone. Then they said their goodbyes and parted ways.

Luke lingered.

She heard Peppi's voice in her head. He recited the poem by Clare Harner that he asked her to read at his funeral. He said a few lines.

"Do not stand
By my grave, and weep.
I am not there."

You're so right, Peppi, she thought, touching the necklace at her throat. Out of sight but definitely not out of mind.

Luke held out his hand, and she joined him at the grave. She clasped his hand tightly. He asked her if she had heard anything new from Shake.

"Toby is still out there, but Doreen is talking, I guess."

Gemma still felt a little sorry for her. Her father was a career criminal, and yet he was the only one who showed up for her trial. Her mother and her pious sister looked the other way. What a messed-up childhood she must have had, lacking in the love and guidance that every child needs.

"If she turns," he said, "she might even end up in witness protection."

She squeezed his hand. "I'm so sorry, Luke. This has all been so awful for you."

"Well, I've talked to Shake again, too. About how I can help."

"Luke—"

He put his forefinger to her lips. "Let's not think about that right now. Let's be happy that I've opened my mind to a lot of things that I never thought I would. I have got you in my life—and I never thought that would happen. It's nice to be half of a couple. It's what I really always wanted."

She chuckled.

"What?"

"Speaking of couples, it appears that our meandering Milo has been up to no good."

"Meaning?"

"Jasmine told me awhile back that she dreamed that Fantasma was pregnant, and she is. She has morning sickness."

He stopped mid-stride. "No way!"

"Yep. You know Milo stayed at my place when I was in New York, and he's been hanging around ever since. Fantasma never tried to get out before, but she scooted out several times after he started hanging around. Clearly, he's been up to no good."

"Fantasma wasn't fixed?"

"Nope. She never went out, Luke. She was a solo cat. I never thought I'd have a problem, and I guess it didn't dawn on me that Milo wasn't . . . you know, neutered."

"So now we are going to have flying kittens?" Luke laughed.

She definitely like the sound of 'we.'

"Around the first of August, according to Theo."

"I can't blame Milo," he said as he took her in his arms. "Entranced by a beautiful woman? Alone with her—just the two of them together with no interruptions?" He nuzzled her hair and kissed her.

He drew back to gaze at her. "Maybe Milo is tired of being alone. Maybe he's ready to shed the black robe and collar just like I was. Maybe he just wants a family. Like I do."

"Maybe," she whispered and lifted her chin and met his eyes. He kissed her again.

Now she laughed. "You had leftover pizza for breakfast, didn't you, Luke?"

"What?" He looked down at his white shirt to see if there was red sauce all over it, then back up at her.

"There's nothing there. How did you . . . did a spirit—?"

She about keeled over laughing. "No, silly. Don't give ghosts all the credit. I tasted it. Rather spicy."

His lips turned up in a wicked smile. "Hmm, you sure? I mean, where's your Sherlock Holmes hat? Don't you want to further investigate to be certain?"

"I do," she said and kissed him again.

Luke stooped down and rearranged the bouquets on the grave. Then he took her hand again.

"Even though Tobin is still out there, maybe she can rest in peace," Gemma said. "Shake will track him down. I'm sure of it."

He put his hands on her shoulders. "That's not enough, Gemma."

She squinted. "What do you mean?"

"I can't quite put it behind me. Bringing Toby Tobin to justice isn't good enough. My father sent him. And besides, he's committed many other crimes."

"But that's not your concern, Luke. Maybe Doreen can—"

"Someone needs to be on the inside. And maybe I'm the one who can bring my father down."

"No, Luke," Gemma said, shaking her head. "It's over."

"It isn't over, Gemma. Not for me."

Judith's voice came through loud and clear, and it echoed Luke's words.

"It isn't over. Not yet."

A word about the author…

Gabriella Lucas is the author of paranormal romances and mysteries. Her first book, The Caretaker, and several romance novellas, have earned her loyal fans in the genre. Writing under the pen name A S Croyle, she has also published a four-book series, Before Watson, combining a Sherlock Holmes theme with young romance.

She has been an attorney for over thirty years in Northeast Ohio. When she's not working, writing, or taking two of her pet therapy dogs to visit local nursing homes, she's making quilts, taking long walks for inspiration, and watching her favorite British detective shows to relax.